one lonely
degree

ALSO BY C. K. KELLY MARTIN

I Know It's Over

one lonely
degree

o o o

c. k. kelly martin

random house · new york

Text copyright © 2009 by Carolyn Martin

Jacket photograph copyright © 2009 by Tracy Kahn Photography

Visit us on the Web! www.randomhouse.com/teens

Educators and librarians, for a variety of teaching tools, visit us at
www.randomhouse.com/teachers

Library of Congress Cataloging-in-Publication Data
Martin, C. K. Kelly.
One lonely degree / by C. K. Kelly Martin. — 1st ed.
p.   cm.
Summary: When fifteen-year-old Finn's world falls apart after a violent sexual encounter,
the only person she can talk to is her best friend, Audrey, until beautiful boy Jersy
moves back to town and both girls develop feelings for him that threaten to
destroy their friendship.
ISBN 978-0-375-85163-6 (trade) — ISBN 978-0-375-95563-1 (lib. bdg.) —
ISBN 978-0-375-85392-0 (e-book)
[1. Interpersonal relations—Fiction. 2. Coming of Age—Fiction. 3. Date rape—Fiction.
4. Love—Fiction. 5. Friendship—Fiction.] I. Title.
PZ7.M3644On 2009
[Fic]—dc22
2008012552

Printed in the United States of America

10 9 8 7 6 5 4 3 2 1

First Edition

Baby girl, stand up and fight.
This is not some paradise.
Oh, it's just where we live.

—"A STORY ABOUT A GIRL,"
OUR LADY PEACE

o   o   o

rage on

one lonely
Degree

one

THINGS DON'T ALWAYS change with a bang. Sometimes they change so gradually that you can't clearly pinpoint the last moment they were truly the same. That's the way it was with my parents. I know they were happy—but I couldn't tell you exactly when.

Audrey says they could just be going through a bad patch and that things could start changing back when I least expect it. *Anything is possible.* That's almost the truth, but it doesn't fill me with hope. *Anything is possible* makes me feel like someone's scraping at the inside of my rib cage with dull scissors. If you kept that idea in your head, you'd never leave the house for fear you'd be crushed by a runaway bus or gunned down in the mall parking lot.

Anything is possible is something I prefer not to think about, but I don't always have a choice. Some nights are just like that. The sick feelings creep up on me until I want to shout so loud that it would make my parents come running. I never do, of course. It wouldn't help, and my parents would cart me off to some highly recommended shrink that would want to know everything.

And there are things I could say, but not anything that I actually want anyone to hear. There are thoughts in my head that I can't get out, but I have my own trick for dealing with them, which is to let other things *in,* as loud and furious as I can. Tonight, for instance, I have to keep pulling off my earphones to listen for my dad's key in the front door. Raine Maida screams "Naveed" in my ears. *Listen.* Then it's "Where Are You," "Innocent," and "Yellow Brick Road." *Listen.* The pounding in my ears, the sound of Raine's voice like burning gold, and the blanket pulled all the way up to my chin is the nearest thing I know to an antidote, but if Dad hears the music he'll open the door and ask why I'm still awake. It's happened before. I used to keep the bedside lamp on, and a couple months ago, around two in the morning, he tapped at my door and asked if I was sick.

"No," I told him. "Just a little insomnia." My face felt like a bleached white sheet, and I was scared that he'd sense my bad feelings and try to put them into words.

"You could try turning down the volume," he said, smiling.

A guitar riff was screeching out of the earphones around my neck, and I furrowed my eyebrows, puffed out my cheeks, and said, "Ha. Ha." Everyone is so sarcastic these days that it's practically boring, but I need all the crutches I can get.

"And turning off the light," he added, still hovering in the doorway in his plaid pajamas and slippers, looking like a sitcom TV father that can solve any problem within thirty minutes.

"You're funny, Dad." I pulled an impatient face. "Anyone ever tell you you're a funny guy?"

"Not my teenage daughter," he said, smile as wide as ever. "Don't go deaf tonight, Finn. You have school in the morning."

I nodded and watched him shut the door, the sickness stretching tight across my face the moment he was gone. My skin feels that same way now. Like a mask that doesn't fit anymore. Like I'm not the person anyone thinks I am—not even Audrey. But if I'm not *that* person, just who am I instead? I'm not the girl who slinks soundlessly through the school hall pretending nothing can touch her. That much I do know.

Listen, I tell myself. *Just listen. Listen.* Everything will be all right, as long as you stop your mind and listen.

And this is the way it goes for a while. Me listening to Raine's voice in my ear. Me waiting for Dad's key in the door. My heels are itchy dry in my socks. My lips are cracking and my fingertips will be next. The air in my room is colder than anywhere else in the house except the basement. My mother says she doesn't know how I can stand it, but I like the contrast. This is me in bed in the middle of winter.

Everything will be all right.

My mother stands at the kitchen counter, eyeing me wearily over her shoulder. She's making Daniel's lunch—or more accurately, packaging it. In fact, it's more of a lunch *kit* than an actual meal. My brother is ten years old and has yet to accept the value of real food. "Are you still taking those vitamins?" Mom asks, pointing to the bottle in front of me. "Your color is terrible."

"I don't have a color," I tell her. "I am the very absence of color." It's true, I'm terminally pale. Much ashier than Daniel, who will look like a Mexican come July. Lately I have problems focusing and forget things too. Sometimes I feel like I don't even know how to breathe anymore and that my brain isn't getting enough oxygen. Mom likes to tell me I don't have enough iron in my diet.

"Where's Dad?" I ask. Normally the four of us eat breakfast together. It's one of those things my parents think prove we're a family.

"Running late," Mom says shrilly, her gaze shooting back to the plastic lunch bag. "You'll be late too if you don't hurry."

Yes, I'm moving in slow motion. I don't operate well on less than eight hours' sleep. My frizzy red hair keeps falling into my face, impeding the flow of cereal from bowl to mouth. I take a swig of orange juice and glance at Daniel in his brown cords, his thick blond hair behaving itself in a way mine never does. Sometimes I wonder what it's like to be him. What happens to him when he leaves this house? Whatever it is, it's probably easier than being me.

For one thing, I don't blend. I'm taller than other fifteen-year-old girls but not skinny or pretty enough for that to be a good thing. For the longest time I didn't even have any boobs. I was like an elongated Pippi Longstocking. Believe it or not, that's not a popular look in ninth grade. Tenth grade either.

Mom is always telling me to "Stand up straight. Own your height." She was an actress for, like, five minutes. Now she's just a woman with extremely good posture. Mom was nothing like me in tenth grade. She was a cheerleader, a regular high school "It" girl. She can't understand why I won't color myself in with lipstick and foundation and do "something" with my hair.

When the three of us assemble at the front door later, Mom's frosted blond hair is swept back into a perfect bun, her lips shimmering mauve. Samsam, our resident furball, crowds into our midst for the daily goodbye ritual. Mom's French-manicured nails dip carefully into her purse for her keys as I press my nose to Samsam's head and inhale. He smells like a damp old blanket, even when he's dry. Some people don't like the way dogs smell, but I'm not one of them. I scratch behind his ears and smooth my hands over his scraggly sandy coat. Fur clings to the arms of my school uniform sweater. Samsam doesn't realize that his hybrid breed isn't supposed to shed much.

Upstairs my parents' closet slides open, evidence that my dad is awake and indeed running late. The rest of our family files out the front door and into the outside world. Or in my case, St. Mark's High School. I'd like to think St. Mark's is nothing like the outside world, but I haven't seen enough of it to know. London or New York. That's where I want to head when I graduate—have regular coffee dates with struggling playwrights and painters, people too cool to even calculate their own cool quotient.

All of that is a long way off, but the last thing I want to think about is where I am: Portable G, its windows facing the frozen football field on one side and Portable F on the other. Homeroom happens to be my favorite class—not only for its brevity but because it's the only class Audrey and I have in common this semester—but it's still St. Mark's.

I slip into the back row, populated mainly by stoners, and slump into the desk next to Audrey's. We're not stoners ourselves, but we're not brainiacs or beautiful people either. It's an interesting geographic problem—everyone has to sit somewhere.

"My dad was out late again last night," I tell her, leaning into the space between us. "I was up for ages and he was still out when I fell asleep."

Audrey tilts her head and looks at me fixedly. "Were you waiting up for him or were you having trouble sleeping again?"

My hands disappear into my sleeves. "I couldn't sleep." The room is rapidly filling up with assorted students, all of them Pack Animals, and I drop my voice. "But it's okay, you know, it's getting better. It wasn't all night or anything."

Audrey nods. Her eyes register concern but she doesn't push it. "Did your mom say anything about him being out?"

I shake my head. "She was in a shitty mood this morning. He didn't even come downstairs." My dad is nonconfrontational at the core. He doesn't raise his voice unless it's absolutely necessary. If you listened to my parents fight, you'd only hear my mother's voice; he makes his point by getting incrementally quieter. What could be quieter than being absent in the first place?

"You know what we should do?" Audrey says, her gold-brown pupils suddenly as wide as Oreos. "We should go to the mall and see Record Store Guy. Screw this. No one will even miss us." Her head cranes towards mine in the aisle, waiting for my reply.

"You don't like Record Store Guy," I remind her. "And it's freezing out there."

Audrey's eyes sharp-focus on mine. "No, I don't like Record Store Guy—you do. Anyway, it's not like a pathological hate or something. Personally, I just can't get into guys in eyeliner and nail polish."

She's trying to help and I'm blocking her. I see that. But I don't know that a trip to the mall will help. I'm not even sure how I feel about Record Store Guy *(Ryan, his name is Ryan)* anymore. Nothing to do with the eyeliner and nail polish. He's still a Beautiful Boy (and they're a definite rarity), but it's complicated. Sometimes I feel like I want to forget about the opposite sex entirely.

"Not today, okay, Aud? I have civics homework due." That's the truth, but it's also true that I don't want her hovering around me in HMV, looking for proof that I'm okay.

"After school?" she adds. "I won't say anything about him. I promise. I won't even go in if you don't want me to."

"It's not that," I say sharply. The guy in front of me turns and stares at me like I've run my fingernails down the blackboard. I give him a wild voodoo stare and turn back towards Audrey. "I'm not sure about him anymore, and you know nothing's ever gonna happen there anyway. What's the point?" I fold my arms in front of my stomach and slide down in my chair, watching her face. "I mean, we can go to the mall after school if you want, but I don't want it to be about Ryan, okay? If we go to the mall, let's just go to the mall."

Audrey frowns like I've nipped her hand, but she recovers fast. "It's okay. We don't have to go to the mall. I just thought you might want to do something—take your mind off stuff."

I feel like a rotten stump, the remains of a tree that fell in the forest while one person was watching. "I know," I tell her. "We should go, you're right." Audrey is my witness for everything, my best friend in the universe for the past four years, the only person under thirty that I trust implicitly—the absolute least I can do is try.

two

THE GIRLS' WASHROOM is painted Pepcid pink. It's supposed to be feminine and pretty, I guess—disguise the gross things happening inside the cubicles and in our *Girls Gone Wild* minds. In my particular cubicle, for instance, I hover over the toilet seat emptying my bladder and reading the following red-pen message: "Drew S. popped my cherry last night."

A concerned silver marker asks: "Did it hurt?"

The reply is in different handwriting yet again: "Not as much as when he . . ."

I grimace as I read the rest. I don't know why I bother looking at that stuff—except that it's there and I'm already late for art class. It took me six minutes to remember my locker combination, which is one of the things that happens when I don't get enough sleep. I should've written the combo down earlier this morning, but I forgot. The result is me in the washroom, reading scrawls on the wall and wondering if any of them are true. I could take out my own pen and ask, but I'd never be able to verify the answers.

I wash my hands, wipe them on my kilt, and head slowly for the art room. Inside, Mr. Ferguson is playing one of his environmental tapes. This one is of the ocean and I'm instantly grateful that I've already peed. Mr. Ferguson nods at me as I walk into the room but says nothing. I've caught him in a good mood, apparently, and I nod back and make a beeline for my usual seat.

Jasper eyes me guiltily from across the table, and then I spot him—another guy sitting in my chair. Jasper is no help. He'd be a social climber if he wasn't a gay guy trapped in a Catholic high school. He's not a true social outcast; he doesn't understand that saving a seat is crucial.

I look over the guy that's filled my space—disheveled light brown hair, a fine scar that must be nearly half an inch long on his cheek, his thin build clothed in the same navy sweater and gray pants that every other guy in St. Mark's is wearing. He must be new; I've never laid eyes on him before. I don't particularly want to make his acquaintance now, but I don't want to find another place to sit either. If I have to shimmy in next to Abel and listen to him plug his Catholic Youth Group, I'll end up stabbing somebody with my pencil.

I walk over to my chair and put my pencil case and books down on the table, right next to the new guy's virgin sheet of bristol board. He glances over his shoulder at me, and it occurs to me that he has no idea who I am yet. I could be winner of the Freshman Science Award or a religious zealot like Abel. I could be the girl who lost her virginity to Drew S.

"You're sitting in my seat," I say. "This is my spot." My finger is pointed down at his bristol board. It's overkill and I'm verging on rude, but I'm extremely tired and slightly panicked. If he refuses to move, I won't be able to do a thing about it.

"I didn't think you were coming," Jasper says, regaining the power of speech. "You're late."

"I know." Everyone is watching our mini-drama and I'm stupid to care.

The new guy's staring at me with an expression I don't recognize. If we could be strangers forever, I'd never know what that look means, and I wish it could stay that way. Why does everyone in St. Mark's feel so depressingly similar in the end?

"I didn't know," the guy says, shrugging. "You're welcome to it." He pinches his bristol board between two fingers and gets to his feet.

"Sorry," I tell him. "I'm a creature of habit." A creature of what? Those aren't my words. Maybe I feel bad now that he's given in. I could be dooming a decent person to the cult of Abel.

Jasper strokes his nose as I sit down across from him. With his wispy blond eyelashes and the glow-in-the-dark veins on his wrists, he could be the only person in the school whiter than me. That complexion helped earn him the nickname Casper. Most people are too polite to say it to his face, but everyone knows.

"So what happened?" he asks. "Where have you been?"

"Forgot my locker combo," I say irritably. "Thanks so much for saving my seat."

Jasper rolls his eyes like I'm being a bitch. "It was a misunderstanding, Finn. I thought you weren't here, okay? Calm down."

"Whatever." I retrieve my rough sketches from Mr. Ferguson's cabinet and examine the clean sheet of bristol board in front of me. I'm not ready to put a mark on it, and there's no time anyway; Jasper spends the entire period talking to me, trying to make up for giving my seat away. I don't take long to forgive him. It's easier on both of us, and besides, I'm distracted by the sight of the new guy glancing periodically over at me from his new seat beside Abel.

"So what's the new guy's name anyway?" I ask Jasper.

"I don't know. He just sat down before you came in." Hmm. Jasper, for the second time today, is no help whatsoever. I flick my gaze back to Abel's kingdom as Jasper drops his voice. "Stop checking him out."

"I'm not," I say, although I suppose I am. For now he's an unknown quantity. "He keeps looking at me. It's creepy."

Creepy isn't the right word. Mysterious, maybe. It doesn't even matter. I pick up my pen and print my locker combination on the inside of my palm, in case my memory shuts down again. The sound of ocean waves breaking against our landlocked classroom makes me want to draw the sea. A river at least. I'm not a future Dalí or van Gogh, but I'm pretty good at putting things together. I figure I could be a graphic designer if I keep it up. London or New York would be the place for that. I don't even care if I'm a poverty-stricken graphic designer, so long as I'm in London or New York.

At the moment, Mr. Ferguson's got us working on a pretend fund-raising campaign for an environmental agency. I was planning something simple. A smiling little girl, sitting cross-legged and holding up a pristine glass of water. But the ocean is very persuasive. It has me envisioning a tranquil forest, a fox lapping up river water at the edge of the scene.

Jasper is way ahead of me, another reason he's talking so much. I don't really mind, only I wish he wouldn't watch so many movies. Half of them sound boring and I don't want to know what happens in the other half, in case I ever see them myself.

"Don't worry. I won't give anything away," he promises. "I'll just tell you the premise."

But there's not enough time for that either. The bell sounds, signaling the beginning of lunch, and Jasper and I pack up our stuff and shuffle through the door, single file. Jasper's waiting for me on the other side of the hall, ready to continue from where he left off, but I never get to him. Somebody touches my elbow and I swing around in the middle of the hall, people buzzing by me on both sides.

"So what's your name?" the new guy asks. He's in no hurry to get the words out, and I'm immediately suspicious. Why does he want to know my name?

"Finn Kavanagh," I tell him. He breaks into a toothy grin that makes my stomach churn. Did somebody put him up to this? I glance over at Jasper, who is taking it all in like a silent movie, and telepathically command him to stay where he is. "What's yours?"

"Jersy," he says happily, smiling wider than ever. "Jersy Mikulski."

Jersy. A familiar feeling ripples through me. Like eating ice cream on your front porch in summer. I say his name over and over again in my head, waiting for a lightbulb to switch on. He's waiting too, and we stand there facing each other, feeling the moment stretch back into the past.

"Yeah," I say slowly, memories jogging back to me in frustratingly small pieces. "Okay." I bob my head and shift my books to my other arm. It's a weird feeling, remembering something you didn't know you'd forgotten in the first place. My brain doesn't know where to put the fragments at first. "Your mom was at Eastman's, right?" My mother still works in their marketing department. Our moms were pretty good friends back in the day. "You guys moved to—"

"Kingston," he says. "Yeah. It's weird. When I saw you in there, it didn't really click, but there was something . . ." He motions vaguely towards my body. "You look different. You're so tall." He doesn't say that like it's a good or bad thing, just a fact.

"Well, six-year-olds are usually shorter," I joke, beginning to relax. "Hair's the same, though." I grab a chunk with my free hand and he laughs. "So what're you doing back?"

He shrugs, his smile beginning to disappear. "What's this place like anyway?" He's two inches shorter than me and his blue-green eyes have to look up at mine. It makes me want to slouch, and because of that I stand even straighter.

"It's okay," I tell him. The kind of information he wants is no good coming from a stranger. The answer's completely dependent on who's asking and who's answering. "But then I have nothing to compare it to, you know?"

Jersy nods like that's just the answer he was expecting. The boy I remember wasn't afraid of anything. He got a concussion somersaulting into the pool at a company barbecue. The next time I saw him, both his arms were bandaged. He'd scraped them something fierce trying out a stunt on his bike, and his mother shouted at him, without raising her voice, when he unwrapped one to show me.

"It all looks the same from here," he says, staring up the hall. I follow his eyes. Kids. Lockers. A sea of uniforms in motion. My eyes zoom back to the spot where Jasper was waiting. He's deserted me, but this time I can't blame him. Lunch never lasts long enough. I concentrate on my kilt, ignoring my own silence. "So I guess I'll see you tomorrow," Jersy continues. "Don't worry, I won't sit in your chair." He blinks at me like he knows he's cute. All the cute guys at St. Mark's know they're cute, but there's not one genuine Beautiful Boy in the entire population.

"Ha. Ha," I say sarcastically. God, I'm an absolute genius. I turn my back on him and point my genius self in the direction of the cafeteria.

"Finn," he shouts after me.

My head whips around to find him. "Jersy," I shout back. My palms are sweaty and I can't explain why.

"Where the fuck's the cafeteria in this place?"

Jersy doesn't sit with us at lunch. He disappears into the crowd the second we step into the cafeteria. I buy chicken nuggets and fries and plop down next to Audrey. Everyone else is already seated: Jasper, Maggie (who isn't quite smart enough to be a brainiac but too quiet to be anyone else), Teresa (Audrey's friend from drama class), and her boyfriend, Edwardo. It's not a pack the way other people have them. We don't do group activities together outside of school. We don't exclude people.

"So what'd the new guy have to say?" Jasper asks, plunging his fork into a plate of macaroni and cheese. "Did he tell you his name?"

Audrey, Maggie, and Teresa stare optimistically over at me. "New guy?" Audrey repeats.

We're all so starved for variety that I'd laugh if it wasn't so sad. "Our moms worked together years ago," I say dismissively. "His family just moved back." I don't want any of them getting too excited, because I know exactly how this will go. He won't be the new guy for long. He'll be just like everyone else, and then we won't even mention him.

But Maggie's already fired up. "And he remembered you," she says. "That's sweet." Maggie's big on "sweet." She uses that word a lot—mostly in relation to romances she reads about in *Us* magazine.

I shrug and shake my head a little. *Whatever, Mags.* That girl needs to get a life. I pop a chicken nugget into my mouth, suddenly feeling too bitchy for words. It's better not to expect too much to begin with. I shouldn't let myself forget that.

Audrey bumps her shoulder against mine, sensing my slip into bad-mood territory. I don't know what I'd do without her. Would I have to start reading *Us* magazine and haunting Blockbuster Video so that I could communicate meaningfully with Maggie and Jasper? "Are we still hitting the mall later?" she asks.

"For sure," I say gratefully.

Jasper's macaroni makes a squelching noise as he stabs it. Audrey and I giggle with our mouths closed. Jasper smiles too. "It lives," he jokes.

"And dies," Audrey says, pointing to the impaled elbow noodles on Jasper's fork.

The six of us are staring down at Jasper's murdered macaroni and smiling like idiots at the lame joke. "It's actually not bad," he says, holding out his fork. "Anyone want to try?"

"I will." I reach in front of Audrey and take the fork. He's right, it's not bad. Macaroni is one of those foods that's hard to ruin. Jasper smiles at me as I nod. Sometimes it seems so easy to make people happy that I wonder why I don't do it more often.

three

∘   ∘   ∘

AUDreY anD I try on nail polish in Shopper's Drug Mart, a different color on each finger, and then shuffle around clothing stores, laughing at all the hoochie outfits. We stuff our faces with flavored popcorn and flip through ridiculous magazines we'd never pay for—magazines that promise to reveal "The Seven Sex Wishes He Wants You to Grant," "The Even Bigger O: What You Need to Know," and my favorite, "Rock Star Sex: How to Turn a Good Girl Bad."

It's hard to believe anyone could take a word of them seriously, but they do. Not the people that I'll know in London or New York, but almost everyone I know by name right now. Without Audrey I'd be laughing at the idiocy of it all practically solo, and how *unfunny* would that be?

There are times I'd swear that I don't know the actual difference between funny and unfunny or wanting to think about the opposite sex and *not* wanting to think about them. The gaps between the viewpoints blend and shift in my mind only to yank themselves apart and shift again.

The part of me that still thinks about Record Store Guy wants to swing by HMV and flick through CDs. He might come and stand beside me, look over my shoulder, and say something like "Buy their first album instead. I promise, it's much better." He's at least four years older than me and a good few inches taller, probably around six foot two. Long sleeves would be hiding his Celtic armband tattoo, but I'd know it was there. I'd look up at him and imagine tangling my fingers into his curly black hair.

"The first one," I'd repeat thoughtfully. "Really?"

"Mmm, definitely," he'd say. "They completely changed direction after their lead guitarist left the band."

And all the time my mind and body would be memorizing him for future reference. To take out and play with whenever I want. Only I can't do that properly anymore, even when I think I want to. It's been that way for months, and I tell myself it doesn't make any difference but I can't make myself believe it. I don't want to walk into HMV wishing everything could feel as easy as it used to.

"We should catch the next bus," I tell Audrey. "You told your mom you'd be home for dinner." Her stepfather is strict about those things, which means her mother is too. It's a pain, but at the same time there are certain aspects of his strictness that I can understand. When you're a cop, you must be hyperaware of all the bad and dangerous things people do. It's like when something nasty happens to you, and the potential for it to happen again stands out in a hundred different situations where you wouldn't have noticed it before.

We pass by HMV as we walk back through the mall, and the

part of me I was telling you about before glances inside hoping to catch sight of Ryan. "Is he there?" Audrey says, her eyes following mine.

"I don't know." I see him the moment the words are out. "Oh—yeah, he is."

"And you're sure—" Audrey begins.

"I don't know," I say truthfully, tearing my gaze away from the record store and looking at Audrey. "I don't know."

Neither of us stops walking.

The atmosphere at home isn't much tenser than usual. My parents are quiet and look tired. Dad asks how Audrey is and I tell him she's fine. Mom's always saying that I need to expand my circle, but Dad just keeps asking about Audrey, like I'm not a complete freak for having only one true friend.

"I almost forgot," I say suddenly. For once I actually have news Mom will want to hear. "There's this new guy, Jersy, at school. Jersy Mikulski. You used to work with his mother, like, ten years ago."

"Anna Mikulski." Mom's eyebrows fly up towards the ceiling. "Did you get her phone number? I'd love to give her a call."

"I barely spoke to him." I can see where this is going, but there's not a thing I can do about it. Mom won't understand why I don't want to ask Jersy for his home phone number. "I didn't even recognize him until he told me."

"Well, you can pass on our number tomorrow," she says, her voice loud with excitement. "I was thinking of her not too long ago, isn't that funny? You two were just the same age." Mom beams at me. "You and her son. He was a real handful. Made me feel lucky that you were so quiet and well behaved."

"Too bad you don't feel the same way now." I say it like I'm joking, but Dad pushes his chair away from the table.

"Come on, Finn," he says. "Give your old man a hand with the dishes." I know this tone. He's trying to head off an argument between Mom and me, but I'm not in the mood to argue anyway.

I help Dad with the dishes, walk Samsam, finish my homework, IM Audrey, and then climb into bed. At first I'm afraid that I won't be able to sleep again, that I'll repeat last night's performance, but then I hear my parents' bedroom door open. My mom's voice is low and strained. Dad says her name like he's reading a police report: *"Gloria, enough."* There's no feeling behind the words, and I shiver under the covers and keep listening. I listen to the silence for so long that the effort of it makes me want to close my eyes. And that's the last thing I remember.

I pass Adam Porter in the hallway nearly every day. His perfect skin and razor-sharp cheekbones make him look like an actor playing a seventeen-year-old. Most of his friends look like actors too—or sports stars. They walk and talk like they're putting on a drama for the rest of us, and for the most part it works. People watch them. People talk about them. Lots of people want to be them.

But not me. I don't even look at Adam Porter, and he doesn't look at me. When the overcrowded hallways force us close together, he turns his face away from mine like it offends him to look at me. I feel queasy when he does that, but it doesn't show on my face. I'm tough. I'm solid steel. Nothing he does can affect me.

I tell myself that every time, but I still break into a sweat. My underarms are damp by the time I get to art class. I'm glad that Jasper won't shut up. I listen to him as I sketch, nodding at all the right moments. This is all right, I think. I can do this. I'm tough. I'm steel. My lines on the page are definite. I know what I'm doing.

Then somebody rushes by me, bumping my back. I jump, sending my pencil skidding across the page. "Whoa," Jersy says, casting a glance behind him as he continues hastily on towards his seat. "Sorry."

The period is already half over, and Mr. Ferguson shakes his head and grabs the attendance sheet. "Jersy," he says, calling him back. "Don't make yourself comfortable yet."

Jersy slides irritably out of the seat next to Abel's, strides back across the room, and leans down over Mr. Ferguson's desk. Their conversation is a whisper and I practice lipreading while flipping my eraser between my fingers.

"It's not too bad," Jasper says, pointing down at my polluted environmental campaign and breaking my concentration.

"I know," I tell him. "It's just pencil."

By the time I'm through with the eraser, you'll never know it happened. If it was that easy to erase bits of my life, I'd be a different Finn.

My eraser streaks recklessly back across the page, leaving rivers of absence that gleam like fork lightning. I can do better than this. My first thoughts are never right; my first thoughts are pure me. Second thoughts aren't much better.

Jasper coughs as he studies my anti-masterpiece, and right then Jersy swings by behind us again, biting his lip. This brainiac-turned-stoner guy named Billy mutters something to him and Jersy nods, his blue-green eyes looking fed up to the teeth. He manhandles the chair before collapsing into it with his arms crossed.

I didn't intend to pass on our phone number anyway, but now I don't have to feel guilty about it. Jersy needs to be left alone.

"It was good," Jasper says, tapping my page. "What'd you do that for?"

I shrug. "Maybe I'm feeling destructive." Sometimes I can't control what I think or feel. Other times I think about Adam Porter just to prove to myself that I can handle it. He doesn't really have any power over me. How can someone who won't even look at you have any power over you?

Across the room Mr. Ferguson is patting down his gray hair. He messes with his hair so much that it's amazing he still has any. It's so annoying that I want to charge across the room and pin his hands down by his side. I do the next best thing—I watch him until he catches my gaze. His hands float down to his desk as his cheeks tighten. The second he does that I feel bad for him. Why stop on my account?

Sometimes I think so hard that it's a wonder my head doesn't fly off. Like before, when Billy Young made that comment to Jersy, I started remembering all these details about Billy. He was the smartest guy in my seventh-grade class, although he never raised his hand. He threw up before the annual public-speaking contest and then won it by a mile with his speech on Nelson Mandela. This dork girl, Tamyra, used to follow him around the schoolyard, but he was never mean to her. In fact, he used to be equally nice to everyone—before he turned stoner and gave up on the rest of the population.

I sneak a look at Billy, wondering why he changed so much, but Jersy catches me. He mouths something, but I'm already dropping my gaze, pretending that I can't see.

Jasper elbows me and motions towards Jersy. "Your buddy wants something."

By now half the table is watching me, turning my face warm, and I force myself to stare at Jersy straight on, but by the time I do he's already turned away. When the bell rings a few minutes later, the entire class moves in slow motion towards the door. No one's ever in a hurry for art class to be over, and that makes it easy for me to wait for Jersy without being obvious. I don't even know why I'm bothering—unless it's for my six-year-old self.

I feel like an idiot the second I step into the hall. My legs want to rush to civics, but Jersy's right behind me and he's saying, "Hey, Finn, hold up a second."

"Hmm?" I stop and face him, casual as anything.

"You owe me big-time," he says, grinning like a kid trying to hold a secret. I'm completely clueless and it must be written all over my face because he tilts his head and adds, "For not stealing your chair again. The guy next to me thinks he's a fucking Mormon—and here I thought this was Catholic school." He motions to my civics textbook, which is thicker than the Bible but even less interesting. "Can I write in this?"

"Write in it?" I repeat.

"My home phone number." Jersy has his pencil ready and is flipping over the cover. "I told my mom about running into you— she wants your mom to get in touch."

"Okay." I stare down at the digits appearing on the page. "Thanks." I'm so hung up on reading the magic numbers that the burst of laughter from across the hall nearly makes me drop my book. I'd know that laugh anywhere; it's the laugh of a high school superstar, and it makes me sick to my stomach.

I don't look up but I see Adam Porter anyway. He's in my peripheral vision for the second time today. Maybe if I didn't have to look at him all the time I'd be better, or maybe I'm just too weak to get past it. I don't know anymore. My saliva's bitter in my mouth and my fingers jerk, just like Samsam's paws do when he's dreaming.

"Thanks," I repeat, carefully closing my textbook.

"Sure." Jersy gives me one last glance before he ambles off down the hall. He's still too much of a mystery for me to understand what the look means, but if I had to guess I'd say he just figured out that I'm the freakiest girl at St. Mark's.

four

∘ ∘ ∘

MOM DOESN'T WASTE any time calling Mrs. Mikulski. A couple of days later they're drinking herbal tea in our living room, all smiles and cheerful voices. Dad pops his head in to say hello and then excuses himself to grade history papers for his senior class at Archbishop MacNeil. Dad's not the most sociable person in the world. For the most part he's happier spending time with homework assignments than with people. My mom thinks that's why I turned out how I did, not that she's ever said it out loud.

I have to admit I'm a little curious about Mrs. Mikulski, though—and not just because she happens to be Jersy's mother. You can forget a lot in nine years, but I remember her sitting quietly next to her husband at an Eastman company picnic. At the time I wished my mom could be more like her instead of flitting around from group to group, thriving on being the center of attention. It embarrassed me to watch her, and as soon as I realized that, I went and stood beside her, feeling guilty for something she probably hadn't conceived of.

"Come on in, Finn." Mom beckons from the couch. "Say hello to Mrs. Mikulski."

"Anna," Mrs. Mikulski corrects, smiling.

"Hi." I dip my head at her as I step into the living room.

"Finn." Mrs. Mikulski pronounces my name like it's a happy surprise. "You're so grown up."

"Tall," I say, because isn't that what she means?

"That too," Mrs. Mikulski says with a gentle laugh. She turns to my mother. "Where did the time go?"

"It's a surprise to me every time I look at her." Mom shakes her head. "I don't feel old enough to have a fifteen-year-old."

Actually, she's one of the youngest mothers around. She had me when she was almost twenty-one. That's why she never got around to finishing drama school and only starred in a single commercial—a tampon ad about a girl in a yellow bikini at the beach. I watched it a zillion times on video when I was a kid. I was so impressed that I wouldn't be surprised if I played it for Jersy all those years ago.

My heart sinks at the thought of him. Why couldn't he have come along? I know I'm an antisocial weirdo, but should that matter to someone who used to pick his scabs in front of you and throw his arms around you all the time when you were six?

The mental burp surprises me. I shouldn't let myself think about Jersy too much. I have a hard enough time trying to deal with my unrequited crush feelings for Ryan.

"Finn, call your brother, please." Mom sips her tea, waiting for me to do her bidding.

I drag Daniel away from some stupid reality TV show he shouldn't be watching, wondering why no one in this house pays any attention to what he's doing. Then I go up to my room, put Sam Roberts on my sound system, and IM Audrey. Our current record is nine hours and twenty-seven minutes, but I'm sure we'll beat it one day. For two antisocial people we do a lot of typing and talking.

Normally I tell Audrey everything. She knows that I would gladly donate my virginity to Raine Maida if he wasn't married to Chantal. She knows I mean it too (or at least that *months* ago I did mean it), and not because I'm a shallow celebrity whore but because Raine Maida is the most beautiful of all the Beautiful Boys, and that's not just a physical thing.

Everyone knows Audrey and I are like two sides of a coin. Our homeroom teacher even refers to Audrey as my "better half." It's true, she is my better half—more confident, prettier, and three times as talented. I'm so proud that she's my best friend that mostly I don't even think I need anyone else.

Considering all of that, you'd think I'd mention some of the things I've been thinking about Jersy Mikulski, but you'd be wrong.

The weekend is as warm as mid-November, although the calendar says February. Audrey has a raging cold, but I get Dad to drive me over to her house, where she sucks on a succession of Popsicles like it's summer. Her parents like me because I'm quiet around them and never seem to get into any trouble. What they don't understand is that all kinds of people get into trouble without ever meaning to.

Getting into trouble doesn't necessarily make you a bad person. It could just be bad luck. It could be a lot of things. But I don't want my mind slipping onto that track again. I want to sit around eating Popsicles in wintertime with my best friend like there's nothing wrong in the whole world.

Audrey's wearing fuzzy duck slippers and hasn't washed her hair since Thursday, but she smiles at me and says, "Thank God you're here. I'm going crazy cooped up like this. Steven keeps telling me I should be in bed." Steven is the cop stepfather that I mentioned before. Her mom worships him, but he has a way of really dragging Audrey down. "I mean, it's not Ebola, it's the common cold. He should just admit he's a dictator—it would make more sense than pretending he's concerned with my health."

Steven understands Audrey even less than my mother understands me. If he was a different kind of person, he'd have already figured out that it's not worth sweating the small stuff. Unfortunately, the chances of him easing up on Audrey are slim, and I nod sympathetically and ask if she wants to continue in her current state of squalor or if I should help her wash her hair.

"Do I look that bad?" she says, tugging her fingers through a mass of tangles.

"You look like a bundle of sickness," I say truthfully. "You look how I look when I'm sick and don't have the energy to take a shower."

Audrey slouches wearily back against the bed. "That's exactly how I feel—and completely bored with everything. Sometimes I feel like I'm going to be stuck here forever."

I'm permanently bored. Everywhere I go, I see people laughing at things they think are supposed to be funny or buying outfits they hope will make them look like their favorite celebrity. The sameness is enough to bore anyone. But since September everything isn't exactly the same as before. *Remember Adam and me in the laundry room.* That ugly voice in the back of my head won't let it go.

"You're not going to be stuck here," I tell her. "Two and a half more years and you'll be miles away at university."

"Maybe UBC." Audrey perks up a bit as she says that. She keeps changing her mind about where she wants to go to school, and the University of British Columbia is clear across the country. In the future most of our conversations will talk place over IM or a long-distance line. A second's sadness whips through me at the thought. I want the next two and half years to pass at the speed of light—except when it comes to that.

I think of the time, two years ago at the lakefront festival, when we spotted this guy who looked like a younger, tanner version of Gerard Way from My Chemical Romance. He was buying a chili dog and we followed him around for about fifteen minutes, until he noticed and pointed us out to his friend. We got embarrassed and took off, but later we couldn't stop talking about him, and we listened to "Famous Last Words," "I'm Not Okay (I Promise)," and "I Don't Love You" at least three times each (even though Audrey usually says she doesn't like guys in makeup).

I can't imagine that day playing out in exactly the same way with anyone but Audrey. Even though we felt like idiots at first, somehow it still ended up being all right, the way it almost always does when we're together.

"So let's fix my hair," Audrey says, standing up on her duck-head feet. "So I don't feel like a tenth-grade bag lady."

We invade the upstairs bathroom, where I battle with her hair. I think I win—but not by much. I have to use so much conditioner to cut through the tangles that I'm afraid her hair will come out oily. I rinse it for ages, Audrey grumbling steadily away underneath me: "My neck's killing me—do you take this long to wash *your* hair?"

When I wash my own hair I do it fast, but now I'm trying to do a good job. "You're lucky I'm doing this," I joke. "No one else would want to touch your head today."

Afterwards Audrey slides a comb easily through her hair. It's not lank at all—just clean—and she thanks me and says it's perfect. I dry it for her like we're at the hairdresser's, and later, when Audrey climbs back into bed to nurse her Ebola, Mrs. Lepage drives me home.

As I step inside my front door, Samsam careens down the hall towards me as though I'm the most important person in the world. He's such a good dog, and I get down on the ground with him and scratch his ears and stroke his back like I have an eternity to do it. Then I kiss him on top of the head, snap on his leash, and bound outside with him. The truth is that I have the best friend in the universe and the best dog. I try to remind myself of that when I'm feeling low, and when I forget, Samsam reminds me. He lies down in front of me at the foot of the couch or nuzzles his head into my lap like the overgrown puppy that he is.

Between the warm air and Samsam jogging along beside me, I feel free. At times like this I absolutely believe everything's okay with me. The feeling's so strong that I'm amazed I ever have any doubt. My face feels like it's bursting with the strength of a hundred smiles. My body's in tune with the entire universe. I run with Samsam until I can't run anymore, until my legs blur beneath me. Then I slow down, sweating in my winter jacket and struggling to catch my breath. I'm an earth girl after all, not a ray of light or a gust of wind.

It's a beautiful day, though. People smile at us as they pass with their own dogs—pugs, terriers, shepherds, Labs. A family of cyclists weave around Samsam and me, and then, before I have a moment to mentally prepare myself, I'm face to face with Jersy Mikulski pushing a dirt bike up the sidewalk. His coat is hanging open, his jeans are flecked with mud, and his hair looks damp. It's a shock and I don't like how it feels, but that's only because I do.

"Hey," he says, a grin biting into his cheeks. "Who is this?" He kicks the bike's kickstand out, crouches down in front of Samsam and loves him all up. Samsam slurps at Jersy's face, but Jersy doesn't flinch or say that's gross; he just laughs like it's all fantastic.

"Samsam." I shake my head and correct myself. "*Samson.*"

"Which one?" Jersy asks, laughing up at me as he scratches Samsam's ears.

"Both. My brother was really young when we first got him." I graze my fingers across the top of Samsam's head, and he looks up at me, like he knows I'm talking about him. "He couldn't pronounce his name. 'Samsam' was the closest he could get, so we all started calling him Samsam too, you know, because we thought it was cute. I guess it kind of stuck."

Jersy nods and I look down at his brown hair and imagine digging my fingers into it, pulling his head towards mine, and burying my nose in his hair like I do with Samsam. I want to do it so much that it feels like temporary insanity. "This your bike?" I croak.

"Yeah." Jersy stands up next to it and looks into my eyes. His own seem more blue than green in the sunlight, and I blink and drop my right hand down to Samsam's head again so I won't feel like a moron for standing there looking into Jersy's eyes like I'm searching for the meaning of life or something.

"Your mom came over," I say.

"I heard." Jersy rubs his eyes like he's tired. "They used to be really good friends."

"I know." Maybe if his family never moved away, they'd still be good friends now. Maybe we'd be friends or something too. But that's a stupid thing to think. I don't even know what he's like—except that he's been sitting with Billy Young in art class for the past few days. Does that make him a stoner?

"So, Finn," Jersy says, abruptly changing his tone and bending his head towards mine, "do you have a thing for Billy Young?"

"Billy Young?" I repeat incredulously. Now I sound like a parrot. A parrot that's searching for the meaning of life in Jersy Mikulski's eyes. "We've said, like, two words to each other since seventh grade."

"So what were the two words?" He smiles widely, all impressed with himself.

I bulge my eyes out at him like he's being an idiot. "Does Billy Young think I have a thing for him?"

Jersy shrugs. "I don't know what he thinks. I've just seen you checking him out lately."

"I'm not checking him out." I don't know where my calm tone comes from, but I definitely appreciate it. "I was just thinking about him. He used to be really different. I just wondered what happened—to make him the way he is now."

"What's wrong with the way he is now?" Jersy asks. The way he says it makes me wonder if I'm acting freakish again, but there's nothing I can do about it. It's not like I can tell him the truth. I'm not ready to feel this way about Jersy. Even if I knew him better. Even if there was a chance he'd feel the same. I just can't.

"Nothing. It's just different." I'm getting tired of explaining. It only makes me sound even weirder.

"People change," Jersy says, cocking his head. "Look at you, you've changed too."

I don't know what he means by that, but I nod. "I barely even remember what I was like back then."

"Man." Jersy shakes his head. "You always wanted to play some wild game. Something with alien invasions or ghosts. It used to scare the shit out of me." He laughs at the memory.

"No way. You weren't scared of anything. You were always doing something crazy—jumping off buildings and holding your breath in the pool."

"Buildings?" Jersy wrinkles his eyebrows. "That's Superman, Finn. It was stairs, wasn't it? That time I messed up my ankle?"

"It was stairs," I agree, the memory shifting slowly back into focus. He tried to tackle a whole flight at his parents' house while we were there for dinner one night—almost made it too. "The point is, you were psycho."

"You were psycho," he jokes, bending down to pet Samsam all over again. "I was a normal kid."

"Yeah, you just keep telling yourself that," I say.

He smirks as he gets up. I don't want him to go yet, but I can sense the conversation coming to an end. Jersy kicks his kickstand up as he grabs the handlebars. "Don't worry," he says slyly. "I won't tell Billy you're crazy and ruin your chances." He starts pushing his bike again, then looks back at me over his shoulder. "See you Monday."

five

○   ○   ○

DAD AND DANIEL are at the Y when Gran calls on Sunday afternoon. My sixty-eight-year-old grandmother has a heart of gold. That's what everyone says about her. She never pries into other people's business or offers unwanted advice, and she has the even kind of voice that makes you want to trust her, especially over a long-distance line. I know because I almost confessed an awful secret to her four months ago. I thought my heart was going to burst out of my chest or that my lungs would collapse. I thought I was standing at a point where everything would change.

Then another phone call came through on call waiting—some woman with a heavy Italian accent wanting me to take a nutrition survey. I was halfway through the thing, in a kind of daze, when I got a call from Gran, wondering why I'd deserted her on the other line.

This is the kind of thing that happens to me a lot, even with the iron pills. But the truth is, I didn't entirely forget about Gran on the phone; I changed my mind and couldn't go through with what I was about to say. Now whenever she calls, I make sure to get her talking about her friend Veronica's Alzheimer's or her other two grandchildren, who live lots closer to her than we do. I don't allow for any quiet time over the phone during which I could get stupid ideas.

But Mom's the one who answers the phone when the original Fionnuala, my grandmother, calls on Sunday. I'm sprawled out on the sofa eating a bagel iced with red pepper cream cheese, half listening to the one side of the conversation I can hear, when Mom walks out of the family room with the cordless pressed to her ear. I think I hear her voice crack in the hall.

Her throat could be dry or it could be my imagination, but I flick on the TV and hike up the volume, just in case. I watch videos for close to an hour, until I'm nearly sure it's safe, and then I head into the kitchen to rummage around for Popsicles. It's deranged to eat Popsicles in winter, I know, but watching Audrey yesterday must've put me in the mood. My head's buried in the fridge when Mom steps into the kitchen wearing her favorite perfume, looking like an Elizabeth Arden ad come to life. I'm afraid to examine her too closely, but I skim a look over my shoulder and say, "So how's Gran?"

"I'm sorry," Mom says absently. "I should've put you on to speak to her." Gran lives five and a half hours north of Glenashton, which means we don't see her very often. Between Veronica, the two cousins I mentioned, plus an unmarried daughter who can barely afford them, Gran has her hands full. My grandmother doesn't like to complain, but my dad must seem like a golden boy in comparison.

Mom swings the top cupboard open and pulls out a box of wheat crackers. "Why don't you pig out on Oreos like a normal person?" I ask. Her snacks are strictly crackers or yogurt. I've never once seen her chomp into a Krispy Kreme doughnut or a Mars bar.

"I'm not fifteen anymore," Mom says. "They'd go straight to my hips."

My mother has perfect hips, not too bony or too big. I think it'd take more than a couple Oreos on a Sunday afternoon to destroy that, but what do I know, I *am* fifteen and I don't have hips like that.

Dad and Daniel burst into the house before I can contradict her. Samsam barks and follows them into the kitchen, wagging his tail like a wild thing. He's happiest when we're all together, and he's so happy now that it makes me smile. It's the happiest I've felt since yesterday's natural high. Seeing Jersy out there was good too. It reminded me of the way I used to feel when Record Store Guy would sidle up to me in HMV. The hair-smelling thing was new, though, and thinking about it makes me feel good-crazy all over again. It feels so fantastic that it seems wrong to be fantasizing about in my kitchen, surrounded by my family.

"I'm gonna call Audrey," I announce, dashing into the hall. "See how she's feeling."

I don't know what I'm really going to do when I get upstairs, only that I'm burning up with Jersy thoughts. My room is cold, how I like it, and I want to savor the good feeling now that I'm alone, but it's already changing.

Downstairs a door slams. I go over to the window and stare down at my father in his black turtleneck, gazing past our melting front yard. My mother comes out after him. She stands directly in front of him, her arms knotted against her chest. It's like watching TV on mute, only there's nothing to hear because no one says anything. My dad turns and goes inside, but Mom keeps staring at that empty space like something else is supposed to happen.

I'm tired of eavesdropping and spying. Whatever's wrong between them isn't shrinking, and I've already seen and heard more than I should. Couldn't they pretend, at least while they're around Daniel and me, that everything's all right? It's like they're not even trying.

"Am I supposed to keep this all a secret?" Mom shouts from her place at the door. "Are you a robot, Alan? Do you feel anything?"

Our neighbors will talk. A familiar gush of embarrassment bobs up and down in my stomach as I stare at Mom's blond head.

I hear the door open and watch her hesitate. Long seconds pass and then she steps inside. I tiptoe to my door and ease it open. My bedroom is closest to the front door, and I hear Dad's voice. "You have no right to discuss any of this with my mother. I don't know what you think you're trying to do, but this is between you and me."

"What's between you and me?" Mom asks. "I don't even know anymore."

"You're pushing me away." Dad's voice is controlled, but I sense the anger. "Everything you do is pushing me. You've made it impossible, and now you're making it unbearable."

"You won't even talk about it," Mom intones. "Emotionally, you haven't been here in months. It's like we don't even exist in the same space. If we didn't have the kids around, we'd never even have a simple conversation, would we?" She lets out a sob that makes my eyes sting. I press my head against the doorjamb and wait for my father's voice. He'll comfort her now, won't he? Otherwise how will this end?

But there are no more voices, just the sound of Dad's footsteps on the stairs. I shut my door so we won't have to look each other in the face. My eyeballs feel like they've been sprinkled with salt, but I don't know whether I'm more angry or sad. How can they be so selfish? Don't Daniel and I count for anything?

I slide Liz Phair into my stereo and play "Good Love Never Dies" as loud as my eardrums can stand, even though I know I don't have an ounce of control over what my parents are doing to all of us. I crawl into bed and sing along in my head as my eyes fizz and my throat swells up. Today "Good Love Never Dies" is the longest song in the world.

Audrey's better by Monday, but not altogether cured. She stands at my locker blowing her nose and explaining that she didn't have the energy to finish her science homework over the weekend. We don't need to discuss yesterday's "Good Love Never Dies" episode. We've already been through it over IM last night, not that there was really anything new to say—except that this time my parents ate dinner in shifts.

"Mr. Savin always comes around and checks our homework," Audrey continues, cramming her tissue into her sleeve. "He deducts two percent if you're not done."

"That's nothing," I tell her. It's not like Audrey to worry about a measly two percent. We're not brainiacs, after all, and your tenth-grade marks don't count for anything.

"I know. But it's so annoying. It's like we're in second grade or something." She frowns. "What does it matter if we finish our homework every single time—so long as we know what we're doing?"

Okay, so now I know what's getting to her. It's too much like something stepdad Steven, obsessed with checks and balances (and common colds and criminals), would do.

"Show him last week's homework instead," I suggest. "I bet he won't know the difference."

Audrey's eyes light up. "You're devious. Have you ever actually done that?"

"Once—and it worked too."

Audrey nods like she's impressed. "It's worth a try."

Of course it is. I shove *The Great Gatsby* under my arm, grab my pencil case, and slam my locker shut. When I look up, Jersy Mikulski's standing beside me, hair falling into his eyes, yawning so wide that I could count his teeth. "Shit, I can't keep my eyes open," he says wearily. "Give me a nudge if I fall asleep in art today, would you? It'll give you a reason to get close to Billy too." His left hand brushes against my arm. "See how I'm helping you out."

I grind my teeth, mostly because this is the kind of reaction he's expecting, and say, "I do NOT have a thing for Billy Young."

Audrey blinks next to me, trying to figure it all out. "She doesn't, you know. You're way off base."

"Off base?" He scratches his head, messing his hair up worse than ever. "Really?" He leans against the locker next to mine and looks at her in a way that makes me jealous. It's not even anything as specific as lust, just interest. But I don't want Jersy to even be aware of Audrey's existence; I want him all to myself. It's completely moronic and I know it.

"Hey, you're in my science class," Audrey notes. "Did you finish the homework?"

"Mostly." Jersy nods. "You want to borrow it?"

"That'd be great." Audrey smiles at him as he hands it over. "Thanks. You're a lifesaver."

"Yeah?" Jersy's eyes land back on me. "Finn says I'm psychotic."

"*Were* psychotic," I correct. *Whatever.* I look over at Audrey, who is smiling at Jersy like her life depends on it, and suddenly feel like a giant on stilts. I'm the kooky friend. That's my function here and I hate it.

"This is Jersy," I mumble in Audrey's general direction. "In case you didn't know."

"Right," he says. "And you're Audrey?" He already knows her name. I want to climb into my locker and close the door behind me.

"Yup." Audrey shows off her teeth: straight and white. She's not pretty in the obvious blond-bombshell way, but what she has going for her is better. It doesn't depend on makeup, hair dye, or lighting. She flips her dark ringlets over her shoulder as she says, "So what do you think of St. Mark's?"

Jersy laughs. "Not much."

I wonder if he means that like Audrey and I do or if it's just the smart-ass thing to say, but I just bite my thumbnail and try not to stare at him too much.

Audrey gives him the benefit of the doubt. She leans against my locker, her posture his mirror image, and says, "Wait till you're here a few months—you'll hate it more every moment."

Jersy nods like he knows exactly what she means. He detaches himself slowly from the locker, giving me a final glance. "Remember, I'm counting on you today," he says. "Don't let me nod off in art. Ferguson already has it in for me."

"See you last period," Audrey says.

"Later," Jersy says, and then he's gone.

"God." Audrey slumps back against my locker, instantly deflating. " 'See you last period.' " She repeats it like it's the lamest phrase in the English language, like she's saying "I just wet my pants." Audrey pulls her tissue out of her sleeve and swipes at her nose. "I'm such an idiot."

"What's wrong with 'See you last period'?" I ask.

Audrey does drama much better than I do. She presses her

eyelids shut and whispers, "I'm sinking." We've used that phrase so much in the past year (for even the most remotely embarrassing episodes) that it's lost all significance, but in this case it genuinely seems to apply.

"It's fine," I assure her. "You're being a drama queen." I could point out that he already knew her name and that I'm so obviously just the wacky friend here that it hurts, but I'm not feeling as generous as I could be.

"It sounds like I'm counting the minutes," Audrey explains.

I fold my arms loosely in front of me and remind myself that this is my very best friend. "So you like him?" *I'm sinking.*

"I don't know him—he wasn't even talking to me. I was practically invisible here beside you." She's completely sincere, and that makes me feel like an evil stepsister. "What was all that about Billy Young anyway? Is that supposed to be a joke?"

"No idea." I shrug. "He's psycho, remember?" I begin to fill her in on all the stuff I remember from Jersy's daredevil years.

"Was he that hot when he was six?" she interrupts, her face scrunching up like she's in physical pain. *"Moron,"* she says emphatically. "Moron question."

"He was every six-year-old's dream." I adjust *The Great Gatsby* under my arm and attempt a straight answer. "He was okay, I guess—I mean, he was just a kid. We went swimming and stuff."

Audrey smoothes down her kilt and looks straight up into my eyes. "Do you like him? I mean, it's not like I'm going to jump him in science last period, but is he available as a lust object?"

"Audrey, I don't even know him. I've spoken to him maybe twice." I make that sound more casual than I feel because I have no intention of standing in her way. The complexity of doing anything more than staring at Jersy makes me feel claustrophobic and defective.

"And you're dedicated to Record Store Guy, right?" Audrey's eyes dance, and I think of all the times I imagined losing my virginity to Ryan. He's not Raine Maida but he's definitely a Beautiful Boy. Even now my chest aches faintly while thinking about him.

"In that pathetic worshiping-him-from-afar way, yeah." I'm only partly joking, but Audrey smiles. "It's cool," I tell her. "Go lust after Psycho Boy."

"Cool." Audrey grins with her whole face. "But if I'm gonna lust after him, he can't be Psycho Boy, okay? It's too weird."

"Okay," I tell her, and the minute I say it I know this is going to be different. Audrey could never all-out fall for someone called Psycho Boy. That's why he has to be plain old Jersy.

six

MY PARENTS KEEP the musical chairs game going for three more days. On the fourth, when Dad sits down to dinner across from Mom, I feel like someone walked over my grave. They keep Daniel and me busy talking to cover their tension, but I feel it anyway. I'm relieved when dinner is over, and as I scoop up plates Mom announces that she's going over to Anna's house for tea. "Finn and I can handle the cleanup," Dad offers.

"Actually, I thought Finn might want to come along," Mom says, raising her eyebrows hopefully as she turns towards me. "You can see your old friend."

"He's not really my friend," I protest. "I barely speak to him."

"But you were great friends," Mom says. "You always used to want to come with me when I stopped by Anna's."

"That was a long time ago," Dad tells her, carrying dirty glasses over to the sink. "Just because you want to go doesn't mean she does, Gloria." Dad never sides with me when Mom's involved; he's usually the one who tries to stop us from fighting. It's a small thing, but the change catches me off guard. Things could get worse. Where does it end?

Mom stands in the middle of the kitchen looking defeated. "Anna said you were welcome to come. I didn't think I was dragging you along—just offering."

"I didn't say you were dragging me." They're not going to fight over this. I may not have control over many things, but this situation is one of them. "I just don't want Jersy to think he has to hang out with me if he doesn't want to. That's all."

"Anna already mentioned it to him." Mom pushes a stray hair back with her palm. "Of course it's up to you, Finn."

Dad's crashing the dirty dishes around in the sink, making more noise than he has to. Daniel's on his feet, hurrying out of the room before Dad can ask him to dry. Anything I say now will be wrong. "Fine." I put my hands on my hips and stare at Dad's rigid back. "Let's go."

Five minutes later we're walking up to the Mikulski house. Mom makes me hold the housewarming gift, ensuring that I feel more awkward than necessary, and rings the doorbell.

"Hi." The girl standing in the open doorway has cropped white-blond hair and is a few years older than me but miles shorter. Her khaki cargo pants have to be three inches longer than her legs, but everything else is in proportion.

Anna appears in the doorway behind her, opens the door wider, and motions for us to come in. "Christina, you remember Gloria and her daughter, Finn?"

"Sure," Christina says. We exchange shy smiles. I'm surprised to see her. I figured she'd be away at university.

I hand over the housewarming gift and Anna takes our coats. "Show Finn downstairs, would you, honey?" she says.

Christina nods and leads the way, glancing over her shoulder at me. "So you go to the same school as Jersy?" She's so pretty that it's hard not to stare. She was always pretty, I guess, but that's not the first thing you notice when you're six.

"Yeah, St. Mark's." My voice bristles with bitterness, and Christina laughs. Her laugh sounds like a female version of Jersy's, and that makes me even more self-conscious.

"Sounds fantastic." She opens the basement door, and I step in after her. Downstairs Jersy's sprawled out on the couch with his eyes shut and his hands tucked into his underarms. Beyoncé's bopping around the TV, "Crazy in Love," and I want to climb back upstairs and sit in the car until Mom's ready to leave. This is the last place on earth I should be after what Audrey told me.

Christina bends down and taps Jersy's arm. "Wake up."

But Jersy must be in a coma or something, because he doesn't budge. A beeping noise chirps behind us, and Christina slides her hand into her back pocket and pulls out her cell phone. "Text message," she tells me, punching the keys. "Hold on a sec."

I balance myself on the couch's arm and stare vacantly at Beyoncé. Jersy's feet are within easy reach, and he's so still that I'm tempted to touch him. I look down at his legs, commanding myself to keep my hands to myself, and when I switch my gaze to his face, his eyes are staring back at mine. "How long have you been there?" he asks.

"Not long." I look at Christina behind me.

"Great," she says, her gaze taking in the now conscious Jersy. "I'll see you later, Finn." Her feet are on the stairs before I can say goodbye.

"Later," I shout after her, and then it's just Jersy, Beyoncé, and me. "This song sucks," I tell him, motioning to the TV.

His hands are still stuck in his armpits, and he blinks like I'm being a pain. "So who do you like—white guys with British accents who stand around with guitars?"

There's nothing wrong with British accents and guitars, but I don't say so. I don't want him to think he knows something about me after two conversations. I watch him root around under the cushions for the remote and hum to himself as he peers under the couch.

"I lose things all the time," he admits finally, collapsing back onto the couch in a semi-upright position. "I still don't know where half my stuff is since the move." He pulls at one of his sleeves, working his entire hand inside it.

A chill begins in the base of my spine as I stare at the disappearing hand. *Everything is fine,* I tell myself. *You're fine. Nothing ever happened in the first place.* But the chill takes hold. It could slide into panic if I'm not careful. *You're all right. Everything is fine.*

And then it is. Christina must've left the door open; I can vaguely make out our moms' voices in the background, and the sound brings a rush of relief. It's true. I am all right.

"So why'd you move anyway?" I ask. I'm terrible at small talk at the best of times. It has nothing to do with lacking iron.

"Are you gonna sit down?" Jersy asks.

I'm so tense I'd forgotten I was perched on the armrest. "Sure," I say, sliding down next to him. One second I want to apologize for being awkward, and the very next I feel defensive. I have no idea how to be alone with guys. I've always been shitty at that, but now rooms become too small. Minutes are endless. On top of that, I can count on one hand the ones worth talking to.

It's all so exhausting and sad that I pull my legs up onto the couch with me, bury my face in them, and mumble, "I think my parents are about to split up."

Jersy's head drops. The basement lighting is so bad that I can't make out the color of his eyes. They still look pretty, though. Some people don't like to use that word for guys, but I swear that's how they look. His body is lean but it looks strong. I'm sure he's stronger than me, and I'm so confused, so full of wanting and bad feelings, that my eyes begin to leak.

I stop myself quick but not quite fast enough to avoid Jersy's detection. His hand grazes my shoulder as his head tilts towards mine. "I thought that about my parents last year. They fought so much I almost wanted them to split up."

"So it's no big deal, right?" I smile bravely. "It happens all the time."

"Yeah," Jersy says, nodding. "But not to you." He leans into the pillows. "If they're really going to do it, they'll tell you."

He's right, but I don't want to be the last to know. If I can get used to it before it actually happens, maybe the reality won't hurt so much. That's too personal to say out loud, though. "So your parents are okay now?" I ask. "It stopped?"

"Yeah, they still fight sometimes, but not like then. There was all this stress they were going through, all this shit." Jersy's cheeks hollow out. "Come on. I want to show you something." He jumps off the couch and waits for me to follow.

Seconds later we're in his bedroom. It's cluttered with packing boxes and smells like a warehouse. The walls are bare, but there's a collection of photos stuck to his mirror—mostly of him and some other guys in a skateboard park. A Chinese girl with long raven hair stars in a row of photo booth snaps. Jersy's in the very last one, with his lips pressed against her cheek. She's beaming into the camera like she knows she's special.

I take all that in during the first few seconds—even before I see the tank. "His name's Gizmo," Jersy says fondly, bending down in front of the miniature habitat. With his leopard spots and orange skin, Gizmo is definitely one of the better-looking reptiles I've seen, but I hope Jersy's not planning on asking me to hold him.

Jersy plucks the metal screen off the top of the tank, herds Gizmo into his hand, and holds him up in front of me. "Wow," I say, looking into Gizmo's blinking eyes. "It's like he can really see us."

"Of course he can see us," Jersy says.

"How old is he?" I skim my fingers across Gizmo's back. He doesn't seem to mind.

"Three." Jersy deposits him carefully back in the tank. "They can live to twenty."

"Wow," I say again. That's longer than my dog. Somehow it doesn't seem fair. I sit down on the bed before I realize what I'm doing. Jersy sits on the far end, rubbing his eyes and yawning.

"So why're you so tired all the time?" I ask. I'm glad that we're not talking about my parents anymore. It feels okay to be up here with him, despite the weird smell and Gizmo's beady eyes blinking at us like he knows exactly what's going on.

"I'm a bad sleeper." Jersy touches his scar, slowly, like he's smoothing away an eyelash. "I get into these phases where I'm wide-awake in the middle of the night. Nothing I can do about it. Just wired, you know? It'd be okay if I could sleep late, but I can't—not during the week. That's why I was late for art that day. Overslept."

"Insomnia," I say.

"Isn't that when you can't sleep at all?" Jersy sits up straighter. "It's more like I have my timing backwards."

"How long do the phases last?"

"I don't know." Jersy pauses to give it some thought. "Maybe six weeks."

"That's a long time to have your schedule inside out," I tell him. "You know what happens to people who don't get enough sleep, right? They go crazy."

"Yeah." Jersy shrugs. "I'm already psycho, though."

"That's true. You could be beyond help." I'd never say that if I thought it was true. He's fine the way he is. Even if he is a stoner.

Jersy smiles. "Could be. Could even be contagious. Maybe you should keep your distance."

"Yeah." I get off the bed and look through his window. Snowflakes the size of golf balls are drifting gently down from the sky. Everything looks so safe in the snow. It's almost like a cocoon. "There are mutant snowflakes out here," I say, turning to look at him.

Jersy comes to the window and peers out next to me. "Feels like Christmas," he says. "We should go outside."

He stands sideways like he's ready to go, and I raise my eyebrows and say, "Seriously?"

"Yeah, seriously," he repeats. "Why not?"

Because I don't like my cold quite so chilly. The controlled cold of my bedroom is one thing; arctic chills that make your bones freeze and break off like twigs are something else. The thing is, I really do love the snow. It makes the ordinary look beautiful and pure, like you're seeing it through different eyes. "Okay then," I tell him.

We shove our shoes on and go out through the sliding door in the kitchen. The backyard has a swimming pool in it, but it's impossible to imagine summer. The snow's coming down so thick and soft that Jersy and I are already covered in fuzz. I fold my arms in front of me and hunch over, doing my best to hold on to my body heat. It's quiet the way only winter can be, and I'm almost afraid to say anything, in case words ruin it.

"It's like the inside of a snow globe," Jersy says, smiling and hunching over next to me. I look at his breath on the air and nod.

We stand silently watching the snow fall for as long as I can stand it. The hazy orange lights from other houses seem miles away. It feels like we're the only people on the planet, Jersy and me. It's weird. He's so quiet next to me, but that only makes him feel more real and near.

I sneak another look at him, for safekeeping. If I had more guts, maybe I'd do something more.

Shit.

Trust me to ruin the moment for myself without even saying a word.

seven

DANIEL AND I are the opposite of twins, whatever that is. He's addicted to *The Simpsons, South Park,* and nauseatingly stupid reality TV shows. He loves wrestling, video games, and rock climbing at the Y and avoids all creative activities like the plague. It seriously makes me wonder about genetics.

If he was a Mini-Me, I'd probably be more worried about how he's handling the situation with my parents, but I don't understand him at all. Maybe I'm a crappy, self-obsessed older sister. That does occur to me from time to time, and when I get back from the Mikulskis' I decide it's time for an official check-in with Daniel.

Because we have limited points of reference, this is clumsy and obvious. I sit next to him on the couch and listen to Cartman screech at Kyle and Stan on *South Park.* The show's actually pretty funny, in small doses, and I laugh and groan at the same time. But the longer you wait to do something, the harder it is. That's why I force myself to say something as soon as the commercials come on. "Mom and Dad are driving me crazy." I spy on Daniel out of the corner of my eye. He's not looking at me; he's staring at a dog food commercial like he's hypnotized.

"Doesn't it bug you?" I prod.

Daniel shrugs and kicks his feet out in front of him. "I don't know."

"But we don't have any peace anymore," I continue. "It's like we never know when one of them is going to snap."

"Dad doesn't snap," Daniel says.

"Not like Mom, no, but he changes." I turn my head towards my baby brother, the Anti-Me, and catch him chewing his lip.

"You shouldn't listen in," he says accusingly, as though somehow this is all my fault. "That's rude."

"You're rude," I tell him, flashing angry eyes in his direction. "I'm just sitting here talking to you, and you're starting to freak out."

"You don't even like this show." Daniel's eyes narrow. "Why're you sitting here?"

"Like I can't sit here all of a sudden. This is my house too, you know." *At least until our folks break up, split custody, and take one of us to live in another town.* It's on the tip of my tongue to say it, just to get a reaction, but I'm not feeling that mean.

South Park fills the screen, and we both face forward and watch the rest of the show without saying another word. What do I expect of the Anti-Me anyway? I wouldn't know what to do with him if he started to cry like I did at Jersy's.

In the lunch line the next day, I tell Audrey about my trip to Jersy's house. I tell her about everything except the snow falling in the backyard. I even tell her about the crying. "At least he was cool about it," she says. "I didn't know he had a sister. He never mentioned her."

So she's been talking to him in science class. If something's going to happen between them, I want to get it over with. I don't want her to go on about him the way I went on about Record Store Guy. Or maybe he could turn into a prick and make us both hate him. That'd be even better.

At our table Edwardo and Teresa are sharing a plate of soggy fries while Maggie flips through *In Touch* magazine. Her head snaps up when she sees Audrey and me. "Aidan Lamb is getting married," she coos, "to his longtime girlfriend." She shoves the magazine at us as we sit down. "Look at her. She looks so normal. She teaches kindergarten. Isn't that amazing?"

"Mmm." I squint at their photo, pretending to be interested.

"He's not really that good-looking himself, though, is he?" Audrey says. "His forehead is huge, and his eyes always look kind of crazy, like he's high."

Sacrilege. Maggie's eyebrows arch. "You're kidding, right? He says he barely even drinks. Did you see *Summer Cold*?"

"No," Audrey says. "Is it any good?"

"Awesome." Maggie's mouth drops. "You have to watch it. Both of you." She fixes her stare on me. "He's the most amazing character in it. So sweet."

"Sweet?" Jasper repeats, sitting down next to her. "Who's sweet this time?"

Maggie slides *In Touch* in front of him and taps the photo. "Aidan Lamb in *Summer Cold*."

"Ugh," Jasper groans, disgusted. "That's such a chick movie, Maggie. Total saccharine. He's completely unconvincing in it. I've seen better performances in infomercials. Honestly, Mags. Sometimes I don't know what we're going to do with you."

Maggie, clearly insulted, reclaims her magazine, but Jasper bumps her shoulder affectionately and says, "Who else is in there this week?"

Maggie's so easily won over. She hands him back the magazine and watches him flip intently through the pages. Jasper is more interested in movies than he is in actors, but there's a certain amount of overlap. Audrey and Teresa, who are both in his drama class, say he's a pretty good actor, but Jasper thinks he could be a *great* critic.

I hope I can be a great graphic designer, but I'd settle for being a good one. Sometimes it feels as much like a compulsion as it does a career choice. I can spend hours redesigning a CD or book cover, just because I think I could've done a better job. My Web page is forever under construction with new color schemes and layouts. At the moment it's minimalist, with a royal purple background and a tiny white font, but that look's already getting old to my eyes.

Edwardo and Teresa are still picking at their fries. At times they can be so into themselves that I almost forget they're around. Other days you'd hardly guess they were a couple. Maybe that's normal, but it feels kind of funny to sit across from two people, never knowing how they're going to be.

"So what are you guys doing this weekend?" I ask tentatively.

Edwardo's working and Teresa has to go to her cousin's engagement shower, but they'll get together to watch a movie or something on Sunday night.

Maggie starts to go gaga all over again at the mention of an engagement. It makes me want to tear her hair out, but I know that's only because I'm bored. Also, my chicken fingers taste like cardboard and I think I'm getting my period.

I spent the years twelve to fourteen dutifully marking Xs on my calendar and then realized my period would roll up any damn time it wanted to. Cramps, check. Bloating, check. *Wonderful.* I'll have to drop by my locker to pick up my stash of sanitary pads.

I excuse myself. Lunch is almost over. I already know I won't make it back in time.

Pads. Bathroom. Period. Yup, I was right. *Wonderful.*

Afterwards I walk slowly in the direction of English class and run into Audrey and Jersy together in the hall. I'm embarrassed about losing it in front of him the other day, but I've already decided that I won't act weird about it and make things stranger. Anyway, the real problem is that he and Audrey look so natural together that I feel like an outsider. Like it's *them* and *me.*

"Hey, Finn," Jersy says. He looks more like a Beautiful Boy every day. He's too short and it wouldn't surprise me if he wore baseball hats, but other than that he's perfect. I can't believe I didn't notice it that first day in art. He's got the good-bone-structure thing going on like crazy, and his gorgeous aqua-colored eyes are killing me. He even makes the gray uniform pants look half decent, and his lips, well, I could spring towards him in the hallway and lick him on the mouth. That's how good he looks.

It's insane.

And then it gets worse. Adam Porter saunters by with Massy at his side. Adam's taller than any of us. His body is more man than boy, and I shrink when I see him, shrink like I'm being squeezed. He smirks in our direction. Just long enough for us to get the point. I freeze on the inside and snap my head away.

Audrey's so angry that I can almost see her shaking. Her hazel eyes hold my gaze. They're the only things keeping me in place. I want to throw up until I feel normal again, but I stand rooted to the spot. Audrey is my courage.

"What's your problem?" Jersy says, cocking his head at Adam.

Adam shrugs like it's no big thing, like he could just as easily let it go. "Hey, man, if you want to hang around with loser girls, that's your business."

Adam falls instantly back into his stride, but Jersy's fuming. He starts off after Adam, and I can see it in my head—kicking, punching, and blood. It shocks me how fast aggression breaks the surface in boys. My heart's racing and the tiny hairs on my arms are standing on end. This shouldn't happen but I can't stop it. My legs have forgotten how to move.

"Jersy, don't," Audrey says, running after him. "He's not worth it."

Jersy turns as she grabs his arm. His eyes are blazing, and I know she won't be able to stop him. Adam and Massy are looking back over their shoulders, and I know they know it too.

"Leave it," Audrey pleads. She's still holding his arm, and she leans her head in real close to his and drops her voice. "Please, Jersy. Don't. Okay?" I can't hear the next part, but I watch his shoulders relax and his eyes go calm. He nods slowly at her and then shrugs lightly, as though he wasn't set on doing anything anyway.

The two of them trek back across the hall towards me. My face feels as white as Jasper's, and for a second I think I really might throw up. Then Audrey stands next to me and loops her arm through mine, feeding me strength.

Didn't I tell you that I have the best friend in the universe?

NINTH GRADE WAS everything that I expected it to be: nothing much, really. A lot of people I knew in eighth grade looked at it as a chance to reinvent themselves. Skaters came back to school as skinny emo boys. Brainiacs tried their best to blend with the dramaheads. Filipina girls suddenly hooked up with gangsta guys. Beautiful people, for the most part, just tried to hold their place. There are a limited number of places at the top of the school chain, and if someone else is suddenly super hot, that means less attention to go around.

Not that all the popular people were shamelessly cutthroat. Some genuinely didn't seem to care about social structure, and according to Audrey, a tenth-grade basketball player named Massy was one of them. Her locker was right next to his homeroom, and by the end of April she was seriously gone on him. "It's like suddenly he's everywhere," she told me. She'd run into him in the hall all day long, see him stocking shelves at the grocery store, even bump into him at the dentist's office. One afternoon her stepdad dropped her off to get a cavity filled, and Massimo was in the waiting room. The dentist was running late, and they sat there talking for an hour, although they'd never officially spoken before.

Audrey hoped that could be the beginning of something, but then summer came and she didn't see him for two and a half months. "All the momentum from that conversation will be gone," she complained. "It'll be like starting from scratch, and he'll probably come back with a girlfriend anyway. Somebody like Kaitlynn James."

"Kaitlynn James has horrible skin," I said loyally. "No way he's hooking up with her. She'd get Clearasil all over his basketball uniform." Mean, sure, but the beautiful people are easy targets—especially when they aren't beautiful to start with. Besides, I'd never say that to her face. I didn't even dislike Kaitlynn James that much. I just wanted Massy to be with Audrey instead.

Truthfully, I didn't even want that. I couldn't see what was so special about him, except that he wasn't an obvious snob. I never really thought there was any danger of him being interested in Audrey, though; I didn't give him enough credit for that. Then September came and Massimo surprised us both. He wasn't with Kaitlynn—he wasn't with anyone—and he asked Audrey if she wanted to go to Sadie and Brian Nielsen's party. Open invitation. Bring whoever you want.

"It doesn't really mean anything," she told me. "There'll be so many people there, we may not even see him."

"Of course you'll see him," I said. "It's not like he's going around asking everyone."

"All those PAs." Audrey groaned anxiously. "Do you really think we should go?"

"You need to keep up the momentum, right?" It sounded like

a nightmare. Pack Animals getting pissed out of their minds, screwing in Mr. and Mrs. Nielsen's bed and then vomiting partially digested beer into the bathtub. Disgusting.

"Yeah." Audrey combed her fingers through her hair. "You're right."

Was I? I wanted to be wrong.

"So you'll go?" she said.

"Yeah, as long as you want me to."

"Are you serious?" Audrey cried. "Of course I want you to go. There's no way I'm even showing up unless you come with me. It'd be a disaster without you. I won't know anybody. There probably won't be that many tenth graders there, and even if there are, they won't be anybody I'd talk to."

She was already nervous, and the party was still five days away. Things were easier for me. I wasn't looking to impress anyone; I just wanted to get through the night.

My mom shone when I told her about the party. She took me out to buy new clothes, even though I protested that I didn't need anything special. I cringe when I remember those details now. How excited Mom was for me. How she made Dad give me a later curfew than he wanted to. She thought it was finally starting for me, that I was on my way to becoming an "It" girl. She seemed prouder about the party invitation than she was of my last report card.

I tried to defuse her enthusiasm by explaining that it was Audrey who'd been invited and that I was only going to keep her company because of Massimo. Then Mom wanted to know more about Massy. I only had to mention the word "basketball" and she regressed twenty years. Wasn't there anybody special I liked? In the entire school there must be someone?

Nope. St. Mark's was full of guys with buzz cuts who spent the summer in sandals and baggy shorts, using the word "shitfaced."

"You're so hard on people," Mom said, frowning. "At least allow the possibility that you might have a good time."

With people I can't stand. Sure.

I just hoped Audrey's stepdad would pick us up before the sex and vomiting started in earnest. Steven didn't want her going to the party, but my mom made it sound so innocent over the phone. She can be very persuasive, and afterwards Audrey raved about how cool she was and how even her own mother hadn't been able to change Steven's mind.

The totally weird thing was that once I was changed and ready to go—full makeup in place, hair supernaturally subdued, and my new B-cup boobs encased in a strapless bra—I was actually almost excited.

"You look fantastic," Audrey gushed, eyeing my black halter-neck and tight jeans. "Whoa, I can actually see your body for once. And your makeup looks amazing. Did your mom do it?"

I nodded. "I love your top." She was wearing a blue crocheted top with navy boot-cut pants.

"Thanks." Audrey chewed the side of her lip. "This is ridiculous. I can't believe we're going. You know what'll happen, right? We'll stand in the corner talking to each other all night long and wishing we weren't there."

It's scary how much she thinks like me sometimes. Because that's exactly what I thought when Kaitlynn James opened the Nielsens' front door. "Hey, girls," she said listlessly. "Bring any beer?"

I laughed and glanced down at her brown legs and flip-flops. For one thing, she obviously had no idea of our names, and for a second, it hadn't occurred to either of us to bring anything other than ourselves. We'd screwed up before even setting foot inside the house.

"No beer," Audrey and I said simultaneously.

"Well." The word stretched out for an eternity on Kaitlynn's disappointed lips. "Come in."

We lurched through the door and along the front hall. In the kitchen a bunch of guys, a beer in front of each of them, were playing Texas Hold 'Em. They stared up at us like we were in the wrong place. "Almost everybody's downstairs," Kaitlynn shouted after us.

We peeked in on the near-deserted living room as we approached the stairs. Sadie was lying across her boyfriend's lap with her eyes shut. "The living room's off-limits," she announced, opening her eyes and blinking tearfully. "No offense. My brother and I just don't want it getting trashed."

"That's cool," Audrey said. "We're on our way downstairs." Audrey made a face at me as we opened the door to the basement. "If we can't find him soon, we'll leave, okay?" I nodded as rap music thumped around us. One minute at the party and I was more than ready to take off.

The basement was packed like Mumbai. I started to sweat as we worked our way through the guys sitting on the stairs. "Audrey," Massy called, grabbing hold of her arm and grinning at her like she was a birthday present. "You want a beer?" He tossed me a smile. "How 'bout one, Finn?"

"Sure." Massy bounded across the room to get us beers. The last normal thing I remember was thanking him as he handed one over.

The beer tasted terrible, like refrigerated pee, but it was too hot down there not to drink. At first I stuck with Massy and Audrey, but after finishing another can I ventured into the crowd and forced myself to mingle. Kaitlynn and I talked about London, where she'd been on vacation two months earlier. The heat was playing havoc with her foundation, and she looked like she was melting in front of me.

Then Sadie came downstairs, rubbing her eyes and complaining that her boyfriend didn't understand the first thing about her. I talked to people without even knowing their names. I talked about things I knew nothing about and nodded and laughed at all the right moments. I danced to OutKast, shaking it like a Polaroid pic. It was me but not me.

People were passing around little purple pills, and Kaitlynn handed me one, explaining that she never took drugs herself. I slid it into my pocket, with no intention of ever swallowing it. When I looked up, Audrey was weaving through the crowd towards me, wanting to know how I was making out.

"I'm cool," I told her, smiling to prove it. "How's it going with Massy?"

"I think there's some momentum happening," Audrey replied, her cheeks flushed. "But I don't know—it could just be the party vibe, you know?"

I bent my head down to answer and felt a finger skim along my bare back, sketching out what felt like a Christmas tree. My head snapped around, and I caught Adam Porter in the act. "What're you doing?" I asked loudly.

"Do you know what that was?" He touched my arm, smiling his flawless Hollywood grin.

"No clue." Adam and I had never exchanged a single word. I had no idea *what* or *why* he'd draw on my back.

"Okay." He swung me around so I couldn't see him and did it again, slower, like he was creating a modern art masterpiece.

I swiveled to face him. "I don't think that's anything."

"It is," he insisted. The cheesy grin was beginning to work on me. Or maybe it was the beer. "It's the Chinese symbol for beautiful."

I snorted and shook my head. "That's so lame," I told him, laughing.

"Yeah?" He hadn't stopped smiling yet. "It got us talking, didn't it?" He wiped the sweat from his forehead.

"This isn't talking," I corrected. "This is . . ." My mind went numb. The whole situation was completely surreal: purple pills, the puddle that was Kaitlynn James, and now Adam Porter practicing the art of calligraphy on my back. I scanned the room for Audrey, who was already halfway across the basement, and shrugged blankly. This is . . .

"This is talking," Adam insisted, moving closer to me. "So how come you never talk to anyone at school?"

"I talk to people at school," I said defensively.

"Not these people." Adam motioned towards the basement population. "You never talk to me."

"You never talk to me either." I was still a little irritated by the accusation, but my voice had mellowed.

"Yeah, well." Adam leaned towards me so that our arms were touching. "I thought I'd finally change that."

He was really good, the way he was staring at me, all soulful and sexy, like he was genuinely concerned that we'd never managed to speak. The fact that I didn't believe him was beside the point; there was something compelling about the performance just the same. And then it occurred to me that Adam was actually quite good-looking and that something needed to happen to me sometime. I was almost fifteen and still wearing virgin lips. Surely I could use some practice. Nothing drastic, just some limited physical contact to stop my body from rusting up before graduation.

"So why now?" I asked, focusing on his mouth. That's what you're supposed to do when you're flirting. I read it in one of those stupid magazines I never buy.

"Well." Adam put his hand up to my neck and brushed my hair back. "You seem a little different tonight. More relaxed."

"Drugged and drunk," I joked.

Adam laughed, his eyes gleaming. For a second I thought I caught a glimpse of the real him behind the bullshit. Then he pressed his body against the length of mine. It felt good. It felt like a wake-up call.

"I don't even think you know my name," I whispered. Not that I cared. It was just another element in the flirting.

"Okay," he said, wincing. "You're right." He drew back, staring at me solemnly. "What's your name?"

"What's yours?" I asked, grinning. The flirting thing was coming so naturally; I couldn't believe it myself. "I'm kidding—I, at least, know who you are."

"Oh, come on," he said lightly, like I was giving him a hard time. "You have to give me points for effort."

"Effort doesn't get you points." I gave him a stern stare, but my mouth was half smiling. "Results get points."

"Yeah," he said breathlessly, bending his head towards me. "Come on, you gotta tell me your name so I know who I'm talking to—and then maybe we could go somewhere a little more private. Get to know each other a little better without all this noise."

"It's Finn," I said in a low voice. "But we're not going anywhere."

"Okay." Adam nodded. "I don't mean leaving."

"Or bedrooms," I clarified.

"No leaving or bedrooms." He threaded his fingers through mine. "Just somewhere a little quieter, all right?" He motioned to the left. "Just over here." I followed him, not only because our hands were attached but because I wanted to.

Then we were standing inside the Nielsens' laundry room, next to an exercise bike that looked like it'd never been used. I straddled the seat and kicked at a pedal like I was in no special hurry. Watching Adam Porter put in an effort was too entertaining to let him stop now. I wasn't used to people doing that for me, even if it was just an act.

Adam grinned at me on the bike and said, "What am I supposed to do? Wait for you to cross the finish line?"

"What's your hurry?" I teased, but even as I said it, I couldn't wait for something to happen. Nervous energy swooshed around in my stomach as I climbed off the bike.

"Life is short, Finn." He still hadn't quit smiling, and I felt my lips tighten with an anxious grin of their own. "And for all I know, you might decide to stop talking to me again at any minute."

I took two steps towards him. They felt like astronaut leaps. "Why would I do that?" I asked.

Adam laid one hand on my back and slipped his fingers through the loop of my jeans. I thought I'd explode. "*Finn*," he said, trying out the word again as he pulled me closer. "I never would've guessed that, but it's a cool name." He buried his fingers in my hair and guided my head up to his.

I was scared I wouldn't know how to kiss him, but the fear didn't last. Kissing isn't something you learn. It's something you're not aware you know until the first time. Adam's tongue was warm and tasted like beer. He kissed my neck too, and the sensation made me want to purr. He slid his hands up under my top and touched my breasts over my strapless bra. I wondered if I should stop him, but I didn't want to. Everything he did felt wonderful and new. He jammed his body against mine, and I pushed back, wanting more.

"Finn," he said huskily, going for my pants.

The first button went. Then the second. I thought I'd die waiting for him to do it. But God, what was the next step? I wasn't going to let him de-virginize me in the Nielsens' laundry room. I didn't even really like Adam.

"Not that," I said, putting my hand down to do up the buttons.

Adam laughed and kissed my chin. It was every bit as hot in there as it was in the rest of the basement. Our faces were sweating and my back felt damp. Adam poked his tongue into my mouth and I kissed him back. My pelvis was bumping against his and I imagined how things would go if I let them. It makes me nauseous to remember how I pictured the act. It makes me shiver, my mouth as dry and disgusting as rust.

Adam massaged my breasts through my top, pinching at my nipples and bending down to kiss them. "I didn't know you were like this," he said.

"Like what?" I whispered.

"Cool." Adam looked up at me. "Sexy." He slipped his hand down between my legs and popped another button.

"Not that," I reminded him, grabbing for his hand.

"Okay." His mouth dipped at the corners as he straightened his back. He took my hand in his and pressed it against his jeans. "Feel that?"

I nodded. It was hard to miss.

"Okay," he said again, unzipping his pants and taking out his penis. He was already hard, and he looked down at himself and said, "I told you that you were sexy—that's proof." He reached for my hand and guided it to him.

But my hand didn't want to move. I didn't even want to look

at his penis. It felt like alien skin against my palm, and Adam was staring at me with small eyes and squeezing my breasts, making me feel even dirtier. "I don't know how to do this," I said, tearing my hand away. "I want to go."

"You're a real virgin, aren't you?" Adam touched my face as I nodded. "That's so sweet, I mean it."

My hands were trembling and I locked them behind me.

"I can teach you a few things," he continued, lips poking up into a crooked grin. "Tricks for the future boyfriend."

"I don't think so," I said, doing up my button as I turned away.

"Hey." Adam gripped my shoulder. "Why are you in such a hurry all of a sudden? We were having fun, weren't we?"

"Yeah, I know, but—"

"We'll do something painless," Adam said, smiling as he draped both arms over my shoulders. "I promise."

"I have to go." My heart was thumping so quickly that I could barely get the words out.

"Finn." Adam coiled his fingers into my hair and yanked so hard that tears came to my eyes. "Be nice. I've been nice to you. I just want to show you something."

I shook my head vigorously, and he yanked again. Adam glared at me as I yelped. For the first time it occurred to me that no one would be able to hear, no matter how loud I shouted. Mary J. Blige was singing "Work That" from the other room. I could hear it clearer than I could hear my own thoughts.

Adam wrapped his hands firmly around my neck, any tighter and I wouldn't have been able to breathe. "Shut up," he ordered. "Get down."

He was stronger than me. I got down on my knees, beginning to cry under my breath. He told me what he wanted me to do. He told me how. "You'll like it once you get started," he said. He smiled at me, but his voice was harsh. "I know you will."

"I can't," I wheezed. "Adam, please. I feel like I'm going to throw up."

He looked down at me and stroked my hair. "Why are you making such a big deal of this? It's insulting."

Insulting? My eyes streamed as I asked him why it had to be me when there were so many girls outside who liked him. "Because you're different," he said impatiently, touching himself and grabbing the back of my head.

I opened my mouth one last time, gagged on air, and heaved up chunks of my pepperoni pizza dinner—onto his hand, his penis, and my hair. Adam's hand flew off the back of my head like I'd knifed him. The taste of vomit in my mouth and the sight of it on his veiny skin made me sick again, worse than before.

"You fucking bitch," he cried, staring down at himself with his mouth open. He brushed secondhand cheese off himself, smearing it against his shirt and pants. "What the fuck is the matter with you?" He rushed over to the sink, turned on the tap, and shoved his hands underneath. "Get up," he shouted. "You're disgusting." The contempt in his voice turned me cold, but I was done crying. Something inside me had changed. "Come here. Clean yourself the fuck up."

I got to my feet and stumbled to the sink. He pointed down, and I stuck my head under the tap, like he wanted. He's going to drown me, I thought, and I don't even care.

But I'm still here, so you know that's not what happened. Lukewarm water rushed over my hair and rinsed it clean. Afterwards Adam grabbed my arm, shoved me roughly aside, and told me to go home.

I did what he said without questioning, and in the moment I reached for the laundry room door my mind vaulted towards safety. It tried, but never really got there. A different version of me walked out of the laundry room with dripping wet hair and the taste of rust and pepperoni in her mouth. That new Finn rubbed her eyes, wrung the excess moisture from her hair, and went to look for her best friend, Audrey.

nine

AUDREY'S THE ONLY person who knows what happened that night. When I found her, I couldn't talk. She dragged me outside with her, into the Nielsens' front yard, beside their yellow rose bushes. We were still too close to where it'd happened, and I asked her to walk with me. I started to cry again as I told her about Adam, and the look in Audrey's eyes made me cry harder. She said we should call my parents, or the police, but the suggestion made me tremble.

Audrey stretched a rubber band around my wet hair and rubbed my back. "It's over," she told me. "You're going to be okay, Finn. *You're safe now.* You'll be home in a few minutes. Then we can think what to do next."

"I don't want to do anything next," I croaked. "I just want to forget about it. Nothing even happened."

Audrey stopped walking and pinched her top lip between her fingers. "It's not nothing. He was trying to force you."

"You can't tell anyone," I pleaded. "Promise me you won't." There was no evidence, just my word against his. How could I look anyone in the eye and explain? I wanted to forget the details, not repeat them out loud. I thought of the way Adam's penis had felt in my hand and the sound of his voice when he'd barked instructions, like the fact that I had no choice but to follow them was part of the fun.

This couldn't have happened to me. Any second now I'd wake up.

"You know I'd never tell anybody unless you wanted me to," Audrey said, putting her arm around me. "Don't even worry about that." Her jaw wobbled a little as she looked at me. "I shouldn't have left you with him. I should've come back to check—"

My head whipped from side to side like I couldn't believe she'd just said that. It wasn't her fault. I didn't want to hear another word.

"Okay," Audrey said softly. "Okay. Just concentrate on breathing, all right? Nice and slow. It'll calm you down."

I took deep breaths and listened to the sound of Audrey's voice. We circled around my neighborhood until my hair was dry and I was calm enough to face my parents. Then we lied to them, told them I'd felt sick and that we'd gotten one of the girls at the party to drop us off. Audrey called home and arranged to stay the night, but I didn't sleep.

I kept thinking about forgetting, and how doing anything else would be worse. I didn't want to be the person this had happened to, and I didn't have to be. Not if I kept it to myself.

Adam wouldn't come near me again; he was disgusted with me. What happened was done and over with, and anyway, it'd never really happened in the first place. Not really. All I had to do was stay quiet, and things would go back to the way they were before.

I listened to Audrey roll over next to me and told myself those same things over and over again until they were the only reaction that made sense. Then I lay there with my eyes open, feeling my wrist ache in the dark. He must've bruised it at some point, but I couldn't remember when. Maybe that meant I was already forgetting.

So nothing happened that night in the Nielsens' laundry room. I didn't make the details realer by sharing them with anyone else—I did my best to make them disappear and stuck with my earphones blasting and the teeter-tottering back and forth between fuzzy viewpoints. Old me. New me. Old me. New me. They're so mixed up now that I'm not sure I know the difference.

Audrey still thinks I should talk to someone about that night, even if I don't want to do anything about it. She'd have let Jersy fight Adam if it was up to her, but she knows I wouldn't like it. We're doing this my way all the way, and Audrey knows I want to be completely off Adam's radar. The less he notices me, the less likely it is that anything really happened to begin with.

It's a system, sort of, and it's more or less worked up till now. Between Audrey and the system I'm mostly doing all right. She's been a therapist, bodyguard, and best friend rolled into one. For three weeks after the party, she raced around escorting me between classes. Then she got a written warning about her lateness. We spent so many hours talking on the phone that my mother suggested we should cut back to allow time for "other activities."

"Friendship isn't meant to be quite so intense," Mom admonished. "You see her every day at school—what could you possibly have to talk about for two hours afterwards as well?"

I lied and told her Audrey was heartbroken over Massy. In actual fact Massimo had stopped registering her existence shortly after the party, without explanation. Obviously he'd chosen to believe whatever bullshit story Adam had fed him, and Audrey told me she was glad nothing had happened between them. "If he's that controlled by other people's opinions, I had him all wrong," she said bitterly. "Especially if he's listening to guys like Adam Porter. He must be a real prick. I can't believe how he had me fooled."

I don't know how you ever really know people—even when you've spent your whole life with them. I thought my dad was the kind of person who didn't have any secrets. Now I wonder where he goes when he's out late. Could there be someone else?

"I can't imagine your dad doing that," Audrey says as we stroll through the mall with Jersy one day after school. "He's too nice. Besides, your mom would kick him out."

That's true and I nod at Audrey, trying to be positive. She's been so happy since she and Jersy made it official that lately I feel extra gloomy in comparison.

Come on, that's not exactly a surprise, is it? The attraction energy was obvious that day at my locker. Honestly, I'm pretty happy for the two of them. It's not like I could handle a boyfriend now, and Audrey isn't the kind of girl who deserts her friends to worship at a guy's feet. I haven't lost her; I haven't lost anything.

Audrey's so sensitive about including me that Jersy's nearly become a second best friend to me in the last four weeks. The weirdest thing about that isn't the time frame, which is a personal record for an anti-socialite like me, but that we're wildly different. Jersy's into any kind of extreme sport you can think of. He's broken more bones than I can name and thinks Beyoncé is a goddess. He's at least as smart as me but twice as lazy. The range of drugs he's into officially qualifies him as a stoner, but he doesn't act like one. Stoners don't have self-proclaimed social outcasts as girlfriends or hang out with brainiacs and dramaheads part-time.

"People don't always split up when someone cheats," Jersy adds as the three of us wander by Old Navy. "Sometimes they work it out."

"Maybe." Audrey shrugs. "Wouldn't be me, I can tell you that. It's disrespect."

"You'd never get the trust back," I add. "What good's a relationship without it?" Listen to me, the relationship expert. Everything I know about love comes from song lyrics.

"Yeah," Jersy says, nodding. "I know what you're saying, but marriage is different." He shoves his hands into the pockets of his baggy pants. "With a long-term thing like that, you have to expect some hiccups."

"Hiccups?" I repeat, unconsciously slowing down as we approach HMV.

Jersy glances at the store as if suddenly remembering something. "I need new headphones—busted mine last night," he says, charging towards HMV before Audrey or I can protest.

Audrey glances apologetically over at me as we cross the threshold. "Jazz section," she whispers, but of course I've already spotted him. As if I could ever in a million years walk into HMV and fail to notice Record Store Guy's presence. For one, he's so keenly edible that he may as well be made of Belgian chocolate. His curly hair and Celtic tattoo are giving me a fever. Not to mention the way his chest fills out his T-shirt. It's all hitting me bad, which is good, but it scares me just the same. Wanting someone that much is dangerous. Somebody should stamp a warning on Ryan's chest for people who don't already have the message stamped into their heads the way I do.

Jersy's already halfway across the store, in search of replacement headphones, and I'm relieved that Ryan's busy talking to a middle-aged woman in a blue hijab. Maybe I won't have to feel weird about making conversation while Jersy and Audrey listen in. Not that they *would*, but the thought makes me edgy anyway. Since September the thought of speaking to Ryan makes me nervous no matter who is or isn't around. It's just not the same.

I scope out the farthest point of the store from the jazz section, which seems to be precisely where Jersy's standing, examining various sets of earphones. When I get there, he looks up at me and then into the distance, like something's caught his eye. "Hey." Jersy knocks his arm against mine. "I think that guy's waving at you."

Sure enough I turn to find Ryan waving casually in our direction, the woman with the hijab striding away from him. As I raise my hand to wave back, the woman swings around to engage him in conversation a second time. Ryan smiles at my return wave before refocusing his attention on her.

"Who's that?" Jersy asks, a pair of mid-priced noise-canceling headphones in his left hand.

"Stop looking at him already," I command.

Jersy's gaze flicks away from Record Store Guy and holds on me. "Why?"

I raise my eyebrows impatiently. Do we have to do this here?

"Do you guys have a thing?" Jersy continues. He says that so easily that it makes me feel more uptight.

"There's no thing," I insist, crossing my arms against my chest and wishing that I didn't feel compelled to answer. My big toe curls up inside my shoe as I lower my voice to a whisper. "I guess you could say I *had* a thing for him once upon a time." I flex my toe inside my shoe and focus anxiously on Jersy's headphones. "But it was nothing really."

Jersy shakes his head but smiles. "You're not a very good liar, are you?"

You'd be surprised. But that's not the answer I give him. My arms fall back into place at my sides as I try to match his casualness. "We used to talk music a lot, but I don't come in here much anymore." I've been going to the record store on the main floor instead. It feels like cheating, but I know that's ridiculous. I'm sure Ryan couldn't care less if I ever set foot in HMV again. He'd wave at anyone he recognized. He's just like that.

My spine starts to tingle. If Jersy grills me about Ryan any deeper, I won't know what to tell him. I can't explain why I don't talk to Ryan anymore. Jersy and I may be friends, but we're not as close as that.

"Are you getting those?" Audrey asks, swooping in out of nowhere and grabbing Jersy's headphones.

He walks over to the cash register to pay for them, and then the three of us go. Regret tugs at me as I walk away from HMV and leave Ryan behind. When will I be able to feel giddy again without worrying where the feeling will lead?

If I was alone, I could get stuck on that question for hours. As it is, Billy Young cuts in front of us with two of his stoner pals outside HMV. "Hey, Mika," he says, calling Jersy by his stoner nickname. "Hey, girls," he adds, nodding at Audrey and me. The days of my rumored Billy infatuation are ancient history and not a problem. I don't even think Billy was aware of the possibility to begin with.

We nod back, and Billy slides his hands into his back pockets. "So, Mika, coming over to Joel's on Saturday to do some damage?"

"Sure thing." Jersy's all smiles.

"What about you two?" Billy focuses on Audrey and me. There's no way in hell we'd ever show up at a stoner party, and Billy knows it as well as we do.

"Maybe," Audrey says politely, answering for both of us.

As the three of us walk away, I can't help but feel surprised, all over again, about being born-again friends with Jersy Mikulski. Sculpting my former feelings into friendship wasn't rocket science, but it took some effort. There's something in Jersy that I want to trust, and that makes this the best-case scenario in the end. Audrey's super happy, and I don't have to worry about fucking things up for myself. Plus, now I have other people to talk to at school, like Billy Young. He's not a bad guy, despite the drug use and general lack of direction. Turns out he's even an Our Lady Peace fan.

Unfortunately, Audrey's current boyfriend status has Mom homing in on my seeming disinterest in the opposite sex more than ever, and when I get back from the mall she calls me into the kitchen, sits me at the table, and says, "Finn, I know you say there's no one you like at the moment, but I'm the last person you'd tell if there was, aren't I?"

"Maybe." She has a point, but I'm sure this is just some new psychological tactic that has nothing to do with the real truth. "But there isn't anyone. Maybe you think it'd be cool if I was having some secret relationship with someone you wouldn't approve of or something, but it's not actually happening, Mom."

"Why would I want you to be having a secret . . ." Mom stops, presses her fingers to her lips, and sighs loudly. "I never felt like I could talk to my mother when I was your age. She was so rigid. I don't want you to feel that about me—that there's no one at home you can speak to about things." She jumps in again before I can protest. "I know you're close to your father, but I thought it might be different when it comes to talking about boys and sex."

I want to cover my ears and run out of the room. "Mom," I say forcefully. "There are no boys and there's no sex, all right? I can't invent things for you. Maybe if you hold on a few years, Daniel will talk about sex with you."

Why does she always have to push so hard? How come Mom's practically begging me to hook up with someone, while Audrey's parents flip at the thought of her and Jersy being alone in the house together? A couple weeks back Steven walked in on them, innocently pigging out on popcorn in the kitchen, and blew a gasket just for that. Mom would've probably congratulated me.

"Can you stop being antagonistic for two minutes?" Mom sets her hands on top of the table and stares at me with determined eyes. "I'm here, whether you want me to be or not. That's all I'm going to say. Now you can stalk off to your room and e-mail Audrey about how your mother doesn't understand you at all, okay?"

"Okay," I reply indifferently, slowly standing. "What's for dinner?"

Mom snatches her hands off the table as though she'd like to strangle me. "I don't know," she barks. "What're you making?"

Hilarious. Both my parents are comedians. Somebody get a talent agent on the phone.

We eat pork chops, cauliflower, and baked potatoes while Daniel slurps on a gourmet creation from Chef Boyardee. Because Dad isn't home, there's tons left over, and Mom packs it all into the fridge in plastic wrap. Supposedly my father is having dinner with a friend tonight. This friend is generic and doesn't have his or her own name.

Dad must still be with said generic friend later in the evening, because he sure isn't here to walk Samsam one last time before we go to bed. Mom and I walk Samsam together instead. We walk quietly, like we have nothing to say to each other, but I don't think either of us is mad anymore. If anything, I'm angrier with Dad for his recurring disappearing act.

In the middle of the night I wake up, stumble out of bed, and stare out the window to where his car should be. Fresh snow has covered up yesterday's tracks, and the empty driveway glows white in the moonlight.

If he's out with someone else, my mom should divorce him. Audrey's right; it's disrespectful. It's not a hiccup; it's wrong.

I climb back into bed, bringing my MP3 player with me. I click on Moby and listen to him sing "We Are All Made of Stars." It's exactly what I need to hear, and I play it over twice before switching to Our Lady Peace. I fall asleep with *Gravity* rocking in my earphones, and when I wake up at eleven-thirty the next morning, I hit Moby again for a final refrain of positivity.

If I could live my life by that soundtrack, nothing would be impossible, but it's hard to keep that energy burning. I feel it slip away as I spy Dad's car in the driveway. Maybe I should feel relieved to see it there, but I just feel edgy. I pull on my clothes and bound downstairs, waiting for something to happen.

Mom's left a note stuck to the fridge, explaining that she's taken Daniel to the mall to pick out a birthday present for his friend. Apparently he has a party this afternoon. He has so many friends that he has a social engagement nearly every weekend. The constant gift buying must cost my parents a small fortune; Daniel would rather stay home than show up at a party with a less-than-stellar present.

Aside from Samsam breathing next to me, the house is silent. Dad must still be in bed, exhausted from his night out. His keys are on the hook in the front hall, like always, and I stealthily free them. Samsam wags his tail, sure we're going somewhere wonderful.

I hate to disappoint him, so I clip on his leash and lead him into the backyard. Afterwards I'll bring him for a marathon walk and let him stop and sniff anything he wants, but I have something to do first.

I unlock Dad's car, climb into the front seat, and ransack the glove compartment. A map of Ontario, car insurance papers, a cable bill, and an open box of Junior Mints are inside. One of my brother's gloves is lying under the passenger seat. The side compartments prove similarly innocent: more maps, a pocket pack of tissues, loose change, Dad's collection of jazz CDs for his ride to work.

I don't know precisely what I'm looking for, but whatever it is isn't inside the car; maybe it's in the trunk. I swing the car door open, set one foot on the snowy drive, and jump at the sound of Dad's voice. "What're you looking for, Finn?" he calls from the front stoop.

I hop guiltily out of the car and slam the door behind me, locking his keys inside. "Shit, I just locked your keys inside," I mutter, pointing to the car.

"Your mother has an extra pair," he says. "Don't worry."

"I'm sorry." I trudge towards him, pulling my gloves out of my pockets and slipping my hands into them. "I was just going to take Samsam for a walk, and I thought I might've left one of my CDs in your car." My dad doesn't like listening to rock music when he drives; he says it makes him speed. "A new one that I picked up at the mall," I add. "But it's not there."

"You have so many I'm surprised you'd miss one." Dad smiles like the same dependable father I've known all my life. It's unthinkable that he'd cheat on Mom, even if they're not getting along. "So where's Samsam?"

"In the backyard. I'll get him."

Dad nods distractedly. "When you come back, I'd like to speak to you, okay?" If he gives me the same talk Mom gave me last night, I'll explode. She was right; there's no possible way I can discuss guys with Dad.

"Okay," I say nervously. "Do you want to do it now?" Either that or I'll spend the duration of Samsam's walk wondering what Dad's planning on saying to me.

"Sure," he says, looking like he'd rather swallow nails. We go inside and sit down on the living room sofa, me picking at a hangnail and him scratching day-old stubble. "I'm sure you've noticed the way things have been around here lately," he begins slowly. "And your mother and I would like to work on changing that." Dad clears his throat and goes for his stubble again. "You're usually home evenings anyway, and we'd really appreciate it if you could keep Tuesday evenings free to babysit your brother."

"For sure," I chirp. "So it's like a standing date-night thing?" Neither of my parents has acknowledged their relationship problems to me before, and a breakup suddenly feels more possible, despite the date idea.

"You could say that," Dad says delicately, his eyes fixed on mine. "Actually, it's counseling, Finn. But we don't want you to worry about it—or us. That's our problem, okay?"

I shove my hands under my legs and lean forward on the couch. How can he mention counseling and expect me not to worry? "Do you think you guys are going to split up?" I gasp.

"Nobody wants that." Dad rests his hand on my shoulder. "We just want to get along better, and we need some help doing that."

"I'm not five years old, Dad," I tell him. "You don't have to sugarcoat it for me. Things have to be bad if you're going to counseling." I cough to break up the lump forming in my throat. "You're never even here anymore."

"That's not true, Finn." Dad looks tired and rumpled. "Sometimes I just need a break." He grips the back of his neck. "It has nothing to do with you or your brother, and even if your mother and I were going to separate—which we're not—both of our relationships with you would continue on the same as always."

That's a lie whether he knows it or not. Nothing ever continues on the same way forever. Something always changes.

"I'm fine with the babysitting," I mumble. "I should go walk Samsam now."

Dad nods quickly, relieved to have the conversation behind him. "I'll let you know if I come across your CD. What does it look like?"

"Don't worry about it," I tell him, and then I'm gone.

ten

○ ▢ ○

SO TUESDAY NIGHTS become my weekly babysitting gig. Mom and Dad trudge soberly out to the car and return hours later with take-out coffee and doughnuts. They sit at the kitchen table slowly sipping their coffees and speaking in level tones. It's a ritual and I don't like to disturb them.

Daniel's in bed by coffee time, and I hole up in my room transforming my Web page into a professional-looking portfolio site. Most of my redesigned CD and book covers look better than the originals. My environmental campaign assignment is up on the site too, in all the variations that occurred to me: the girl with the glass of water, a tranquil forest scene, and my personal favorite—the one I actually handed in to Mr. Ferguson—a close-up of a child's legs, frothy ocean waves breaking against them.

Our latest assignment is pointillism, and it's making me crazy. When I close my eyes, I see dots. I'm seeing them now, in homeroom, as I nestle my head into my arms on top of my desk.

"Finn, I'm totally craving fries and a shake," Audrey says, breaking my trance. "Wanna walk down to McDonald's for lunch today?"

"Sounds good," I tell her. It's mid-April, and the local McDonald's seems a lot closer now that the snow is gone.

Jasper and Maggie jump at the idea when we head them off outside the cafeteria later. Teresa and Edwardo are in studious mode, wanting to bone up on Canadian history before their test next period, so it's just the four of us. Jasper starts up the celebrity sex game as soon as we're out the door, and Maggie's eyes light up, thrilled at the possibilities.

"Chris Martin or Jake Gyllenhaal?" Jasper asks. "Who would you rather sleep with?" You have to choose one. That's the rule. Even if you find them equally untempting.

"Jake all the way," Audrey says. "Those eyes. And you can tell by his movie choices that he's the kind of person who's thinking all the time, so you'd even be able to have a cool conversation afterwards. Who could resist Donnie Darko?"

"He's hella cute," Maggie adds. "No comparison."

Jasper nods vigorously in agreement. "After *Brokeback Mountain*, I'd even forgive him for *The Day After Tomorrow*."

"What's wrong with *The Day After Tomorrow*?" Maggie squeals, but Jasper and Audrey have already spun towards me.

"It'd have to be Chris Martin," I announce, breaking the consensus. "For the English accent and the song 'Fix You' alone." Yeah, the lyrics are kinda sappy, but the sincerity in his voice makes you believe him. It's as simple as that.

Jasper waves dismissively. "Girl, you're as bad as Maggie." He presses his lips together and arches his neck up to the sunny sky. "How about . . . Jack Nicholson or Angelina Jolie?"

Audrey, Maggie, and I all wince. It's an interesting question.

The three of us are straight, but Jack Nicholson is old and disgusting.

"Angelina," I admit. "Even if I kept my eyes closed, there's no way I could do it with Jack." I shudder for effect. "He'd be all heavy and sweaty on top of you, and he'd probably want you to talk dirty." I don't know that for a fact, but he definitely looks like a pervert. It's funny, but I have no problem talking about sex during the celebrity sex game, maybe because it has such little resemblance to reality. In a way, it almost makes me feel better, like if I can kid around about Jack Nicholson squirming around on top of me, maybe I'm not so screwed up after all.

"Yeah." Audrey grimaces. "It's gotta be Angelina."

Maggie picks Jack, refusing to cross into bisexuality territory, but Jasper takes a long time to answer, and when he does, he opts for Angelina too. "She has amazing skin," he explains. "And she's a very talented actor and great humanitarian."

"You'd change your sexual orientation to sleep with a good actress with nice skin?" I tease.

"Not change it," Jasper says, putting on his gay voice. "Bend it. For one night. Same as you, Finn honey."

"True," I say with a shrug. "Okay, between Superman on *Smallville* and . . ." I rack my brains for suitable competition. Josh Hartnett? Paul Walker? Usher? None of them seem up to the task.

"Hey, there's Jersy," Maggie says, stopping in the middle of the sidewalk. The rest of us turn to catch sight of Jersy, Billy Young, and a third stoner sauntering in our direction, obviously on their own McDonald's run. Jersy and Audrey aren't like Edwardo and Teresa; they stick with their own crews at lunch. This meeting is purely coincidental, but now that it's happened it makes seven of us for McDonald's and puts an abrupt end to the celebrity sex game.

Audrey and Jersy hold hands and I trail behind them, next to

Billy, complaining about the strange effect pointillism is having on my brain.

"And what do all these little dots do when you see them?" Billy grins, his top teeth gripping his bottom lip. "Form a conga line and dance? Sounds like you've been indulging in some serious hallucinogens. Want to share with your brother Billy?"

"If I was taking drugs, I'd expect better hallucinations," I tell him.

He laughs and starts talking about a new horror movie opening on the weekend. It sounds like a real bloodfest, and Jasper, Maggie, and the third stoner jump enthusiastically into the conversation too. Soon we're all talking over each other's voices and finishing each other's sentences. You'd think we were all friends or something.

We even sit together at McDonald's, and I chomp on Billy's fries, despite my burger and shake. None of us are in any hurry to get back to school, but soon it's time to go just the same. We walk back outside and begin crossing the parking lot. Jersy and Billy lead the way this time, and Audrey hangs back, clutching at my arm. "Come with me," she whispers.

"Where?" I whisper back.

Audrey stops walking and yells, "We'll catch up to you guys later."

Maggie wants to wait, but Audrey waves her on. "I have to go to the drugstore," Audrey tells me, pointing at the plaza across the street. "It'll just be a minute."

"What's the big secret?" I ask, crossing the street with her.

Audrey squints up at me, shading her eyes with her hand. "I don't want you to make this into a big thing, okay? Because I don't really think that it is, but you're my best friend and if I can't tell you, I can't tell anybody."

"Okay, fine," I say, although her speech does a pretty good job of making whatever it is sound like a big thing.

"I just want to pick up some condoms," she whispers, pulling the front door open. "While we're here. It's, you know . . . like a proactive thing." Audrey's cheeks are turning red, and I feel the color drain out of my face as I stare at her. Jersy's the fifth guy she's made out with but the first one you could count as a boyfriend. I can't believe they've reached this point so quickly.

If I'd guessed what she wanted beforehand, I'd have made some excuse not to go to the drugstore. This isn't like the celebrity sex game; it's not something I want to think about.

"Don't look at me like that, Finn." Audrey turns and leads the way down the shampoo aisle. She stands in front of a collection of styling products and says, "This isn't a bad thing."

I nod slowly, and after a couple seconds of us standing there pretending to look like we care about hair products, I manage to say, "Why doesn't he have any? I mean, if you two are going to do it . . ."

"We're not." Audrey tucks one of her hands under her chin and looks at my kilt. "That's not what I'm talking about." My gums feel cold against my teeth. I will warmth into my face and continue down the aisle. Why should I care what she wants to do to Jersy? It has nothing to do with me.

"And maybe he does have them," she continues, her right hand plunging into her hair. "But we haven't talked about it, and I just wanted . . ." She sucks in air and then pushes the rest of the words out with one long breath. "I'm not even sure I'll go through with it. But I really like him, you know? I think it'd be okay."

She sounds like she knows what she's doing, but the more she talks about *we* and *him*, the worse I feel. "What do you want me to say?" I fiddle with the hem of my kilt, and I know this isn't what she wants to hear from me, but at the same time I can't be any other way. "Maybe you should talk to him about it before going ahead with all this." The words are sandpaper on my lips. I could use another shake.

Audrey smiles but her eyes are hard. "It's not like I can do it without him, Finn. And somehow I really don't think he's going to have a problem with it. Sure, I could leave all the details and timing up to him, but why should I?" Her head drops in frustration. "Why are you acting like it's wrong for me to want to do this? He's not like everyone else. I thought you'd get that."

I do.

"Audrey." I touch her sleeve, sorry that I've reacted badly. We've always been able to talk about everything; I don't want to ruin that. "You're right." I'm not entirely convinced, but I don't trust myself either. My head's spinning, trying to work out what's wrong with this picture, and when I shut my eyes, pointillism specks flash across the insides of my eyelids like a hundred and one miniature tattoos.

"Let's just do this," she says, moving in the direction of the family-planning aisle.

Seconds later we're eyeing a wall full of condoms. I don't understand why there have to be so many different types, but I start picking them off the pegs and flipping them over, trying to process their differences. Studded. Extra-sensitive. Flared design with roomy tip. Ribbed for her pleasure. Ultra-thin for his. Form-fitting. XXL. Extra-strong. Extended pleasure.

Audrey selects a package of mint-flavored as casually as if she's picking out chewing gum. "Come on," she says. "We'll be late for class."

I think we already are.

The woman at the cash register looks just a few years younger than my gran, but she stuffs the condoms into a bag and recites their cost without giving it a second thought. Audrey smiles politely and hands over a twenty.

"Have a nice day," the woman says, pressing Audrey's change into her palm.

"You too," Audrey tells her, and I wish we could rewind the last thirty minutes and go back to McDonald's or the celebrity sex game, but I wonder if any of it would feel the same now or if I'd have to rewind all the way back to August to be the Finn I'm supposed to be.

What would that Finn say to Audrey in the drugstore?

eleven

MY MOM'S FAVORITE restaurant is Sottoprova. It's the most expensive restaurant in downtown Glenashton, and if you're not fast enough a waiter will discreetly drop your napkin into your lap for you. The food is delicious, and I swear I always shuffle out of there at least five pounds heavier than when I went in. Even Mom, who hates to splurge, usually eats too much.

It's not Mom's birthday today—it's not any special occasion I can think of—but we're sitting in Sottoprova, a cream-colored napkin draped across my knees, listening to our waiter, Matteo, recite today's specials like they're odes by Keats. Matteo's black curls remind me of Ryan, but his skin and eyes are much darker. I'm spending too much time staring at him, and when I convince myself to look away, I find that Mom is doing the very same thing.

Once we've ordered, Dad takes hold of Mom's hand like they're contestants on one of those bachelor reality shows. He's been acting like that a lot lately—like he's trying to impress her.

Maybe that means the therapy is working, but it's awkward to watch.

"Can you drive me over to Caleb's house if we're finished early?" Daniel asks, pulling at his best shirt. "He got a new racing video game for his birthday, and when you crash—"

"You're gonna go to Caleb's in your good shirt and dress pants?" I cut in, smirking. My mom made us dress like royalty tonight, despite the absence of any special occasion.

"We just got here," Dad says. "Let's not rush it. His video game isn't going anywhere."

My brother's face falls, and I suddenly remember what it felt like to be ten years old. The game won't be quite so new anymore by the time he gets around to playing it. Some of the magic will have worn off, and no matter how good it is later, the game will never be as good as it seems at this moment. It's probably not even that good now. It's all perception. Like how in pointillism our minds fill in the spaces between the dots.

"Audrey and I are thinking about getting summer jobs this year," I announce. My mouth's watering at the assortment of zesty smells in the air. I may have to devour my napkin to stop myself chewing my own arm off before the antipasti arrive. "Maybe at the same place. At the mall or something."

"I doubt you'd find a place that would hire you both," Mom says.

"You should try the bookstore," Dad suggests, smoothing one hand over his tie. "You could get us all discounts." Dad is a nonfiction nut, while Mom sticks to the lighter side of the bestsellers list. I've never seen Daniel read anything other than a comic book.

"The comic bookstore would be cooler," I say, thinking out loud. "That bookstore's always dead." The great thing about Dad being a teacher is that he's home all summer long. He'll be able to chauffeur me to and from my work every day—Audrey too if we can get fixed up at the same place.

"An art supply store." Dad smiles as he points at me. "That'd be your perfect summer job."

"Or a record store," I add, because Audrey doesn't know the first thing about art.

"Mmm." Dad nods. "We'd need one of those hearing dogs for you come fall."

"She needs one of those already," Daniel says, ogling a piece of chocolate chip banana cake destined for another table. He'll eat five bites of the simplest thing on the menu and gorge himself on dessert. It's the same every time; he doesn't know what he's missing.

My rigatoni with asparagus and blue cheese is a gift from heaven. Mom finishes every bite of her grilled salmon and roasted potatoes, and Dad wolfs down veal like he's spent the last six weeks in jail. It's the best family night we've had since last summer. It's easy to be in a good mood when surrounded by fantastic food, but it's not just that. Once my parents finish with the hand-holding part of the evening, they seem at ease. It puts me at ease too, and I smile as Matteo approaches, forgetting to be awed by his Mediterranean good looks.

Matteo smiles back and plants himself beside me like he can read my thoughts but is too much of a gentleman to comment.

For a night out with family, it's just about perfect.

Audrey rushes up to my desk in homeroom the next day, dark circles under her eyes and the metallic blue nail polish on both her thumbs half chipped off. "I need to talk to you," she says urgently. "Can we go?"

"Yeah, come on." I'm already up, following her towards the door and away from Portable G. "Are you okay?" I touch her arm as we climb onto the bleachers. The only other place to talk is the bathroom, which is even less private. Someone's always holed up in there, crying about being two-timed by her boyfriend or bragging about who she hooked up with over the weekend.

"I wanted to call you last night, but they wouldn't even let me do that." Audrey presses her fingers into her forehead and hunches over, on the verge of tears. "They confiscated my cell. They have me completely cut off. No Internet. No telephones."

"What happened?" I lean towards her on the bleachers so that our shoulders are bumping.

One of Audrey's fingers works over her blue thumb as she looks at me. "Steven came home early and we didn't hear him. We were in my room . . ." Her voice trails off and I know why. She's afraid I'll disapprove of what she's about to tell me. I nod like she doesn't have to worry about that and listen to her say, "Me and Jersy were on the bed, practically naked." Audrey's face crumples. "It was so embarrassing. He saw us . . . together. I mean, he saw *everything*. He stormed out, slammed the door shut, and started shouting at us from the hall, totally flipping out."

I nod again so she'll know I'm following every word, and she folds her hands over her belly. "I can't even look at him now because I know we're both thinking about that moment. But the worst part is, he told my mom that Jersy and I shouldn't see each other anymore because we're out of control. And she's listening to him, like she always does. She says we need some time apart."

"Time apart?" I repeat. "What does that mean? For how long?" Now that she's put that picture of the two of them into my head, I can't get it out. It's like the pointillism all over again.

Audrey wipes her face, but the tears are coming fast. "They say it's indefinite. Until I've proven myself."

"Have you told Jersy?"

Audrey drops her head back into her hands and rubs her bloodshot eyes. "He was late this morning—you know he's never here on time. And I had no way of getting in touch with him last night."

"What're you going to do?" I've never seen Audrey this upset; it makes me feel helpless. I put my hand on her back and try to conjure the words she'd use in my place. "You have to talk to him. What does he have first period?"

I know his schedule by heart, but I'd never admit it. "Com Tech," Audrey confirms, touching my hand. "But Finn, you know I can't stop seeing him now. They'll make me wait too long. I'll lose him."

"You don't know that," I say, but I'm not as certain as I sound. Jersy likes her a lot, but he doesn't seem like the waiting-around type.

"It'll take me months to get Steven to trust me again," Audrey squeaks. "You know the way he is. It only takes one wrong step to set him off for days—and this was huge. If you'd heard the things he said to us . . ." She folds her fingers around mine and squeezes. "You have to help me, Finn."

I squeeze back. "What do you want me to do?"

"I'm grounded for two weeks." Audrey turns towards me. Her pink-lined eyes are painful to look at. "But after that I have to try to see Jersy when I can. Could you cover for us? It won't be for forever, just until Steven calms down."

Steven won't calm down in a hurry—Audrey said that herself—but of course I'll help. I'll do whatever I can for as long as she needs me to.

Audrey throws her arms around me when I say yes. "What would I do without you?" she cries. "Thank you! Thank you! You're the best!"

Jersy says roughly the same when he hears. He doesn't show up for art, but he catches up with me in the hall the next day, looking windblown and smelling like a carton of cigarettes. "You're really helping us out," he says. "Without you we'd be stuck."

"Her stepdad sucks," I say, breathing in the smoke still clinging to Jersy's uniform.

Jersy leans back against the nearest wall. "You know, I don't think he's ever even smiled at me."

"He doesn't smile that much anyway," I say. "He's like a military type. He just does the basics—no small talk or unnecessary facial expressions. He probably took an oath to save all his energy for 911 calls."

Jersy smiles and pushes himself away from the wall. "Are you gonna be in art later?"

When am I ever not in art? I begin to smile back, but then I see Adam Porter. He's sauntering up the hallway like we're invisible, and I freeze for a millisecond, damaged all over again. Adam doesn't care about me. I'm no one and nothing, and he'll never come near me again, but he still makes me shiver. He makes me sick with him and sick with myself. It's the worst kind of sickness; it sticks to everything.

Adam walks towards us and I stare down at the wall, counting the seconds until it's safe to look again. One–one thousand. *Go away.* Two–one thousand. *I am steel.* "Finn," Jersy says, forcing me to look up. He's got this weird expression on his face. I can't tell whether he's about to say something serious or not. "What is it with you and Adam Porter?"

I gape at Adam's back as he fades into the distance, my heart pounding with relief. "Nothing," I reply, my voice shaky.

Jersy opens his mouth like he's about to say something, but I speak first. "I have to go to my locker. I'll see you in art, okay?"

Jersy pulls both his hands inside his sleeves like he's physically incapable of keeping still. "I'll be there."

I turn before he can say another word, rushing down the hall on my way to nowhere, my lungs sucking in air like an industrial-strength vacuum cleaner, like I could never in a hundred years get enough. And for the first few seconds, I can feel Jersy's eyes on my back, wondering about me, possibly even noticing that if I walked any faster I'd be full-out running.

twelve

○ ○ ○

MY LITTLE WHITE lies are simple and painless. I don't feel guilty in the least because Audrey and Jersy are as sweet as ice cream and almost as mushy. In fact, with all their PG-13 making-out-in-the-hall scenes and soulful stares across the cafeteria, they'd make me cringe if I didn't like them both so much. It's worse when they come over to my house after school, because it's obvious how much they want to touch each other. Being around them is like standing next to an electric fence; you don't know quite where to put yourself.

If it weren't for Daniel, they'd want to take over my bedroom for hours at a time, but everyone knows he can't be trusted to keep that kind of secret. With all the reality TV he watches, he'd guess what was going on in an instant. The best I can do is ten minutes' privacy here and there—fetching snacks and taking extended pee breaks in the upstairs bathroom. Even then I knock at my own door before entering. One time Audrey was still straightening her kilt when I walked into the room. My face turned as red as a cherry tomato, and Jersy sat up on my bed and said, "Can we just have five more minutes, Finn?"

I don't blame them, but it's hard for me too. If I thought God would listen, I'd be tempted to pray for Steven to change his mind. Maybe Audrey and Jersy would calm down if their relationship was allowed into the open air again. Then again, maybe they're just "Crazy in Love" like Jersy's number one goddess.

The best times for all of us are when the two of them go to Jersy's house after school. In some ways it's equally stressful, because Audrey tells her parents she's at the mall with me and then I have to switch my cell off and either hang out at the mall solo or screen landline calls (thank God for caller ID) at home, in case they decide to check up on her via me. The bonus here is that I don't have to catch sight of them getting horizontal. Her mom and stepdad call to check up on her about a third of the time, and Audrey regularly complains that she feels like she's under surveillance. "You must be getting so tired of this," she says apologetically. "All the stupid phone calls to your house and us coming over to invade your bedroom."

"You'd do the same for me," I tell her.

"I would," she says readily. "But that doesn't mean it isn't a drag."

There she goes again, thinking so much like me that we might as well share the same brain. "Steven's gotta change his mind sometime," I say. "You've been proving yourself for a month."

"Yeah," she says ironically. "I've been some angel lately."

I laugh, but I have no idea exactly how much of an angel she's being or not. I haven't asked for any details since that day at the drugstore, and Audrey hasn't offered. It's as though we've both decided it's better for me not to know, which is strange because

Audrey and I talk as much as ever. Once the dinner hour hits, the presence of parents makes it nearly impossible for Audrey and Jersy to see each other. Our lives go back to normal until the following day at school, when the two of them are all over each other like a virus again.

I know how that sounds, but I really do like them both a lot. Sometimes I just wonder if maybe I like them better separately than together. Constantly covering for them makes me feel like an accomplice who isn't getting her cut. It's not the kind of thing a friend should think, but I do, and every day I get just a little happier with thoughts of summer.

I'm not a bikini-on-the-beach girl like my mom would want, but I'm happy that the breeze is warm these days, and when I'm out with Samsam, I grin at the other dog walkers, glad to be in the sunlight. Everything feels better in the sun, even when you have red hair and singe in ten minutes without a hat. Partly it's because I know my after-school covering days are almost over, and Adam Porter, the person who turns my stomach on a daily basis, will soon graduate and go away to university. Partly it's because school is mostly useless anyway and a summer job will net cash for my growing CD collection. It's every single thing really. I have two years of high school down and two more to go. London and New York are inching steadily closer, and after graduation I'll get on a plane and find a flat/apartment there I can barely afford. I'll take art courses part-time and work in a secondhand record store that still sells vinyl. My free time will be spent strolling through Hyde/Central Park, and the people I don't know there yet will comp me tickets to their fringe-theater/Off Broadway plays. After a year or two, when I've gotten enough of London or New York to tide me over for a while, I'll come home and do a graphic design degree. Maybe, if I'm lucky, I'll eventually be able to work my way back to either of those places and design theater posters, CD covers, and cereal boxes.

Summer's a step closer to the future. That's a big enough reason to like it, even without the heat.

Audrey's equally enthusiastic about the season but for different reasons. She'll be able to jump Jersy's bones at his house all summer long while his parents are at work. There are plenty of ready alibis she can use during the day while their parents are out of the picture—her future job, the mall, random bike rides, and long walks, you name it.

"Just don't lie about being with me," I remind her. "My dad could answer the phone at home and spoil everything." Dad usually spends summers carting Daniel and me around to various attractions, but this year Daniel's going to day camp with two of his friends. Dad says he plans to spend hours sitting under the umbrella on the patio, catching up on his reading.

"I know," Audrey says. "The main thing is that we have to get out there and find jobs before school's out. University students have probably snagged most of the good ones already."

So I design résumés for both of us on my computer. Neither of us have much to put on them, seeing as we've never been employed before. I could practically fit the info onto a business card, but Audrey uses her drama skills to pad them out. Between our two creative minds, the finished products look and sound quite respectable. We even use each other's parents for references—who could be more respectable than a history teacher and a police officer?

Afterwards we complete the first wave of our find-employment crusade, flooding the mall and surrounding area with résumés. If none of our first choices get in touch, we'll do another circulation run and keep on going until we hit the bottom of the barrel—fast-food chains. One of the last things I want to do this summer is sport an ugly orange uniform with matching name tag (the look would clash with my hair, and I'm pretty sure the smell of sizzling fat would make me nauseous within two days), but I'll do it as long as Audrey does.

Unfortunately, our working-together plan quickly proves shaky. Play Country, a warehouse-size toy store across from the mall, calls Audrey two days after we submit our résumés. She did practically all the talking to the assistant manager, so that doesn't surprise me. I just tell Audrey to put in a good word for me when she has her interview in ten days. Play Country employees wear green rugby shirts with the Play Country logo emblazoned across the front. On chesty girls it looks like a dirty joke, but maybe that's just my freaky mind working overtime. It's not the coolest place in the world to work, but not the lamest. There's zero chance of encountering sizzling fat and an equally small chance of colliding with Beautiful Boys.

The more I think about it, the more ideal it seems. No commission stress and no remotely cool guys hanging around, making me nervous. And my boobs are probably too small to make their stupid logo look perverted; you'd hardly notice them in a big old rugby shirt.

By the time Play Country finally gets around to calling me nearly a week later, I'm convinced it's the perfect, hassle-free summer job I've been looking for. The manager and one of the assistant managers want to interview me on the exact same day they're talking to Audrey. My interview is two hours later, meaning Audrey can spoon-feed me all the questions beforehand. It feels like everything's falling into place, and the feeling scares me by getting my hopes up. I get more anxious in the car, thinking about how I've never had an interview before and how on the rare occasions that I go to confession I never know what to say except that I never go to church on Sunday.

Mom appraises my nervous presence in the passenger seat and advises me not to worry. "It's a nothing summer job. It doesn't matter whether you get it or not. Just be yourself." She takes another look at me and revises her last statement. "Be confident. People like confident people."

Even if they lack confidence themselves? "I'm okay," I tell her. "Just wait in the parking lot in case it's over really quickly."

"I'm getting my nails done at the salon," Mom says. "I'll be back in about an hour."

So what am I supposed to do in the meantime—wander through the aisles like a confident reject? But it turns out there are two people ahead of me waiting for interviews—a gangly guy with the face of a thirteen-year-old and a girl named Nishani who was in my French class last semester. The guy keeps picking at a humongous pimple on his neck, and Nishani and I exchange subtle glances of revulsion, afraid he'll begin to bleed or ooze at any moment.

His interview is over in less than ten minutes, and then they call Nishani, who's gone for at least twenty. At first the waiting makes my nerves worse, but then I'm just bored. I'm still bored when a twenty-something-year-old woman calls me into the manager's office, smiling like she's a department store catalog model. "I hope you haven't been waiting too long," she says. "We're running a bit behind."

"It's okay," I lie. *I enjoy watching people perform minor surgeries on themselves.* "It looks like you're interviewing lots of people today." My sucky attempt at small talk.

"We have a few different positions to fill." The woman's smile eases up. "Are you more interested in stocking or being a cashier?"

"Uh . . ." God, I'm stuck already. My nerves are back full-force. "Stocking, I guess." It sounds marginally more independent than standing in the same spot for three or four hours at a time.

She leads me into the manager's office, where a bald man in his thirties is reclining in his chair, feet up on the desk and everything. He jerks his feet off the desk as the woman sits down in the chair next to his. "This is Fionnuala Kavanagh." She points to the bald guy. "Gerald Goldmann. And I'm Suzanne Eckebrecht."

"It's Finn," I say, pointing to myself. "Everybody just calls me Finn."

"Finn," Gerald repeats, reaching across the desk to shake my hand. "I don't think I've ever in my life met someone called Finn—or Fionnuala, for that matter."

I smile, figuring I'm supposed to. "It's an Irish name—my grandmother's."

Suzanne isn't one for small talk after all. She purses her lips like I'm wasting their time. "We have a few short questions for you, Finn. Our aim here is to try to get an idea of how you'd fit in with the Play Country team."

My mouth drops a little, dismayed at the suggestion. I don't want to fit in with the Play Country team; I just want a hassle-free summer job. Then Mom's advice pops back into my head, and guess what? She's absolutely right. This is a nothing summer job. It doesn't matter whether I get it or not. Sure, the money would be good and it'd be cool to work next to Audrey for the summer, but whatever, it's not life and death.

That makes it easier, and I manage to answer all of Suzanne and Gerald's questions without looking like a total anti-socialite. Gerald puts his feet back on the table and tells me they'll be in touch in a week. I don't know whether I should shake his hand again or not, so I don't.

"Thanks," I tell them. Audrey would probably smile and say something witty, but trying to impress people takes a lot out of me and I'm already spent.

Mom's car is in the parking lot when I go outside, and she gives me a hopeful look and asks how it went. I repeat Suzanne and Gerald's pseudo-corporate questions, and as soon as we're home I call Audrey. When she picks up, I put on a fake business tone and tell her I want to discuss our future bosses and roles on the Play Country team. Audrey laughs and says, "What I remember most was that Suzanne looked like she was dying to knock Gerald's feet off his desk. All through my interview her eyes kept zooming over to them with this pissed-off look."

"She didn't seem too happy in mine either," I tell her. We promise to give each other a call as soon as we hear something definite, and I hang up and swallow the daily vitamin that I forget to take every morning.

Later we do our family-dinner thing, and afterwards I help with the dishes. My hands are in the sink when the phone rings and Dad picks up. "She's not here at the moment," he says, eyes narrowing as he listens. "Not as far as I know," he adds. "Would you like to speak to Finn?" I grab a towel and dry my hands, staring pensively at Dad. "It's Steven for you." My throat dries up as he hands me the cordless. "He's looking for Audrey."

"Steven?" I say into the phone. Audrey's mom is always Mrs. Lepage, but Steven, for some reason, is just Steven.

"Finn." I hear his firm military voice in that single syllable. "Audrey said she was riding her bike over to your place. I take it this is the first you're hearing of it?"

My brain's jammed. I can't invent a lie fast enough. "Well . . . I've probably just forgotten," I stammer. "But I'll tell her you're looking for her when I see her. I bet she'll be here any second now."

"She left over an hour ago." He sounds like he's reading a police report. "Where would she have gone instead?"

"I don't know." I'm so afraid to say the wrong thing that my lips barely move. "Maybe she bumped into someone from school."

"I have a good idea who that could be," he says. "Is there anything you want to tell me, Finn?"

"No." I sound baffled, and I am. I can't believe Audrey would use me as an excuse without mentioning it. Is it possible she's really missing? "Can you let me know if you find her?"

"I'll find her," he says confidently. "Don't you worry about that."

I tell him goodbye and hang up. Goosebumps are popping up on my arms, and I stand next to Dad, who wants to know what's going on. I give him the official version of the story, same as I gave Steven, my voice thick with genuine worry. If Steven finds Audrey and Jersy together, she'll never have another chance to prove herself. Her parents will ground her for the entire summer, possibly longer. They'll confiscate her computer and take the phone out of her room, and that could be just the start.

I can't imagine a summer without Audrey, and I feel panic bang at the inside of my chest. It grows stronger with every hour, until I can't stand it anymore and dial her house, my mouth full of marbles.

"I'm sorry?" Mrs. Lepage says. "Who is this?"

"It's Finn," I blurt out. "Is Audrey home?"

Mrs. Lepage sighs into the telephone. "She'll speak with you at school on Monday, Finn." The dial tone hums into my ear, telling me everything but the details.

I was wrong about this summer.

Freaky girls don't have good summer vacations.

thirteen

○   ▫   ○

THE LAST WEEK of classes rushes by in a blur of tears and hushed voices. Audrey and Jersy disappear every lunch hour and return looking flushed and frustrated. I hardly have a minute to speak to Audrey alone, and when I do, she won't stop talking about Jersy and how she doesn't know how she'll get through the summer without him. "Or you," she adds hastily.

Or me. Yeah, I'm an afterthought. I'd be angry if I wasn't missing her so much already. What am I supposed to do with two empty months of sunshine without her?

We have the same conversation every morning in homeroom, until Friday when I lose it and say, "What were you thinking? You would've had all summer long to be with Jersy, and you had to go and mess it up. You never even warned me that you were using me as an excuse to go over to his place. And my entire family was home! There's no way I could've covered for you anyway." I'm practically shouting, and the guy in front of me swivels around in his seat and raps on my desk with his knuckles like he's calling a courtroom to attention.

"Fuck off," I tell him.

"Fuck you," he says back, smiling. "Gee-zus, chill why don't you. It's the last fucking day of school."

I give him a Medusa stare until he turns away and then sneak a peek at Audrey. Couldn't she at least have hidden her bike in Jersy's garage? She made it so easy for Steven.

"You don't understand what it's like, Finn," she says. "We've hardly had any time alone since April. I thought they were easing off with the phone calls. I'd never have done it if I thought they'd call you." She pulls her hair down around her face. "I know you were sick of all that. I wanted to leave you out of it."

Her explanation sounds like a half-truth. Mostly she was just in a hurry to get over to Jersy's house and mess around while his parents were out. I was the last person on her mind—just a convenient alibi.

Now the three of us have to suffer all summer long. Steven's already arranged to ship Audrey off to her aunt's house in Gatineau, Quebec, for the summer. He and Mrs. Lepage are going to drive Audrey over there two days after her last exam. Audrey's mom tried to pass it off as a holiday, but Audrey protested that holidays are usually optional. Then Steven started yelling that they obviously couldn't keep track of her twenty-four hours a day in Glenashton.

"I want to be out of it," I cry. "But it seems like every single aspect of our friendship now is just about you and Jersy."

Our homeroom teacher strides into Portable G before Audrey can reply. My hands are shaking, and if I wasn't sitting in homeroom I'd already be crying. I don't want to be mean to Audrey. I want to work next to her at some nothing summer job for the next two months, joking about our shitty bosses. I know she'd be with Jersy every chance she got, but there'd still be some time left over for me—especially if we worked together.

I glance over at Audrey, but she's looking straight ahead, pretending to listen to announcements. We stand for prayers and I stare straight ahead too, hoping she's glancing over at me and that she's not angry.

Then I realize I've forgotten my locker combo again and that I threw away the scrap of paper I'd written it on two days ago, thinking I'd never need it again.

My gaze shoots over to Audrey, who is dedicated to the idea of not looking in my direction, and then down at the corner of my desk where someone has carved the letter "G." I never noticed it before, and now I don't know if I've been missing it all year long or if it's brand new.

The bell rings and Audrey's halfway to the door. I'm both missing her and mad, and I have no idea what to do, except follow her out of Portable G. She's waiting outside, her lips puffy and her eyes small. "What you said is not true," she protests. "I've never forgotten about you."

"These last couple of months have sucked," I say honestly. "I feel like your pimp." Audrey's mouth drops, but I keep blabbing. "And now you don't even care that we're not going to be together this summer. It's all about Jersy. It's completely gross the way you guys are always crawling all over each other." I want to bite back the words, but they're already gone, and Audrey yanks her head away like we were never friends to begin with.

"I'm sorry." I grab for her arm, and then I'm crying, like a complete moron, blubbering away in the space between Portables F and G like I'll never be able to stop.

Audrey sucks in her breath and hugs me. "Calm down, Finn.

It's okay." She smoothes her hand over my back. "This isn't fair, you know. I'm the one that's being sent away for the summer like some kind of juvenile delinquent. You should be comforting me."

"I know," I mumble. "I'm sorry. I didn't mean it."

"Yeah, you did," Audrey says. "You think I don't know you?" She pinches my arm. "Look, we're both going to survive this summer. You can work your ass off and buy your own record store." I smile at her through my tears, disgusted with myself for being such a suck. "Hang out with Jersy," she adds. "Make sure he hangs on to a couple of brain cells."

"What about you?" I sniffle. "What're you going to do in Gatineau?"

"I don't know." Audrey pouts. "My cousins are thirteen and twelve, and my aunt and uncle are the kind of people who go to church every Sunday. Maybe I can join Abel's Youth Group when I get back."

"This summer is going to set a new record for shittiness," I say vehemently.

"Yeah." Audrey shakes her head. "I can't believe you said we were gross—after all the drooling you did over Record Store Guy. You would've been on him like a rash if you'd had the chance."

"I know," I say humbly. "It's just—being around it all the time is weird. Every time I'm with you two, it's like you'd rather be alone."

"That's only because we can never *be* alone. You know it wasn't like that before my parents banned me from seeing him." Audrey tugs at my sleeve and gets us walking in the direction of the main building. "Anyway, it's not something you'll have to worry about anymore. They're never going to let me see him now."

I stop walking and stare at her. "So that's it? You're giving up."

"I'm not giving up." Audrey stops too. "But what can I expect?

You think Jersy's still going to be waiting for me come September? And even if he was, we'd be caught again by October. So I don't know what's going to happen, but this feels like we're saying goodbye. That's why . . ." She turns, crossing her arms in front of her. "That's why it's so hard. You and me won't have this summer, but me and Jersy might not have *anything*."

I'm the worst friend in the world; I've only been thinking about myself. I'd never have survived this year at school without Audrey. Then it hits me that this is the final day of class. I could still run into Adam during exams, but it's unlikely. After today I'll probably never see him inside these walls again. An enormous weight lifts from my shoulders, and I apologize and wrap my arms gratefully around Audrey.

At lunch she disappears with Jersy as usual, and later in art class he shuffles by me. "Hey," I say, grabbing his arm. The stupid thing is that I have nothing to follow it.

"Hey," he says blankly. "I'll talk to you later."

"Sure." I'm surprised he bothered to show; Billy Young and the other stoners are nowhere to be seen. I feel bad for Jersy, sitting there in art on his own, and I lean over and whisper to Jasper that I'm changing seats.

Jasper gives me a puzzled stare, but I slide out of my chair, cross the room, and pull up a seat across from Jersy. He eyes me expectantly, but I have nothing to say. "Audrey wouldn't skip class," he complains, shifting his legs restlessly under the table. "She's been warned by her parents."

"What'd yours say?" I ask.

"That going behind her parents' backs isn't right and we have to respect their decision." He shrugs as he squints in Mr. Ferguson's direction. "It's bullshit. What do her parents think they're going to do—lock her up every time she meets a guy?"

It's weird to hear Jersy mention future guys while he's still in the picture, but I nod, trying hard to be good and make up for my outburst this morning. "I can't believe they're sending her away. It totally sucks, but it's just one summer. You can make up for it in September."

Jersy stares past me like he's thinking something that he's decided not to share. He folds his arms in front of him and slumps in his chair. "I don't want to talk about it anymore, Finn. Audrey and I have been through it a hundred times already. There's nothing else to say."

"Sorry." Doesn't he know he's supposed to let me be big about this? "I just thought—"

"I know. It's okay." He shifts in his seat. "I think I'm gonna take off anyway."

"Are you sure?" I don't know if I'm supposed to let him go or not. It's a basic thing and I have no idea. "Where're you gonna go?"

"Anywhere," he mutters. "Wherever." He stands up and brushes past Mr. Ferguson without saying a word.

Mr. Ferguson pats his hair and stares after Jersy, bewildered. I feel every bit as confused as he looks. One minute I'm so relieved about Adam that I could kiss the ground, and the next I feel lonely, thinking about the two months ahead without Audrey.

When I get home, there's a message from Play Country telling me that they'd like to hire me for the summer, if I'm still available, and to give them a call to let them know when I can start. That messes me up even more, because I'm sure they've contacted Audrey too, and I stay up flicking through late-night talk shows long after my parents have gone to bed, trying to shake myself out of it. Samsam naps on the floor in front of me, his paws twitching lightly, as I watch *David Letterman,* then *Conan,* and finally the second half of *Casino Royale.*

I'm so exhausted by the time I go to bed that I fall asleep instantly, but when I wake up I'm already thinking it: I'll be alone this summer. Maybe it's my own fault for having one friend at a time, but this is what I've always been like. My old best friend, Josephine, moved away near the end of sixth grade, and the one before that, Linnea, started hanging out with all these popular kids that I hated halfway through fourth grade. That time with Linnea was really hard. For about two months I didn't have anyone to eat lunch with or hang out with at recess. One of the popular girls felt sorry for me and asked me to eat with her and her friends one day, but the next day I couldn't do it; I didn't feel like myself when I was with them. It's not easy being alone but it's not the worst thing. The worst thing is to be surrounded by people that you don't feel true around.

Audrey is the closest friend I've ever had. Closer than Linnea or Josephine. I'm the closest friend she's ever had too, the only one aside from her mother that knows her real dad isn't MIA like she tells everyone but an alcoholic who still comes to visit once a year or so, always with a gift she's years too old for. I wonder if she told Jersy, and I wonder if he knows about that day back in sixth grade when we found out that our substitute French teacher of seven days had drowned in her pool. Every girl in our class cried— except for Audrey and me. It was *seven* days; we hardly knew her. The boys didn't know what to do with all the emotion in the room, and we didn't either. How could it possibly be real?

Later that day I went up to Audrey in the parking lot while she was waiting for her mom to pick her up. We haven't stopped talking since, and summer feels like a waste without her, like something to rush through to get to the other side.

I start by calling Play Country and telling them when I can start. Then I study like a brainiac for my English, civics, and science finals. Not so much because I care, but because it gives me something to focus on.

On Saturday Dad gives me an illegal driving lesson (I'm four months too young for a learner's license) in a public-school parking lot. It's supposed to be a thrill, I guess, and it's okay, but Daniel's more impressed by the experience when he hears about it later than I am. Some nights I watch *South Park* with him, and I must be losing it because Cartman seems funnier every time.

Because I've studied so much, the exams are no hassle. I easily recognize the formula for calcium hydroxide and faithfully sketch out a diagram detailing the stages of mitosis. Explaining the main features and functions of the various branches of government is a snap. If it's possible to lose it and get smarter at the same time, that's me. If I get any more diligent, I'll have to invest in a better calculator and sit with the brainiacs next year.

I don't run into Adam Porter at school during finals. If I'm lucky, I'll never lay eyes on him again. The relief of that is still with me, but the other feelings stay too. If I could claw them out of my skin like a tumor, I would.

Once Audrey leaves, I'll be the only person who knows what happened that night. It makes me extra lonely, and thinking about Play Country doesn't help. Dad's right, I should've applied at an art supply store. I could call Play Country and tell them I've found another job, but the thought of putting out another round of résumés solo is even more depressing, and if I stay home with Dad and Daniel all summer I'll turn into one of those people who write Internet fan fiction and don't get out of their pajamas until three in the afternoon.

I'm sinking.

But I try to be supportive when I'm around Audrey, like she'd be in my place. I've already screwed that up once. Her parents let me come over a few times before she leaves, and we paint her room pastel orange, to cheer her up when she gets back. It looks Willy Wonka–esque, without the candy, and her parents hate it but they don't say anything.

The last time I see her, we both start to cry and Audrey says, "I'll e-mail you as soon as I can." She's leaving early the very next morning, and her mom's suitcase is open beside the bed, waiting for last-minute items.

"I'll e-mail you so much you'll be bored with me," I tell her, trying to smile. "And I expect detailed responses to all my pathetic Play Country news." Tomorrow's my first day as a trainee team member. I cringe as I picture the next nine weeks, my boobs bouncing around in a Play Country shirt as Suzanne frowns at my lack of team spirit.

"Oh, God." Audrey winces. "Why did we apply there?"

"Because it's across from the mall," I remind her. "It seemed like a good idea at the time."

"A lot of things seem like a good idea at the time." Audrey's face is blotchy, and I bet mine's the same. "My mom let me talk to Jersy earlier. To say goodbye. I think she knows I've been calling him while they're at work anyway." She wipes her damp cheeks. "But today was so sad that I wish I didn't call."

"What'd he say?" I ask.

"He said summer's short and that I should just try to have the best time I can. He told me he'd see me when I get back and that I should e-mail him when I can." Audrey's shoulders sag as she looks into my eyes. "It wasn't what he said, so much. It was how his voice sounded—like things were different."

Between the two of us, I know I'll miss her the most, and I get this twinge of sympathy for Audrey, wondering if maybe she was right about Jersy not hanging on until September.

Mrs. Lepage's voice zooms up the stairs, jolting us out of the moment. "Finn, your father's here to pick you up."

Audrey pulls the door open and shouts, "She'll be down in a minute." She kicks her mom's suitcase as she shuts the door. "Stupid thing won't even close." Her fingers tug at the zipper, but it only shifts a couple stubborn centimeters. "You see." She presses her lips sourly together and looks up at me. "Maybe I'll get knocked up with twins by some French guy while I'm away. That'd show them."

"Some guy in his forties," I add. "With a wife and five kids."

"Yeah." Audrey chokes out a laugh. "They'd probably ship me to Greenland."

"Yeah." I peer at the door, but my feet don't move.

"So I guess you have to go." Audrey stands up next to the suitcase. You'd think we'd be smiling, what with the overwhelming amount of pastel orange in the vicinity, but her bottom lip is shaking and that makes me feel worse.

"Yeah." I blink back tears and murmur, "It's only two months, right? It'd go by in a flash if you were here."

Audrey nods doubtfully. "I know." She reaches out and folds her arms around me. "Thanks for everything."

I hug her to death, feeling guilty for every negative thought I had about her and Jersy. The room is so bright that I have to press my eyelids together to keep from going blind. It feels exactly like the summer neither of us will have.

fourteen

○   ○   ○

DaD Frowns as I climb into the front seat. His hands are gripping the steering wheel like it's a life preserver, and one of his live jazz CDs is on the stereo. "It's one lonely degree out there tonight," a woman says, introducing the next song. "So let's keep the atmosphere warm." Her voice hangs on the last word, melting it into honey. There's a smattering of applause as I buckle my seat-belt and watch Dad back expertly out of Audrey's drive.

My eyes smart and I'm sure I look like shit, but Dad is silent, concentrating on the route he's taken a zillion times. I wait for him to ask how it went or tell me I'll be fine, but he just keeps staring out the window like he's drugged.

"I can't believe she's really going," I say finally. "Now I have all summer alone at that stupid toy store." Dad gives me two seconds of his full attention and then fixes his stare back on the road. "And we were gonna take the train to Toronto this summer and walk around Chinatown and Queen Street and check out cool second-hand record stores."

"You can do that anytime," Dad tells me. "The city's not going anywhere." That's the exact same response he gave Daniel that night in the restaurant, and a lightbulb flicks on in my head: this is no different to him. This is me wanting to play some useless video game.

"That's not the point." My voice is prickly. "The whole summer is ruined, Dad. We were gonna go to Ontario Place and Wonderland and the sidewalk sale here and everything." I can't believe I have to spell it out for him. He knows Audrey and I were Siamese twins until Jersy came along.

"It's two months," Dad snaps. "Get a grip, Finn." My skin burns as I turn away, shocked. He was always the one who understood about Audrey. "She's not moving to New Zealand, for God's sake."

His words sting so much that I want to rip his CD from the stereo and fling it out the window like a Frisbee. What I do is different. I scowl and stare decisively out the passenger window, ignoring him with all my energy.

When we get home, I unbuckle my seatbelt and slam the car door shut behind me. Dad marches upstairs without another word, and I hold my head high, pretending I don't care. Samsam's sitting in the family room with my brother, and he gets up and comes over to me like he knows better.

"Your face is all red," the Anti-Me says, glancing up from his video game.

"Shut up." I sit cross-legged on the floor and bury my face in Samsam's fur. "How come you're not in bed? It's almost ten-thirty."

Daniel casually guns down an assortment of mutant soldiers. "I don't know."

It's not like my parents to forget. That's one thing they're actually strict about when it comes to Daniel. He always has to be in bed by nine-thirty.

I get up and go into the kitchen, Samsam trailing behind me. I fill his empty water bowl and head upstairs. The hallway is dark and my parents' bedroom door is closed. Someone's pulling dresser drawers hurriedly open inside. "I can't be around you at the moment," my father says. "Just let me do this without another argument." The bed squeaks and the closet door opens and shuts as I stand frozen in the hall, listening to the sound of my mother crying. Her sobs are ragged and low, and the desperation in them makes me tiptoe back downstairs and into the room where my brother is mercilessly annihilating an entire army.

"You told them, didn't you?" he says, his voice full of blame.

"I didn't tell them anything." I stretch out on the couch and fold an arm across my face. "I think they're asleep."

"They're not asleep," he says scornfully.

Of course they're not. "Just play your game," I tell him. "They're not coming to get you." Mom's sobs echo in my head, filling me with dread.

"They're not asleep," Daniel repeats. The firing from his video game has stopped, and I swing my arm away from my face and look at him.

"Whatever," I say. "They're not coming."

Samsam barks from the kitchen as the front door slams shut. Daniel and I turn instinctively towards the hall. Samsam barks again, and I call his name, the real name we never use anymore. He pads anxiously into the family room, but he won't sit down. I have to push his ass down to the ground like when he was a puppy.

My heart's beating fast, like something bad is about to happen. I wait for the sound of footsteps on the stairs, but they don't come and finally I look at Daniel. He's watching me, waiting for me to take charge somehow, and that freaks me out almost as much as everything else.

"Maybe you should go to bed now anyway," I say, throwing a hint of authority into my voice.

"Okay," he says, his eyes worried.

I watch him go and then lie on the couch with my hands folded over my stomach, waiting for Dad to come home. I thought they were doing okay, even with the weird hand-holding and stuff. I thought Tuesday nights were working, but now my stomach's churning. Samsam stretches out on the carpet beside me, and I think about switching on the TV or going up to bed but I don't. I shut my eyes and dream I'm an Egyptian mummy, my bones dissolving into dust. My legs won't move and my eyelids won't open. An eternity settles over my body, and when I wake up it's five-thirty and coffee's gurgling in the kitchen.

I stumble into the hall, following the noise. Mom's leaning against the kitchen counter in yesterday's clothes, and the second I see her I realize that I expected to see Dad. "What're you doing?" I ask numbly.

"Finn." She has dark circles under her eyes and looks older than yesterday. "Please. We'll talk in the morning."

It is morning. "Did he come home?" My voice sounds ancient.

"No, he didn't," she says unsteadily.

I blink in slow motion, still half paralyzed. Then I go up to bed without another word, my feet heavy on the stairs and my eyelashes sticky. I lie on top of my bed, wide-awake, waiting for my mother to pull herself together enough to tell us the bad news.

* * *

Just before nine I remember about Play Country. My training starts at nine-thirty, and Dad said he'd drive me. Now there's just Mom, having a nervous breakdown in the kitchen. I put fresh clothes on my ancient mummy body and scrub my face and underarms.

Downstairs I peek into the kitchen and spy Mom nibbling a chocolate chip cookie. I've never seen her with anything that fattening in her hand, and she blinks up at me like she's expecting me to comment. "I'm starting work today," I say. "Can you give me a ride?"

Mom's eyes glaze over. "Daniel's still in bed. Why don't you take the bus?"

"I don't even know what time it comes. I can't be late on my first day." I blink back tears, feeling like an idiot. Most of me doesn't care if I ever get to Play Country, but some small part won't let it go. Anti-Me has a summer of day camp with his friends—what do I have?

"I can't do this right now, Finn," Mom says. Her arms are thin in her sleeveless top, and I think I see them shake.

A wave of sympathy rushes over me. Dad should be here to talk to us. It's not fair. We don't even know where he is. What if there's an emergency? What if Mom plans to sit here eating cookies for the rest of her life? "It won't take long," I plead. "It's just across from the mall."

"You can walk then." Mom gets up from the table, pours me a glass of orange juice, and slides the vitamins towards me.

I down the glass of orange juice in seconds and ignore the vitamins. "If they fire me on my first day, it's your fault," I say bitterly, and then I'm off, jogging towards Play Country in the summer smog.

My pores clog instantly, and my hair frizzes like a novelty store wig. By the time I get to Play Country, fifteen minutes late, I'm a puddle of sweat and red fuzz. My throat's on fire, and I don't have a cent on me. Suzanne's eyebrows jerk together when she sees me. "Are you all right, Finn?" she asks disapprovingly.

"I had to walk," I rasp. "Is there any water around?"

"There's a water cooler in the staff room," she replies. "I'll take you there after we pick you up a uniform. Another girl's starting today. We've been waiting on you."

So much for first impressions.

Suzanne leads me into an office supply room and rummages around in one of the boxes. "What size are you, Finn? Most girls take small."

Yeah, I noticed. "Large, please," I tell her. "I have really long arms." I hold them out to demonstrate.

Suzanne's eyebrows spring back together as she holds out a large in front of her. "I think you'll drown in it."

"It's fine," I assure her. She points me in the direction of the staff bathroom, and I take off my top and pull the Play Country shirt over my head. I look like a nine-year-old in her father's shirt, which makes it just about the right size as far as I'm concerned. At least my boobs aren't advertising their desire to play.

In the staff room I gulp down water and nod as Suzanne introduces me to my co-workers. Nishani from French class is sitting at the table too, and she smiles up at me. She's the other girl starting today, and I feel my shoulders relax a little. Nishani was really quiet in French class. She shouldn't be any trouble to work with.

Suzanne makes us watch a boring safety video and then gives us a whirlwind tour of the store, offering brief descriptions of each aisle. The stockroom is gigantic, and I wonder how I'll ever be able to find anything. Suzanne taps employees on the arm as we pass, making quick introductions. She has a printed list of items we need to shelve and guides us back to the stockroom to start. My head's pounding and my stomach's rumbling, and Nishani and I trail behind Suzanne, wondering aloud when we'll get a break.

"I'm not even supposed to be doing this," Nishani whispers. "I'm supposed to be training on cash."

"So what're you doing here?" I clutch my stomach as it roars again.

"I'm not sure," she admits. "You sound like you're about to explode."

"I know." It's embarrassing, but there's only one thing I can do about it and it doesn't look like that'll be happening anytime soon. "And I forgot my lunch too."

"We can go to the mall," Nishani suggests. "I didn't bring one either."

My stomach purrs at the idea. "I don't have any cash on me. I slept in this morning. I thought I was getting a ride, and then I had to walk . . ." My voice trails off.

"That's okay," she says. "It's on me. You can get it next time."

Suzanne turns, hands on her hips, and shouts, "Come on, girls. This isn't a short list."

She's right. A ton of seasonal items have to be shelved: jumbo sidewalk chalk, jump rope, plastic baseball sets, water guns, beach balls, pail and shovel sets, yada, yada. The list is infinite, and we're not even a quarter of the way through when she finally informs us we can go for lunch.

We tear off in the direction of the mall and have pizza slices with french fries drowned in ketchup. The fries are actually Nishani's, but she tells me she'll have to make herself throw up in the Play Country bathroom if I don't help out. "Kidding," she adds, slapping her left thigh. "Do I look like a bulimic?"

She looks like she could lose ten pounds and still not be too skinny. In other words, she looks completely normal. My skin goes cold as my mind skips back to Mom eating chocolate chip cookies this morning. Has she spoken to Daniel already, or are they waiting for me? I don't want to hear what she's going to tell me. I don't understand what happened between the hand-holding and last night, but I don't want to know. Wondering about it makes me angry with both of them, especially Dad because he's the one who left.

After lunch Nishani and I wear ourselves out finishing another quarter of the list under Suzanne's watchful gaze. I'm so exhausted that I feel like I'm in some kind of trance, but it's for the best because when I get home I don't care what happens.

I don't care that Dad came home especially to talk to Daniel and me. I don't care that he and Mom are having a difficult time and need some time apart. I don't even care that he won't be able to drive me to work because he'll be staying at a friend's cottage in Orillia for the summer. Nothing my father says feels real. I'm actually relieved when he announces that he's leaving.

"I'll be back and forth to see you two," he says. "I left the cottage phone number on the fridge. Call anytime."

I hang back and watch the Anti-Me hug him goodbye. The two of them look sad, but I just feel stuck. Audrey's in Gatineau, Play Country's one step up from legal slave labor, and my parents are separating for the summer.

I have never been so tired.

This can't be my life.

fifteen

○   ○   ○

UNDER THE COVERS Raine Maida sings "Clumsy" into my ears and I almost believe him. *Maybe I should sleep . . . Maybe I just need . . .* I roll onto my chest, my arms doubled up underneath me like a folding chair, and he sings me to sleep with that golden Beautiful Boy voice of his. Once I'm there, I don't want to come back. I don't want to call Dad at some cottage in Orillia I've never been to. I want to live down behind my eyelids with the music charging through me like a force of nature.

I sleep for a long time, but when I wake up at noon I'm still spent. My stomach's in knots and I feed it strawberry Pop-Tarts while watching *Scooby-Doo*. The more wakeful I feel, the more my stomach tightens, and I rush upstairs and type out an e-mail to Audrey, telling her everything that's happened in the past day and a half. Her e-mail from Quebec yesterday was eleven sentences, and mine is endless and full of gloom.

If Audrey were here, I'd be sitting in her pastel-orange room now. I wouldn't want to move, but she'd try to drag me over to HMV to stare at Record Store Guy or convince me to take the train downtown with her. That way I wouldn't spend the day glancing at Dad's phone number on the fridge or dreading tomorrow's shift at Play Country.

I can already feel the worry taking over my bones, fusing them to my ergonomically incorrect chair. Audrey's right. I have to get out of here before it's too late.

I drag my ass away from the computer desk, shower, and throw on cutoff denim shorts and a faded Beck T-shirt. I don't have a clue where I'm going and I don't have anyone to go with, but I can't hang around here decomposing. Samsam's at my heels in the hallway, and I grab his leash and take him outside. God knows when Mom or Daniel will remember to walk him again; Dad and I are the primary dog-walkers.

Samsam's ecstatic the moment his paws hit the park. He strains at the leash when we spot a squirrel but sits politely as two kids stop to pet him. I jog him for another ten minutes or so before it occurs to me that we're only a few minutes from Jersy's house. I haven't seen him since that last day in art class. He probably won't be home, but I start heading for his neighborhood anyway. With Audrey out of the picture, I'm not even sure we'll have much to say to each other, but I kind of miss having him around.

A couple minutes later I'm standing on his front step with Samsam, listening to the doorbell peal through the hall. There's no movement inside, and I'm halfway to deciding no one's home when I hear heavy footsteps on the stairs. Jersy pulls the door open, blinking into the sun like he's going blind. He's wearing a rumpled yellow T-shirt that says "Road Crew" and black sweat shorts that stretch down to his knees. "Hey," he says, his voice dusty.

It's obvious that I woke him up, and I'm about to apologize

when he bends down and rakes his fingers energetically through Samsam's coat. "You coming in?" he asks, cocking his head.

"Sure." I follow him inside, Samsam's lead gripped in my right hand.

"It's okay," Jersy says. "You can let him go."

Right. I unchain the leash and watch Samsam pad nosily around the Mikulski kitchen. It's the first time I've been inside Jersy's house since that winter day, but this time I know I won't panic.

"Have you heard from Audrey?" Jersy asks, leading me through the house and out to the patio.

"Yesterday," I tell him. "I just sent her an e-mail this morning."

"She e-mailed me too." Jersy collapses into one of the wooden lounge chairs beside the swimming pool. "She sounds okay."

"Bored," I qualify. The water's sparkling like a Caribbean coast, coaxing me forward. I take off my sandals and stand with my toes curved over the edge. This place was a snow globe a few months ago, and now I can't stop thinking how I haven't been swimming since last summer.

"Go ahead," Jersy urges, motioning to the pool. "You know you wanna." I swivel around and catch him smiling. His hair's fierce mountain man on one side and stuck flat to his head on the other, and he yawns a little as I smile back.

Right then Samsam bounds out the sliding door and towards the pool. I grab him by the collar and command him to sit. "It's okay," Jersy says. "He can go in if he wants."

"The chlorine is bad for them." I stand by Jersy's chair. "He's thirsty. I should get him some water."

"I'll get it." Jersy jumps up and heads inside.

I sit in the chair closest to his and watch him return with a pail of water and flop back into place. Samsam immediately starts slurping, and the sound makes us smile. "Man," Jersy says, rubbing his head with both hands. "I was at Joel's place with Billy last night and we . . ." He stops mid-sentence as though he just remembered who he was talking to. "Forget it. You don't want to know."

"What, you got totally wasted or something, right?" My tone's impatient. I don't get the fascination with frying your brain. Personally, I'd like to hold on to mine for a few more years.

"Yeah." Jersy scratches his knee and leans over the side of the chair towards me. "I know you guys aren't into that—you and Audrey. But you probably never tried anything either, right? Did you ever even smoke a joint?" He looks into my eyes, making me feel like a total kid.

"What difference does that make?" I cross my ankles on the sun chair and hold his stare. "It's not like I've been brainwashed by my parents or anything. I just don't like the idea of messing myself up."

Jersy nods. "I knew you'd say that. You and Audrey are exactly the same."

"Whatever. I just don't get the drug thing." I shrug. "There's a lot of stuff I don't get about people. Sometimes I feel like an alien." I can't believe I just told him that. I'd never have said that forty-eight hours ago. "I don't even know what people are talking about half the time or what to say to them." I look over at him, unembarrassed about my freakishness for once.

Jersy reaches out to touch my arm. "You feel human."

"Sensory illusion," I say.

Jersy gives me a lopsided grin. "Nobody gets anybody, Finn. It's a miracle I can even understand what you're saying."

"Maybe you don't." I roll onto my side. "Maybe you only think you do."

"Yeah." Jersy's blue-green eyes bug out at me. "You sure you're not stoned right now?"

Just numb.

Jersy keeps blinking his long brown eyelashes in my direction. "I was wasted last night, but that doesn't happen as often as people think it does. I don't go looking for situations, you know? They just happen."

Obviously he doesn't avoid them either, but I didn't come over to rag on him. "So what else is going on with you?" I ask. "Audrey said you got some job in a factory."

"Shit job in a factory," he clarifies with a shrug. "But the pay's all right. They hire a student to cover vacation time every year. This week I'm filling in for a guy on midnights. How's Play Country?"

I roll my eyes and complain until my throat hurts, but the worst thing about this summer sticks to my insides like Krazy Glue. I go over to the pool, park my butt on the side, and dip my legs in.

"I know you can swim," Jersy says, peeling off his shirt and striding by me. He cannonballs into the pool, soaking my T-shirt and shorts. "And now you're already wet." He breaststrokes over to my side of the pool, grinning like his six-year-old self.

"I don't feel like it," I tell him. "Some other time, okay?"

Jersy lowers his head into the water and swims off, Aquaman-style. He holds his breath for so long that you'd swear he has gills and then pulls himself out of the pool in one swift motion.

"Show-off," I tease, but I'm not smiling.

Jersy smoothes his sopping brown hair back with his hand and stares at me for so long that I have to look away. "Are you okay?" he asks.

"Yeah." I should've told him when he opened the front door. Now I don't know how to explain. "It's just . . ." I bend over and dip my hands into the water, next to my legs. "You remember how I told you about my parents before?"

Jersy's dripping on the patio in the shorts he probably slept in, his eyes solemn. "They broke up?" he asks.

"For a while anyway. My dad left the night before last." My hands flutter through the water as I look over at him. He really is my second best friend. I had to tell someone. "He's staying at his friend's cottage for the summer."

"His friend?" Jersy repeats suspiciously.

"Some English teacher guy from his school." I yank my hands out of the water and wipe them on my thighs. "I don't think he's having an affair or anything. I think things just aren't working out with them." My parents act like two people who don't like each other anymore. If someone asked them why, I bet they wouldn't even be able to answer.

Jersy looks down at me like he doesn't have a clue what to say, and I smile and add, "You don't have to say anything. There's nothing to say anyway. These things happen all the time." Our eyes lock, and for a second I know we're thinking the exact same thing: *But not to me.*

Jersy sits down beside me and plunges his legs into the pool. His silence reminds me of the last time we were in his backyard. Maybe he's one of those people who actually know when to keep quiet. We sit by the pool for a couple minutes, our legs making circles in the water. Then Samsam begins slurping away again, instantly changing the tone.

"You seem okay, though," Jersy says, knocking his arm against mine.

"Yeah, right. If I seem okay, why would you ask?"

Jersy tilts his head to the side and squints over at me. "This is shit timing. Did you tell Audrey?"

I stare at my knees. "In my e-mail this morning." I don't want to go to pieces on him like last time, but it's happening. Fresh sadness hurts the worst, and I feel a new wave wash in, taking me over.

Jersy slides his arm around me and squeezes my shoulder. "It's okay," he says, and I start to cry, under my breath and into his skin. I bury my face in his shoulder as he wraps his other arm firmly around me. He smells like chlorine and the salt of my tears. There's something so sweet about the mix that it hurts even deeper.

"I hate crying," I say vehemently into his neck.

"Are you sure? You seem pretty good at it," he kids, and I smile and cry at the same time, feeling better and worse. Maybe I shouldn't have come here. Maybe I'm worse off than I think.

"Hey," he says softly. "Any more and the pool will flood."

I pull myself away and press my palms against my eyes. "I should go," I announce. I've weirded him out enough for one day.

"Where?" Jersy stands up next to me.

"Home, I guess." That's the last place I want to go but the first thing that popped into my head.

"Why?" he asks.

I stare at him, the taste of my tears in my mouth.

"If you're not doing anything, why don't you guys stay awhile?" He smiles over at Samsam. "I won't even rag on you about being afraid of the pool."

"I'm not afraid of the pool," I counter.

He smiles wider. "Yeah, whatever, Finn. You're not psycho. You're not brainwashed. You're not afraid of the pool. Whatever you say."

I put my hands on my hips, and he touches my elbow and says, "I'll make popcorn or something. We'll just chill."

That sounds pretty good, and I stay for another two hours. We don't talk much about my parents or Audrey. We don't even talk about school. Jersy talks about getting money together for a motorcycle, and I tell him about my top-secret driving lesson. Then we try to talk about music, but we only like three of the same bands: Bloc Party, Green Day, and Pearl Jam. Jersy's into all this shitty rap stuff, and I tell him that rap hasn't been any good in years. He says I'm crazy and that Raine Maida loves to pretend he's some huge rock star, but nobody even knows who he is. I should know better than to argue music with somebody who likes Beyoncé, but I tell Jersy he's only into her because she never wears anything more than a silver babydoll with matching monster stilettos.

Jersy hides his smile behind his hand. "And there's something wrong with that?"

"Your taste sucks," I tell him. "Except for Audrey."

He laughs and scratches his sun-dried hair. "That situation's so fucked. I don't know where we're at. I can't even get her on the phone for the next two months."

I frown and furrow my eyebrows. "You said you just got an e-mail from her."

"Yeah, I know," he says with a laugh. "Does that make us pen pals?"

I study Samsam lounging on the grass and envy his canine calm. I know I never thought Jersy was the waiting-around type, but if he tells me he's breaking up with Audrey after forty-eight hours, I won't be able to forgive him. "You make it sound like it's over," I tell him, not bothering to hide my disapproval. "After two days."

"I never said that." Now he's pissed. "I'm just saying that it's a shit situation." He throws up his right hand. "You completely twisted that around. Why are you in such a hurry to think the worst?"

He's right, and I feel like a fly on a windscreen—a very

relieved, partially squashed fly on a windscreen. "I'm sorry." I fold my arms in front of me and grasp my elbows. "I'm all messed up about yesterday."

"Don't worry about it," Jersy says, instantly reverting to calm. "I just meant that it's rough." He hooks his fingers around the end of the armrest and stares at the pool. "It's probably rougher on you than it is on me, with what's going on at home."

That's true too, but I feel like I have to make it up to him somehow. "Maybe I can call Audrey for you, give you guys a chance to talk. I could do it now if you want. She might be home."

Jersy smiles at my peace offering and says, "You should talk to her too, you know."

We take Samsam inside with us and go up to his room. Audrey included her aunt's phone number in the e-mails she sent us yesterday, and I punch in the digits as Jersy recites them.

"Do you think her parents would've given them your phone number?" I ask, wishing I'd remembered my cell.

He shrugs. "I guess we'll find out."

Jersy gives a thumbs-up when I make it past the screening process and get her on the phone. Then he steps out of his room and closes the door behind him, letting me have my turn first. I talk Audrey's ear off and let her tell me everything will work out. The tension flows out of me as I listen to her voice. I could easily make some kind of long-distance record, but this is Jersy's quarter.

"Let me get your favorite boy," I say.

"Great." I can practically hear her smile from three hundred miles away.

sixteen

○   ○   ○

MOM DOESN'T TELL me I have to take Dad's phone calls. Most of the time she's too tired to care what I do. I think some small part of her is also relieved to have me on her side. Not that I ever really took sides before. It was just easier for Dad and me to understand each other. We're both back-of-the-room people, while Mom usually prefers the spotlight. I say "usually" because she's spent the majority of the past two weeks sequestered in her bedroom. If it weren't for me, Daniel would be massacring soldiers until midnight.

Mom's new eight o'clock bedtime doesn't help her get out of bed any. She hits snooze five times every morning, and when she finally leaves for work she looks unfinished, like the same raw version of herself that emerges from the bathroom at seven in the evening after her shower. It's obvious she's depressed, but I don't know what to do about it. How are my parents supposed to work things out when they're never around each other?

Maybe if Dad would spend more time with Mom on the phone instead of letting Daniel monopolize the conversation, we'd get somewhere. Maybe I wouldn't feel like a third-class passenger on the *Titanic*. Because right now that's what it seems like.

I'm sinking.

And no one's around to stop me. Dad's drinking beer on a lawn chair up north, ripping through a stack of nonfiction, Audrey's playing sleepover with her French cousins, and Mom's hiding out under a queen-sized pillow.

If it weren't for Play Country, I'd go insane. That sounds certifiable, I know. Suzanne keeps doling out impossibly long lists and I have a ladder phobia that makes the high stuff a nightmare and Nishani still isn't on cash like she's supposed to be and this nineteen-year-old guy named Kevin constantly stands too close to you like he's about to smack his lips against yours. It's terrible, but it's *there*.

Gerald Goldmann flashes smiles at everyone, afraid to come off like a big bad boss. Suzanne thinks he's a wuss and rides everyone extra hard to make up for it. That makes all the employees hate her, especially the cute customer-service-booth girls with the tiny Play Country shirts that Gerald smiles at the widest. Actually, I don't even think he knows he's doing it. I think Gerald's one of those guys who never got near a pretty girl in high school and is still in awe of them.

Nishani laughs when I explain my theories. "You should be a psychoanalyst. You've got it all figured out." She tosses her thick black hair back and hurls a bundle of M&M's into the candy bin. "So what's Kevin's story? Let me guess." Her teeth poke out from between her lips. "His mother didn't breastfeed him."

"Exactly." I shudder and look over my shoulder. Kevin loves to sneak up behind you and earwig. I don't know what he thinks he's going to do with the information. Nobody in Play Country has anything useful to say. The job makes you stupid if you weren't already.

Take this exact moment, for instance. Two boys are bouncing a basketball behind us while a third circles erratically around on a bicycle two years too big for him. Kevin left his ladder out in the action-figure aisle, an accident waiting to happen, and one of the customer service girls has just paged for cleanup in Arts and Crafts. I'm not sure precisely what needs to be cleaned up, but I'm afraid to find out, and the baby screeching a couple aisles over is killing my will to live.

It's mind-numbing, but like I said, it's *there*. Most of the people aren't bad, and Nishani's cooler than I ever would've discovered in French class. Suzanne keeps matching our work schedules together because we're both in training.

"Did Suzanne say when they're going to start training you on cash?" I ask. This is a sore point with Nishani, who detests heavy lifting about as much as I fear ladders.

Nishani balls up her shoulders. "She said maybe next week. If nothing happens by then, I'm going to Gerald."

"This isn't so bad," I tell her. The best thing about being a stock person is that there's always somewhere to hide. I could spend the next hour in the stockroom and no one would notice.

"It'd be okay if we were working together all the time," Nishani says. "But they won't keep scheduling us like that. We'd have our own sections to stock."

I nod and, from the corner of my eye, catch Courtney from customer service bouncing over to us. "Hey, *chicas*," she sings, sliding her hands into her back pockets. Wavy blond hair trails halfway down her back, and her chest juts out like a *Maxim* pinup.

She'd be a typical Hooters wannabe if she weren't so indiscriminately friendly.

"Hey, Courtney," we sing back.

"Finn." Courtney's baby blues shoot over to me. "Some totally hot guy was looking for you here last night. What's the situation?"

"Huh?" Goosebumps pop up under my rugby shirt. She couldn't be talking about Adam. He wouldn't do that.

"Light brown hair," she continues. "Not real tall." Courtney's hand slices through the air at roughly five foot nine. "Tiny scar on his cheek. Kinda grungy but totally hot. He's not your boyfriend, is he?"

"No." That's a definite description of Jersy. He must've been next door at Sport Mart and decided to stop in. "That's not my boyfriend."

"Hmm. Didn't think so." Courtney lowers her voice. "Shit. Don't look now, but here comes Kevin. Catch ya later, *chicas.*" She swivels on her heels and rushes back towards the safety of the customer service booth.

The insult sinks in as I watch her go. She didn't think it was possible for me to have a boyfriend who looked like Jersy; I'm geek-boyfriend material. Nishani makes a clucking noise and whispers, "Who is this totally hot not-your-boyfriend person?"

"I didn't know you had a boyfriend," Kevin booms from mere inches away. His six-foot frame means we're almost on eye level, unfortunately.

"It's scientifically impossible for you to have heard that," Nishani protests.

Kevin ignores her completely. "I thought you were available." His eyes are drinking me in like a six-pack at a frat party.

"I'm not available." I take a step back, catch sight of the

basketball boys, and will them to lob the ball at the back of Kevin's head.

"C'mon," Kevin says smugly. "You are. You both are. It's written all over you in invisible ink."

Nishani and I turn towards each other and then back to Kevin to scowl at him. Invisible ink? Does that make *any* sense?

"Excuse me, folks." An old man in a plaid shirt interrupts, giving Nishani and me the perfect excuse to end the conversation.

I smile at the old guy as I take another step away from Kevin. Nishani follows my lead, leaving Kevin stranded alone in the middle of the aisle. "Can we help you?" I ask.

The man scrutinizes the piece of lilac notepaper in his hand. "Where, within this monstrosity of a store, would I find such a thing as the Fisher-Price Little People Airplane?"

Play Country policy dictates that you always accompany customers directly to the product they're searching for. Reciting aisle numbers is a big no-no, along with leaving your ladder unattended. "I'll show him," I tell Nishani. Kevin, in no hurry to help anyone, has already disappeared.

I escort the old man down the toddler aisle and grab one of the blue and white airplanes from the bottom shelf. "How much is it?" he asks, wrinkling his nose.

It's obvious he's going to buy it—somebody's gone to the trouble of writing it down on pretty purple paper for him—but I politely quote the price.

"Thank you." He takes the box from me.

When I meet Nishani back at the candy bin, she still wants to know about the not-my-boyfriend person. I tell her he's Audrey's boyfriend, Jersy Mikulski, and she knows who I'm talking about but she doesn't think he's good-looking. In fact, she only likes

South Asian guys. "My sister's the complete opposite," she says. "She likes everyone but desi guys."

Her sister is seventeen and going into twelfth grade at St. Mark's. Last I heard, she was seeing this Scottish guy, Maxwell, who put on a perfect American accent to play Biff in the school production of *Death of a Salesman*.

"That's ancient history," Nishani tells me. "Aneeka has a short attention span. She always loses interest before they do. We're going over to the mall tonight after work. She wants to get a full Brazilian for summer." Nishani and I wince in anticipation of the pain. I tried to wax my legs once last summer and only made it halfway up one knee. "Why don't you come with us?"

Not like I have anything better to do. The more time I spend away from home, the less likely I'll be there when it plunges to the bottom of the ocean.

After our shift Nishani and I wander in and out of clothing stores as Aneeka has her pubic hair methodically torn out by the roots. Then Aneeka drags us cheerfully into swimsuit stores looking for the tiniest bathing suit she can find and decides on a minuscule fire-engine-red thong bikini. Nishani declares Aneeka too afraid of their parents to ever wear it out of the house, but the sparkle in Aneeka's eyes tells me otherwise.

"It could be good for indoor recreation too," Aneeka says.

Nishani flicks her gaze up to the heavens. "You're such a skank." If it's possible to say that with love, I've just heard it.

Aneeka reaches around me and pinches Nishani's arm.

"Ouch." Nishani yanks her arm away and whirls towards me. "You see? She's crazy." She massages the sore spot, her jaw and shoulders tight. "That's going to leave a bruise."

"It will not," Aneeka intones. "You're such a baby." She gently strokes her sister's hair. "Did they put you on cash yet at that ridiculous place?"

I answer for her. "No, she's keeping me from going insane stocking."

Nishani and I describe the crazy day we've had, including the interruptions from Courtney and Kevin. Aneeka's immediately offended on my behalf. "Who does she think she is, implying you're not good enough to be this guy's girlfriend?"

"Courtney's too blond to realize when she's being insulting," Nishani adds.

"It's true." I smile so hard that my teeth hurt. Maybe the Play Country gig won't be so bad after all. Maybe I'm even making new friends.

That happy thought gets me as far as the Kavanagh kitchen, where Daniel's holding a dripping ice cream sandwich in one hand and the telephone in the other. "Do you want to talk to Dad?" he asks, shoving the phone in my face.

"Later," I tell him, pushing it away.

I dive into the bath minutes later, making that impossible. If I spoke to Dad, I'd only say the wrong thing. He'd try to defend himself, but he'd fail. Mom is here and he isn't. Mom was trying and he wasn't. I heard enough from the hall the night he left.

My throat swells thinking about it, but I won't give in. I've bawled enough for one summer.

seventeen

○　　○　　○

AUDREY E-MAILS ME every day from her cousin's computer. She's been spending a lot of time on the paddleboats at the park down the road and has become a pro at mini-golf. Her twelve-year-old cousin, Justine, is completely enamored with Audrey's Shakespearean-style love affair, and as well as allowing access to her computer any time of day or night, eagerly soaks up whatever Jersy details Audrey will share. Audrey says she wishes she were at Play Country with me, despite how bad I make it sound, and that she's so tan from paddleboating that she could be Daniel's Mexican sister.

She understands exactly how I feel about my dad and tells me it's only natural that I'm not in a hurry to talk to him. "Don't worry about him," she says. "Just take care of yourself."

I e-mail her daily too, sometimes twice. I'm forever stumbling across Internet stuff she'd be interested in, like today's Sagittarius (her sign) horoscope: "Recently forces have been mobilizing against you, leaving you feeling defeated. Be patient and let the drama play itself out, and you'll be surprised how the battle ends."

The last thing I should be doing on a summer day is surfing the Internet for astrological predictions I don't believe in, but my days off are long and boring, and Saturdays are the worst. Mom alternates between pacing restlessly around the house, her hair in a limp ponytail, and napping on the living room couch. The ever popular Anti-Me's over at the waterpark with friends, his favorite summer activity. In the past Mom would've nagged me to get off the computer and do something, but now she can't even muster the energy to pick up the ringing telephone.

I eye it warily as it rings for the fourth time. It could be Dad again or the woman who keeps calling to say Mom's won a free gym membership at the Women's Health Club two blocks away. I could pick up and explain that Mom's eleven-hour sleep schedule doesn't leave much time for a gym membership, but I let the answering machine do the job for me.

Afterwards I play the message back. Anna Mikulski wants to set a dinner date with Mom. I wonder if Jersy told her about my dad leaving. It's not a secret. Maybe a night out with Anna would do her good. I leave her a note on the kitchen table and take Sam-sam for a walk down to the lake. He doesn't chase geese like he does squirrels; he stares distastefully at them as they honk. It's the weirdest expression, and I giggle to myself as I pull him towards the water. His retriever half is genetically programmed to obsess over sticks, and I toss them repeatedly into the lake and let him play out his genetic destiny.

Behind me a group of younger guys are playing hacky sack. A teenage couple at the nearest picnic bench are kissing heatedly, the girl straddling the guy's lap. My head wants to turn and watch them like a pervert. They remind me of Audrey and Jersy on my bed, and embarrassment wells up inside me, dragging me away.

Before September, I used to think about sex a lot. Sometimes I still do, but it's different when you have to police your mind so that the thoughts don't mutate into bad memories. And now I get nervous when guys make dirty jokes or wolf-whistle from cars. Conversations with Kevin from work have the potential to make me queasy. Of course Kevin makes all the girls he works with queasy, but there's absolutely no way I should be visualizing my best friend with her boyfriend.

"C'mon, Samsam," I tell him, fighting a blush. "Let's go home and drag Mom off the couch."

When we get there, my mother's clearing stale food out of the fridge and sanitizing surfaces. She hasn't plucked her eyebrows since Dad left, and tiny hairs are growing in under the previously perfect arch. "Wet dog smell," Mom notes. "You let him go in the lake?"

"It's hot. You know how sluggish he gets in the heat."

Mom purses her lips, a bead of sweat gathering between her eyes. "Now that you're home, maybe you can help me clean up a bit. The living room needs vacuuming."

Mom takes a shower as I vacuum. When she comes back downstairs to check my progress, the tiny hairs under her eyebrows are gone and she's wearing salmon-colored nail polish with matching lipstick. "Your dad's on his way over for a visit," she says. "He's picking up Daniel along the way."

"What?" I scrunch up my eyebrows. "How come you didn't say that before?" The makeover's more than coincidence. She's still trying. Unlike me. I have no intention of hanging around to make nice.

"I thought you might try to take off somewhere," she admits. "He really wants to see you." So now she's an accomplice to the guy who made her miserable? Dressing up for him and making the house gleam? Does she have an ounce of self-respect?

"If he wants to see me so much, he shouldn't have taken off to Orillia," I retort.

"You know that had nothing to do with you or Daniel," Mom says in a high-pitched voice.

Of course I do. "I'm going out later anyway," I lie. "Over to Jersy's. He dropped by the store looking for me yesterday." That last part's the truth, at least.

"You never mentioned that." Mom glances at her watch. "Talk to him for a few minutes at least, Finn. He should be here soon."

Dad walks through the door with Daniel over thirty minutes later. Anti-Me rushes towards the fridge, but Dad hangs back, waiting for Mom to invite him in. "Can I get you something to drink, Alan?" Mom asks. She looks nervous around him when she should be giving him attitude.

"That'd be nice." Dad smiles at me as he follows her into the sparkling kitchen. "How you doing, Finn? I've had a hell of a time trying to get you on the phone. Every time I call your cell, it goes straight to message."

"I've been busy with work," I grumble. "We have to leave our phones in our lockers." Daniel sticks a purple freezie in his mouth and sucks at it like a vampire. He's the only one who doesn't look tense, and he flashes Dad a purple grin before careening out of the room.

"I know you're busy." Dad nods sympathetically, trying to make up for his impatience that night coming back from Audrey's.

"Uh-huh." My tone's edgy. In my mind I'm leaping away from the table and sprinting over to Jersy's. There's no way he'll be home on a Saturday night. I should've phoned Jasper and Maggie and begged them to go to the movies with me. They'd be surprised to hear from me outside of the school year, but they might say yes. Aidan Lamb's starring in a new action flick. Maggie wouldn't be able to resist that.

"Well, I'd like to put together a schedule of when the three of us can see each other," Dad continues doggedly. "You, me, and Daniel. We can juggle it around your work schedule. With school out and Audrey away, you must have some time."

Mom sets an iced tea down in front of Dad and edges discreetly out of the kitchen. "The thing is, I don't have time to go over it right now," I say. "Me and Jersy are hanging out tonight. I'm already late."

Dad clasps his hands together on the table. "You're avoiding me." He rubs his forehead and sips his iced tea. "It's not easy for me being away from you and Daniel, Finn. It's not the way I wanted things, but your mother and I—we're not good for each other right now, and that wouldn't be good for you and Daniel."

"What about the counseling?" I ask bluntly. "You guys were going every week. I thought things were getting better."

Dad sighs. "It's not as simple as that, Finn."

"Okay, fine," I say, like talking about it's boring me. Dad looks discouraged, and I'm glad. He can't tear our family apart and expect everything else to stay the same. *It's not as simple as that.* "Can we do the schedule thing over the phone? I have to go."

Dad doesn't answer. His cheeks sink into his face as he takes his hands off the table.

I blink down at him as I stand. "I'll call you, okay?"

It takes all my strength to pretend that I couldn't care less how he feels. If he knows me at all, the way I'm acting should make it clear how wrong he was to leave.

"Will you?" he asks quietly.

It's the saddest thing I've ever heard. It breaks my heart, but I'm going just the same.

"I'll call," I tell him. "I said I would."

I run most of the way to Jersy's house. My chest's pounding and my throat hurts like I just had my tonsils scraped out with a jagged piece of glass. I can't catch my breath, but it doesn't matter. Jersy won't be home, but that doesn't matter either. Nothing matters much. Except getting away.

I slow down about a block from Jersy's house and smooth my hair into place. I don't want the Mikulskis asking me what's the matter. I wish I could sneak into their house unnoticed, like the Invisible Woman, and just be somewhere calm and normal for a change. I could sit on the edge of Jersy's bed and stare at him and he'd never know.

The thought jumps up and down inside my head, making me shudder. I shouldn't think things like that. He's Audrey's. *Don't be crazy,* I lecture. *You're just sad. You're reaching out in any direction. It didn't mean anything.* The shock lasts for about ten seconds, and then I'm back to being miserable.

Christina sees it in my face when she answers the door. "He's out on his dirt bike," she says apologetically, her eyes squinting with concern. "Why don't you come in and wait awhile?"

"No thanks." I push my lips into a rigid smile. "Just tell him I stopped by." It was a bad idea to start with. I should've called Jasper or Maggie. Nishani might've wanted to hang out with us too.

" 'Kay," she says. "I'll let him know."

I walk purposefully down the driveway, in case she's watching, but my shoulders slump at the end of his street. It's too soon to go home, but where do I go? I'm kicking myself for not getting Nishani's number and simultaneously trying to choose a first runner-up (Jasper or Maggie) when I spy a guy pushing a dirt bike up the road in the distance.

It has to be him. My hand shoots up to wave, and he hesitates a second before waving back. I keep walking and meet him halfway, sadness coiled so tightly into my lungs that it aches to breathe.

"Hey, Finn," he says, coming to a stop in the middle of the sidewalk.

"Hi," I say back. "I didn't think you'd be home."

"Not much point in coming to visit me then, is there?" He smiles and starts walking again. His strides are longer than mine, despite the fact that his legs are shorter, and I practically have to jog to keep up.

It's obvious that he's not going to ask me what happened. He can't read my mind like Audrey. He probably doesn't even know something's wrong.

"Did you bring your swimsuit this time?" he asks. "You didn't, did you?"

"No." I shake my head. "I didn't really think you'd be here. I was having a crisis moment." Suddenly I can't stop talking. "And I just ran over here, thinking you'd be out. Not actually thinking, if you know what I mean. Just running. And then your sister answered the door and—"

"What happened?" Jersy cuts in. His eyes are pure blue in the evening light.

"My dad came over and I didn't want to talk to him. Seeing him just makes everything feel worse." The coil squeezes as I continue. "I don't want to worry about my parents or us as a family anymore. It's too hard. I wish I could've gone away for the summer instead of Audrey. I wouldn't even care about being bored. At least I'd be gone, you know? I'd be out of it."

"Yeah, but you can't really be out of it, can you?" Jersy says. "They're your family."

"I know. That's the problem."

"Yeah," Jersy repeats. We stop at the end of the street, and he adds, "I dropped by your work a couple days ago to see how things were going, but you weren't around."

"I heard."

"So." Jersy cocks his head. "You coming in with me? I have something to do later, but I have a couple hours."

I want him to ask me a second time. To make sure he really means it. "Does your mom know what's going on?" I ask.

"Yeah, she talked to your mother earlier today." I'm glad to hear Mom called Anna back. She hasn't been returning most of her friends' calls these days, but she needs someone to talk to.

We start walking again as though I've agreed to go with him. Jersy puts his dirt bike in the garage, next to a snowboard, and charges through the front door with me in tow. The smell of tomato sauce wafts forward to greet us. "Fifteen minutes, Jersy," Anna shouts from the kitchen.

He glances over his shoulder at me. "You hungry?"

"Not really." I'm starving. I just don't want to sit around the dinner table making polite conversation with the Mikulskis.

"I'll get something later," he yells back. "Finn's here. We're gonna hang out for a while."

Anna emerges from the kitchen looking homey and together. My mom looked together earlier too, but it was a lie. "I spoke to Gloria this afternoon," Anna says gently. "I was sorry to hear about the trouble with your parents. Are you doing okay?"

"I'm fine." I fix my eyes on the tile floor.

"If you ever need anything, just give me a call, will you?" I look up at her and see that she means it. That chokes me up and I nod, unable to get the words out.

"Upstairs or downstairs?" Jersy asks, tugging at my sleeve.

"Upstairs, I guess."

We leave Anna behind and go up to Jersy's room. I surprise myself by closing the door automatically behind me. It feels all right, and I sit down in front of his computer while he flicks on his docked iPod. "I know what you'll want to hear," he says, scrolling through the menu.

"American Idiot" blasts through the speakers. I know the words by heart, and I bob my head along, singing in silence. Jersy smiles as he stretches out on his bed.

"You're not gonna fall asleep on me, are you?" I ask.

"I'm not that kind of tired," he tells me. "My body's tired, but my brain's completely alert." He props his head up with his hands. His hair looks soft, like it's never been subjected to a styling product. "I'd ask you to come to this thing tonight, but it's not your scene."

"What thing?"

"My birthday thing. A few of us are driving over to Joel's brother's place in Windsor. He says there's always a party going on somewhere."

"I didn't know it was your birthday," I chirp. "Happy birthday."

"It's tomorrow."

"Well, 'Happy birthday' for tomorrow then." That makes him a Cancer: intuitive but changeable. I seriously have to cut down on the bullshit astrology sites.

"Thanks." A grin carves into his cheeks. "When's yours?"

"Not until October." Libra. Supposedly that makes me sociable and well balanced with amazing taste but a tendency to be lazy. It's about half right, which is enough to keep someone with a lot of time on their hands checking their horoscope.

We both tune into "American Idiot," absorbing the lyrics. I don't understand how somebody can appreciate Green Day and listen to crap like 50 Cent. It blows my mind.

Jersy blows my mind, and I'm trying to fit the pieces together, watching his head move to the beat of the song, when someone raps loudly at the door. Mr. Mikulski swings Jersy's door open and stares over at me. He switches his gaze to Jersy and motions for him to turn down the music. I reach over and turn it down myself. It's really not all that loud. We could understand each other just fine.

"The door was closed," Mr. Mikulski says sternly.

That's my fault, but Jersy's eyes bug out at his dad. "It's Finn." Jersy points at me like his father's being ridiculous.

"That doesn't make any difference. You know the rules." The crisscross lines on Mr. Mikulski's forehead make him look like Frankenstein. "We want this to be a safe place." Mr. Mikulski's heavy stare makes Jersy blink.

Twenty seconds ago I was comfortable in my own skin. Now the dread's back. What does Mr. Mikulski mean about wanting this to be a safe place?

"Okay," Jersy says quietly. "Sorry. Leave it open."

His dad stands in the doorway for a few seconds before turning and walking away. I get up from my chair, check to make sure he's gone downstairs, and then sit penitently down again. "I'm sorry," I tell him. "That was me. I didn't think."

"It's okay. You don't know the house rules." Jersy smiles as he continues. "I guess Audrey didn't tell you everything."

"Yeah." I slide my ass to the edge of the chair, ready to fly. "I should get going anyway. You need to rest up for later." My palms are moist and my jeans are sticking to the backs of my knees. I'm amazed my voice sounds normal.

Jersy rolls off the bed and turns up the volume again. "Don't let him throw you. He's like that with everyone. It's a family policy." The bed creaks as Jersy leaps back onto it like a skydiver. "No members of the opposite sex allowed behind closed doors."

My parents don't have house rules like that; I never needed them.

I check out Gizmo and find his beady eyes staring back at me. *"He can see you,"* Jersy teases, quoting me from that first time at his house.

I roll my eyes at him and then sweep my gaze around his room. It doesn't look any more finished than it did four months ago. Actually, it looks more like a walk-in closet than a bedroom. Jersy's cell phone's on the hardwood floor next to a jumble of mismatched running shoes, socks, and a deodorant spray. He's taken the pictures off his mirror, leaving it blank, and I wonder if the Chinese girl's smiling secretly away in his desk drawer.

"Your photos are gone." I point at Jersy's reflection. "Do you still keep in touch with your friends in Kingston?"

"We IM," he says. "And I'm going up there for a week at the end of August."

"That's good." The nerves haven't gone, and neither have I. There's nowhere better to go, and Jersy's pretty easy to deal with, for a guy. I slide down in my chair and concentrate on Green Day. If you listen closely enough, you lose the separation between yourself and the music. I won't get there now, with Jersy in the room, but I can feel it in my pulse and that's good enough.

Jersy's head is down on the bedspread, his arms at his sides. I watch the calm rhythm of his breath and barely even mind that he lied about staying awake.

eighteen

○   ○   ○

I DIDN'T LIE about phoning my dad; I just haven't gotten around to it yet. I'm not in any hurry to listen to his hurt voice over a long-distance line, asking why I'm mad at him. Why do I have to explain myself? He should already know that things were difficult enough when he was around. With him and Audrey gone, there's nothing left holding me in place. Mom's lost in her own sadness, and she never understood in the first place. She's always blamed things like bad posture, vitamin deficiency, and my aversion to cosmetics. She thinks I could be normal if I tried harder.

You'd think I'd be relieved now that normal has lost its currency, and in some ways I am, but I can't stand to see her so deflated. Mom was a talented third-year drama student when I came along. She was meant to be a career actress, not just some random girl in a tampon commercial, but my parents, acting more responsible than their years, decided to get married. Mom never finished university, and Dad, who'd been aiming for grad school, swerved into an education degree instead.

They told Daniel and me the truth about their history and never sounded like they regretted it; they had each other, and they had us. I guess it seemed like enough, but now Mom doesn't care about anything. The day after Dad's visit she went back to lying on the couch like someone with a permanent case of the flu.

If Dad came back, she'd be better. They could try harder and make it work. I know they could. But Dad doesn't want to give it a chance.

So why should I buckle and give in the second he seems unhappy? Besides, I'm busy, busy, busy. I have things to do. E-mails to send. A Web site to update. Long hours to put in at Play Country with that stupid logo busting across my chest.

Somehow Mom managed to shrink one of my uniform shirts in the dryer. I got ketchup down the other one on break yesterday, which leaves me no choice but to put on the former large and current medium. It's a typical Monday-morning thing, along with Mom making us ten minutes late for the start of my shift. She screams at Daniel in the car because he forgot to tell her he was supposed to show up early for a bus trip to African Lion Safari.

Lucky for him the bus waits. A harried camp counselor ushers Daniel onto the bus, pausing to frown critically at my mother.

"I can't keep this up," Mom says to herself as we pull away.

"Seatbelt," I prompt. She must've been driving without it since we left the house. Daniel's usually the one who notices, but he was too busy being yelled at.

Mom snaps on her seatbelt, worry lines spreading across her face. "It's just too much running around with your father gone. How am I supposed to keep this show on the road on my own? He's off having a vacation while I run myself ragged."

Someone who averages eleven hours' sleep a night is a better candidate for bedsores than exhaustion. I chew my thumbnail and avoid Mom's eyes. If she starts doing the pity-fest thing, I'll have to throw myself out of the car and hope for the best. It sucks that Dad left; I don't need her reminding me how shitty she feels.

"Couldn't you take the bus to work in the morning?" Mom asks, her voice gooey.

"It's not even ten minutes from Daniel's camp," I cry. "What're you going to say when I start night shifts—buy some pepper spray and sit next to the driver?"

"Of course not." Mom's tone hardens. "I just thought it would give me some extra time in the morning, what with all the running around."

"Getting out of bed when your alarm goes off would give you some extra time in the morning," I retort.

That stops Mom cold. She doesn't even say goodbye when I get out of the car in the Play Country parking lot. The car speeds away, leaving me to wonder whether she intends to pick me up at the end of my shift.

Gerald claps his hand on my shoulder as I stomp through Play Country's sliding doors. He's smiling, as usual, but he must be aware that I'm late. "So how're you settling in here, Finn?" he asks. "Feeling at home yet?"

"Getting there," I tell him.

"Good, good," he says jovially. "We like to see our employees happy."

I smile like an idiot, but it's only half fake. There's something so clueless about Gerald that you don't want to disappoint him.

"Nishani's in eight this morning," he adds. "Why don't you join her there and continue on?"

"Sure. Thanks." Nishani won't be ecstatic about being stuck in stocking. I sail towards aisle eight (home of Barbie/Bratz dolls and accessories), trying to scout her out. She must be in the back, loading up a stock cart. I push up my sleeves and head into the bowels of the stockroom, where Kevin's standing by the recycle bin, a stack of collapsed boxes at his feet. Courtney's about ten feet away from him with her hands on her hips and her bottom lip jutting out. "Just frigging pick up line three," she says impatiently, turning on her heel. "Or don't—I don't frigging care either way."

"Hey," Kevin says, showing off his weird Chiclet teeth. "Don't be that way. Ya know I love ya."

Courtney doesn't care; she's walking away as fast as her summer-bronzed legs will carry her.

Kevin winks at me as she goes. "Little Miss Serious," he calls after her.

I don't know what that was about, but I take off before he can get in another word. It's better not to talk to Kevin for too long. Conversations degenerate fast.

Nishani's in the middle of filling her cart with doll clothes. She hears my footsteps and looks up at me. "You're late. I was afraid you weren't going to show."

"I can't believe you're still stocking," I tell her. "Are you gonna speak to Gerald or what?"

"At eleven o'clock," she says. "I tried to ask him about it first thing, but he said he had some notes to go over for a conference call."

We haul our load to aisle eight and start restocking Barbie/Bratz clothes. It's bizarre—they have bigger wardrobes than I do, and I'm a real live person. Nishani and I take turns playing fashion critic. Conclusion: Barbie is a skank-princess with a white-bread smile and no fashion sense, while the Bratz are a race of alien-skank hybrids with urban attitude. The common skank element is hard to miss.

Hanging out with Nishani is the part of Play Country that I actually like, and I tell her that being a stock person's going to suck without her. "We can still take breaks when we're on together," she says. "We should exchange numbers so we can compare schedules."

We swap phone numbers then and there so we won't forget, but by ten after eleven Nishani's standing in aisle eight next to me again. "Gerald asked me to give him another week to fit me into the cashier schedule," she says. "It's like trying to have a conversation with one of those yellow smilies." Nishani sighs. "He had a grin frozen on his face the entire time, and he kept saying what a good job I was doing with the stocking, which is a joke because I still don't know how to find anything in the stockroom."

"Me neither," I admit. "I'm amazed I found you."

"I'm amazed there's anything on these shelves," Nishani says. "Somebody around here must know more than we do." All the stocks guys know more than we do. Nishani and I are summer surplus. Anything we manage to get done is a bonus. "How long are you sticking around anyway?" she asks. "I want at least two weeks off before school starts."

I was planning to stay right up until September. Otherwise Dad might try to invite me to the cottage. "Do you want to do something after work tonight?" I blurt out. "I had a fight with my mom in the car on the way in. I'm not in a rush to get home." Nishani doesn't know about the situation with my dad. This is the most personal thing I've confided.

"Sure." She nods like it's a good idea. "What do you want to do?"

"Do you like Aidan Lamb? He's in that new action movie."

"I saw the commercial." Nishani's eyebrows wiggle unhappily. "It looks like all car races and explosions."

"We can see something else." I don't care what; I just need

somewhere else to be. I can't keep running over to Jersy's every time something goes wrong.

Nishani suggests some Italian movie about four girls on summer vacation. That's fine with me, and she calls Aneeka at lunch to invite her along. "She can drive you home afterwards," Nishani explains. "Then you won't have to call your mother to pick you up."

I leave a message on Mom's voice mail telling her I'm going out with friends after work, and she doesn't call back to ask where these friends mysteriously appeared from. She'll probably be asleep by the time I get back. I'll have to walk Samsam because she'll have forgotten, and Daniel will be glued to a repeat of *The Surreal Life.* He'll tell me Dad called and whine when I send him off to bed. Then, once I finally have a minute to myself, I'll e-mail Audrey to complain about how shitty everything is.

Well, almost everything. The movie turns out to be pretty cool, and after a while my brain forgets it's reading subtitles and believes it's conquered the Italian language. Aneeka, Nishani, and I sit in the center of the middle row, which means I have to disturb the old couple near the aisle on my way to the bathroom. They look Italian anyway, so they most likely understand what's happening despite my ass blocking the screen.

Coming back, I spot Billy Young in line at the concession stand. I can't remember seeing him out of school uniform since eighth grade, and it takes my eyes a second to adjust to his dark jeans and black T-shirt. If I didn't know he was Billy Young, I might even think he looked good. He's got nice arms (not beefy but not thin), wide hazel eyes that look like they never quit thinking, and a rangy build he hasn't finished growing into. Billy nods hello and I nod back, wondering if Jersy was right about me liking Billy, if maybe he just realized it before I did. Then Jersy steps out of line next to Billy—and suddenly I know that's not true.

Jersy's wearing a navy T-shirt that says "I'm with the Band," and his hair's shaved down to the tiniest fraction of an inch from his skull. For the first three seconds I'm outraged. Then relief sets in. His hair isn't soft and tempting anymore. I'm saved.

"How's it going?" Jersy asks, sauntering towards me.

"Okay. How was your birthday thing the other night?" And what's going on with me anyway? I shouldn't be thinking about his hair; I shouldn't be thinking anything.

"No party." He smiles. "We drove around most of the night and ended up crashing at Joel's brother's place."

"Your hair," I say incredulously.

"Yeah." His hand skims across his shorn head. "It was too hot."

"Wow." I should shut up about his hair already, but it's so weird. He's like a whole different person, almost a stranger.

Jersy laughs. "Good or not good?"

"I don't know," I say truthfully. "Just weird. Who are you again?"

Jersy slides his hands down into the front pockets of his jeans. "So which movie are you catching?" he asks. If he'd walked into St. Mark's with his hair like this, I would've recognized him straight off. He's flashback Jersy, all lips and eyes.

"*È Così*. It's Italian." I motion in the direction of the theater. "What about you?"

"*Liar's Restitution*." That's the Aidan Lamb action flick Nishani wasn't impressed with. Jersy glances over his shoulder at Billy's second-place spot in the concession line and adds, "Looks like I gotta go, but when're you coming over for a dip?"

"I definitely have to do that," I tell him.

"How about tomorrow night?"

"Sure." Really? I thought it was one of those things we'd never get around to. "I guess tomorrow's good."

"You gotta go in the pool, though, you know." Jersy's smile is infectious enough. He doesn't need the T-shirt. "This time you definitely have to go in."

"I know." A blush starts at my ears, quickly working its way across my cheeks. Why does my brain instantly convert the most harmless phrase into something dirty? *Don't worry, this time I'll get wet.* Shit. *We can get wet together.* Oh, shit.

I have to get out of here fast. Before smoke starts piping out of my ears like an overheated cartoon character. "Enjoy the movie," I add quickly.

"See you tomorrow," he says.

"See you, Jersy." I turn and spin away, my crazy cartoon legs blurring underneath me like wheels.

I am anything but saved.

nineteen

o o o

THE NEXT MORNING Mom drives me to work without any mention of taking the bus. The three of us are quiet in the car. Daniel's tired from staying up late last night, Mom's always tired these days, and I'm tired because my brain refuses to leave things alone. *I should call Dad. I shouldn't go swimming at Jersy's. I should stop wasting so many hours surfing the Internet. I should practice sketching instead.* It's exhausting.

The rest of the day isn't much better. After work Daniel asks me why I never talk to Dad on the phone. "You said you'd call him," he adds. His right hand's clutching the remote, and he's riding the channels like a maniac with a wicked nervous tic. It takes every inch of my willpower not to snatch the remote out of his hands.

"How do you know?" I ask. Anti-Me's been eavesdropping. I thought I was the only one.

"He's always asking to speak to you," Daniel continues

heatedly. "He wants to take us up to the cottage with him for a few days."

"It's not even his cottage."

"So what?" Daniel's eyes are as wide as hubcaps. "It'd be cool. There's a canoe and we could go swimming all the time." I'm already going swimming. Tonight at Jersy's. I can't get out of it now. He'd think I was making excuses.

"Just go without me," I say. It's not like Daniel will miss me. The only thing we ever do together is stare at the television. Mostly not even that.

"It won't be the same." He looks at me like I should know that without him having to say it.

"It'll be better," I tell him. "You'll have Dad all to yourself."

Daniel fixes his eyes on the screen. His knuckles are white, that's how hard he's gripping the remote. "Why do you always have to be like this?"

"Like what?" I'm being the crappy, self-obsessed older sister again. Don't think I don't notice. "Look, I'm going to call him when my schedule gets worked out, okay? But I probably won't be able to go to the cottage. I have to work one shift every weekend." This is true. It also happens to be an excellent excuse. "But you should go. It'll be fun."

"You can still talk to him next time he calls." Daniel stops flicking and stares at me like some demon child out of a horror movie.

"Chill, okay?" I fix a Zen stare on his agitated presence.

Daniel's head twists back towards the television. If he starts levitating and talking backwards, I'm leaving the room. Mom can deal with the exorcism on her own.

"Daniel?" Mom pops her head into the room, saving my immortal soul. "Set the table for me, please."

Daniel glowers at me again as he gets up. Five minutes later the three of us are eating hot dogs and Pringles at the kitchen table, despite Mom's aversion to junk food. I munch Pringles in stacks of three and four and wash them down with swigs of ginger ale. Mom concentrates on her hot dog, which she's dabbed with mustard and relish, and Daniel shoves a bit of everything into his mouth at once.

My appetite's gone before I start on my hot dog. I don't know what time I'm supposed to be at Jersy's for swimming. Maybe he's forgotten. Who wants to go swimming with a pound of Pringles lining their stomach anyway? I'd probably sink straight to the bottom.

I'm tapping my feet anxiously under the table and telling myself not to be such a moron when the phone rings. Daniel, who has the chair closest to the phone, reaches behind him and grabs the cordless from the wall. The eager look in his eyes tells me he's expecting Dad, but his face falls as he cradles the phone. He hands it wordlessly to me, and I take it. There's no way it can be my father; Daniel's not that good an actor. It's gotta be Jersy. I know before I even press the cordless to my ear.

"Finn?" Jersy's voice is deeper than it was last night.

I stare at the wall, ignoring Mom's and Daniel's presence. "Hi, Jersy." The slurping sound behind me is instantly replaced by incessant crunching. Daniel sounds uncannily like Samsam when he eats potato chips. Actually, Samsam's neater. He never leaves crumbs.

"I'm gonna have to cancel tonight," Jersy says. "It's not a good time. There's some stuff going on here. I called your cell and left a message, but I wanted to make sure—"

"It's all right," I cut in. I'm more relieved than disappointed. "Don't worry about it." But his voice doesn't sound all right. He's restless or moody or some other thing I can't pinpoint. Audrey would know. "Is everything okay, though?"

"Yeah," Jersy says hesitantly. "It is . . . it's just . . . not a good time to use the pool and stuff, you know?"

No, I don't know. "Okay, don't worry about it. We can do it another time." Of course, we never will. This is probably the last I'll hear from him until September. Maybe now I'll be able to finish my hot dog. Maybe I'm saved after all.

"For sure," Jersy says. "Another time." He hangs out silently on the other end of the phone line, waiting for me to pick up the slack.

"I better go." I glance behind me at Daniel, Mom, and the dwindling supply of Pringles. "We're in the middle of dinner."

"Okay, see you later," Jersy says.

"Yeah, see you." I hang up the phone and immediately reach for another stack of Pringles. Now I sound like Samsam too. I bet he sits at the table and devours garbage like this in his doggie dreams. Or maybe he's happy enough chomping down the contents of a torn garbage bag with no one standing over him to yell at him.

"Was that Jersy?" Mom asks, studying me.

"Yup." She knows it was. The question's redundant. "I was supposed to go swimming at his place, but he had to cancel."

Mom doesn't ask why, and I wait for Daniel to make some bad-seed comment. For once he's quiet. He must be totally pissed off with me to be so quiet, and I wish I could reach over and tousle his hair, but making friends with the Anti-Me wouldn't be that easy. He'd think I was making fun of him.

After dinner Gran calls, and I cram the conversation with trivial details about work so she won't think we're all falling apart without my dad. Then I e-mail Audrey and fool around with stock photos I've downloaded from the Internet. One of the photos is of a teenage girl on a pier, her hair tied back in a ponytail. The other is a wide shot of the Milky Way, twinkling purple and black. Merging the two images could create something beautiful. In my mind I see a dreamlike vision of a girl surrounded by the mysteries of the universe, but not all my ideas work. I crop, scale, color, blend, and blur for hours, trusting that I'll know when it's done and ultimately whether to junk it or save it.

Like always, I forget to blink when I stare at the screen, and like always, my eyeballs are as dry as starched napkins. That's what you get for concentrating too hard, and I take a break to rest my eyes and walk Samsam. When I get home, Mom's telling Daniel to go to bed. My ears perk up in surprise. Is this a one-time thing or a hint of recovery?

"Finn," Mom says, stopping me in the hall, "I'm going up to bed now too. Don't stay up too late, okay?"

She says that like the last two and a half weeks never happened, like life without Dad is entirely normal and doable. Is this the same woman who ate a hot dog for dinner and only plucked her eyebrows again because Dad was coming over? Am I losing my mind?

"I won't," I lie. "Good night." I kiss her on the cheek and feel my stomach clench. What was my family actually like before? I can't remember. There's only this constant weariness and layers of webs.

I'm in a fog.

I don't understand why things went wrong. I don't know how to make them right, and it's too exhausting to try.

Like with Jersy. We're friends, but he'll never know me any better than he does at this moment. Any more and he'd stop liking me. He'd think everyone else was right after all. And that would be that.

I don't know how much of that kind of thinking is me and how much is Adam. That scares me, and now there's more. There's our whole family breaking apart and me floating away like a balloon someone let slip from their hand.

Audrey would say she'll be back soon. Dad would tell me he misses me and that I should come up to the cottage. Why can't those things be enough?

Why am I crying again?

At first I fight it. I sit at the computer and continue working. Tilt. Resize. Change transparency. The tears keep coming, blurring my vision. Drops snake down around my nose, making me sniffle. Then my cell phone rings. It's nearly twelve-thirty, and I jump before reaching over my bedside table to pick it up, sure that Dad would never call this late.

"Hello?" a male voice says. "Is that you?"

"Who?" I ask. My voice sounds warped from crying.

"Finn?" The voice is flat, almost mechanical. "It's me, Jersy. You awake?"

"Yeah, I'm awake." And panicked. Why does he sound so strange? "What's going on?"

"Nothing." Jersy pauses. "Sorry I scared you. I was just thinking about coming over—if you're not just about to get into bed or something."

It's after midnight, and he hasn't been to my house without Audrey since he was six. I hold the phone firmly in my right hand, my brain stalling.

"Bad idea," Jersy says slowly. "Okay."

"No, it's fine," I tell him. "You just caught me off guard." I can't say no after running over to his place like it was an emergency room—twice. Somehow I'll have to snap out of this crazy meltdown; somehow I'll have to act semi-normal and smile when he makes a joke.

"Just say no if you want, Finn. It's like one in the morning, I know. I just thought since I had to cancel earlier—"

"Just get over here, Jersy." Something's obviously going on. "It's cool."

"Okay." He doesn't give me another chance to change my mind. "I'll be there in two."

He hangs up first and I shut my computer down, slip quietly onto the front step with Samsam, and watch Jersy tear up my driveway on his skateboard, summer wind tugging at his oversized sweatshirt. "My mom and brother are asleep," I say. The entire neighborhood's asleep. Trees rustle and air conditioners hum. If an alien landed on my driveway, he'd think this was a peaceful planet. How could people with such green grass possibly be unhappy?

Jersy bows his head like he's about to say something. Then he looks into my eyes, steady and serious. "Can we go inside or do you want to stay out here?"

Samsam doesn't pad forward to greet Jersy like he normally would. He sits by my side and watches us like he's sizing up the situation. "We can go in," I say. "I just didn't want you to ring the bell."

I open the front door and let Samsam in first. He turns and stares back at us in the hall, waiting for us to catch up. I lead Jersy into the family room, where we automatically occupy opposite ends of the couch. The empty middle seat feels like an awkward reminder of Audrey's absence; if Samsam were allowed on the furniture, I'd call him up to fill the gap. Jersy reaches for Samsam, scratching his ears and running his hand down his back.

I watch the two of them the way Samsam was watching us a minute ago. I don't know what to do or say or if I should even ask Jersy why he's sitting on my couch at nearly one o'clock in the morning.

"Do you want to watch TV?" I ask finally.

"Sure." Jersy's hands disappear into his sleeves as Samsam sits down in front of him.

"He really likes you," I say. "He likes pretty much everyone, but he likes you a lot."

"I like him a lot too." Jersy nods, but thick lines pop up on his forehead. "He's your dog, isn't he?"

"Mostly. Me, then my dad." I turn on the TV and flip through *Blind Date, MTV Cribs, The L Word, Bones,* yada, yada, yada. I'm as bad as my brother with his mad anxious tic.

Jersy slides his hand loosely over his head like he's still adjusting to his new buzz cut. "We used to have a dog too. Silver. She was an escape artist. Half the time my parents couldn't figure out how she got out. The last time we couldn't find her. We drove around for weeks, called all the shelters, posted flyers everywhere—but we couldn't find her."

I stop flicking and rest the remote on the arm next to me. "You never found her?"

"Never found her," Jersy confirms. "She could be somebody else's dog now."

"That's so sad." I can't imagine losing Samsam; he's practically part of me. "What kind of dog was she?"

"Australian shepherd." Jersy's right hand slips out of his sleeve. "The blue merle kind. Her eyes were blue too."

"She sounds gorgeous."

"Yeah, she really was." He's using the past tense, I notice. Maybe he doesn't believe she's someone else's dog now.

Jersy touches his scar with his fingertip. "My parents were kinda losing it earlier," he says. "That's why we couldn't go swimming. Christina does this thing where she takes off, and it freaks them out."

"You mean she runs away?" Why would Christina Mikulski ever run away? She has the perfect family.

"Not really." Jersy squints at the television, where some vaguely familiar blond actress is talking up a kitchen gadget that'll change our lives for only five installments of $19.99. "Usually she goes to see her best friend at Western for a couple weeks. Just to get away from things."

"What things?" Christina Mikulski could have anything she wanted. She's one of those girls. You can tell just by looking at her.

"My parents, for one." Jersy's hand climbs back into his sleeve. His voice is flat, like it was over the phone. "They worry about her all the time. Even worse when she's gone and they don't know what she's doing every second of the day." Jersy blinks slowly. His eyes focus on mine, then peer away.

"Her and her best friend are like you and Audrey," Jersy adds. "She's fine there. They just freak."

I press my lips together as I stare at him. He's worried too. He has to be. What else would he be doing here? "Can you call her?" I ask. "To check up on her? Will she e-mail you or anything?"

"Sometimes she does." His body sinks into the couch like someone let the air out of him. "Finn." His voice turns stern. "Don't ask, okay? I shouldn't even be telling you any of this." Pink patches bloom on his cheeks. "Everything's fine. She'll be back soon."

"Okay," I tell him. His ears are turning pink too. I'd never have noticed that before the haircut. "Don't worry. I'd never say anything anyway."

Audrey must know what he's talking about. Maybe the Chinese girl too. But you shouldn't share your secrets too freely. I never do.

A shiver pinches at my insides, stealing my breath. Mr. Mikulski said he wanted their house to be a safe place. Why would he say that? My neck prickles cold as I gulp in air.

I know without anyone needing to tell me. I don't want to know, but I do. I can't look at Jersy; I can't get the words out.

"I know you wouldn't," he says. "It's not that."

What happened to Christina is dense in the air between us. My gums taste like rust and rot. Jersy and I shouldn't be talking about this, even though we're *not*. I don't want to fill in details with my imagination. I want him to go.

"What about your dad?" he asks. "Have you talked to him?"

"I told you I didn't want to talk to him," I snap. The prickles creep over me like fur. I could scratch all my skin off, but it wouldn't quit creeping.

Jersy's brown eyelashes blink in surprise. "I know, but you have to talk to him sometime."

"I don't have to do anything." I glare at his chin. "Why does everybody keep telling me to talk to him all the time?"

Jersy's silent next to me. Then he hunches over to pet Samsam. "Maybe they think you'll be sorry if you don't." Jersy stares up at me, his eyes wide.

I turn away, feeling raw. If I opened my mouth, my jaw would click with tension.

"Can I?" Jersy motions to the remote. He must be the most clueless person alive. Anyone else would know they should leave.

I let him take the remote and flip over to videos. What does that make me?

"Hard Road" fills the TV screen, and we watch Sam Roberts

rock away like a musical Jesus, his shaggy dark hair spilling down to his shoulders. We sit quietly for another thirty minutes or so, watching video after video, barely looking in each other's direction. After a while I calm down a little and begin to remember that Jersy has his own problems. I haven't been the most sympathetic person in the world.

"Do you want something to eat?" I ask. "I can microwave some frozen pizza."

"Nah, it's late. I should go before I fall asleep on you again." He stands up, arms hanging loosely at his sides. His gaze shifts as I stand too. "Thanks for letting me come by," he adds, flashing a hint of a smile.

"Hey, no problem. I had to return the favor." I clasp my hands tightly behind my back. "We should still go swimming sometime." That's a nervous tic too. The night's been so strange that I don't know what else to say. "Later, when it's okay."

"Oh, yeah." Jersy nods. "Anytime."

That sounds a hell of a lot less definite than tomorrow night, but I can't let it get to me. I walk Jersy to the front door, Samsam a step behind me. I'm about to tell him goodbye when he steps up and folds his arms around me. "Thanks," he says.

His sweatshirt smells like the same fabric softener Mom uses. It's safe and warm, and my arms wrap snugly around his back as I press my face into his neck. I'm bigger than him all over, but somehow we feel right together.

"I'll call you when it's safe to come swimming," he says, suddenly letting go.

"Okay." My face is hot. I want to hide or climb into his sweatshirt with him. I can't decide which.

Jersy crouches down and runs both hands through Samsam's coat. That's the way I always say goodbye to Samsam too—on eye level. Strands from Samsam's sandy coat affix themselves to Jersy's sweatshirt like a second skin, but Jersy doesn't notice. Or maybe he just doesn't care. He looks at me as he gets to his feet. "I'll talk to you soon," he says.

"Bye," I warble.

Jersy stands in front of me in the doorway for so long that I imagine I can smell his sweatshirt, even with the distance between us. He stands there for so long that it seems like one of us will have to say something.

But nobody does.

One Mississippi. Two Mississippi. Three Mississippi.

Jersy swings my screen door open and pushes off on his skateboard. He flies down my driveway and onto the road, his sweatshirt billowing up behind him. I watch him until he disappears, until it's just me standing there with Samsam, staring off into the summer night, listening to the grass grow.

twenty

o o o

THE PHONE RINGS four times before Dad answers. He sounds out of breath, and I'm so nervous that I almost hang up. I picture him rushing indoors, a thick hardcover under his arm. He's wearing his blue striped polo shirt or the gag gift T-shirt his students bought him last year. The T-shirt says, "What if the Hokey Pokey is really what it's all about?" Dad thought it was hilarious—he still does.

"Dad," I say hesitantly. "It's me."

"Finn, how are you?" He sounds outright cheerful.

"Okay." He's not mad at me for taking four days to call. How come that doesn't make this any easier? "Tired. They work us really hard at the store. Break's the only time you get to sit down. I'm getting blisters on my feet." Both of my big toes are wrapped in bandages. I'm so delicate that it's not funny.

"It sounds like Audrey lucked out," Dad says.

"Maybe." She doesn't think so.

The two of us are quiet, each waiting for the other to speak. It reminds me of last night. Then I remember what Jersy said about me being sorry if I didn't talk to my father. It's true, but talking to him hurts too. He's only been gone three weeks, but he's changed everything.

"Are you coming back?" I ask.

"I don't know, Finn." That horrible sinking feeling whips at me. "I might start looking for somewhere else to live in a few weeks. Somewhere around Glenashton."

"Have you told Mom that?" She wouldn't have plucked her eyebrows if she knew. I can't believe he's doing this.

"Finn." Dad's voice is calm. "This might be something we can't resolve. Right now I just need some time to myself to think things through." I've heard all this before. He can call it what he wants, but he's giving up. "But I'd love to have you up here with your brother for a few days. There are bunk beds in the second bedroom, and it's just a five-minute walk down to the lake."

"I can't. I never have two days off in a row." I could ask, maybe, but I won't. "Daniel will come, though. He's all excited about it."

"I know." Dad's tone isn't lighthearted anymore. "That's too bad about your schedule. Are you sure you couldn't swing something for next weekend? Swap shifts with somebody?"

"I don't think so." We're talking, aren't we? He can't have everything. Besides, even if I wanted to go, even if I wasn't mad at him and found someone to trade shifts with, I couldn't leave Mom alone. She might spend the whole weekend in bed.

"Okay," he says. "I'll be driving down to pick up your brother next Friday. Can we at least have dinner then? The three of us could catch a movie."

"I can do that." I'll let Daniel do all the talking. I'll be a shadow. That's the closest I can come to satisfying everyone.

"Good," Dad says, halfway back to lighthearted. "You know this is only temporary—the distance. We'll be able to see each other much more in the fall."

He wants this summer to be over as much as I do. It's an unpleasant end, but he can see past it to a new beginning. He's looking forward to the fresh start. That's the big difference between us. I don't want to get used to this emptiness. Even Mom shouting on the doorstep was better.

"Finn?" The emotion in Dad's voice makes me flinch.

"What?"

"I'm really glad you called."

Massy and Kaitlynn James come into Play Country together a couple days later, his arm possessively around her bare shoulders. Nishani points him out to me from the bottom of the ladder. "Another one of Aneeka's conquests," she remarks. I'm halfway up and afraid to look down in case I go vertigo and fall over the side.

"Who?" I say, but I'm already turning to look anyway. My head spins when I catch sight of them—Massy's tangle of dark hair and Kaitlynn's tan midriff. They were both at Sadie and Brian Nielsen's that night in September, but I've seen them a hundred times since. Maybe the fact that we're not at St. Mark's makes it different, or maybe it has something to do with hearing about Christina. I don't know why they suddenly remind me with a vengeance, but *it's not fair*. I scratch at one of my eyelids and stare at the ceiling.

"Come down," Nishani calls. "I'll do it."

"It's okay. I just shouldn't have looked down." I steady myself and keep climbing, turtle-like, up the ladder until Looney Tunes Monopoly is within reach. I grasp the box between my fingers and work my way slowly down, reminding myself to breathe.

On the ground Nishani smiles at me. "Good girl," she says proudly.

Yup. Somebody give the girl a medal.

"I didn't know your sister had a thing with Massy," I say. It must've been before he showed up on Audrey's radar.

"Uh-huh," Nishani says nonchalantly. "For about three weeks."

Next thing we know, Massy and Kaitlynn James are walking up the board game aisle towards us. Kaitlynn's crazy high heels are tilting her forward, and Massy's stuck on her like moss. Her foundation's as thick as Liquid Paper, but her skin's as bumpy as ever. How does Massy kiss her without streaking her paint job? I bet he goes straight for her boobs, afraid to look up.

If Audrey were here, we'd kill ourselves laughing the minute they cleared the aisle. Massimo and Kaitlynn James hooked up after all. It's too stupid.

"Hey," Kaitlynn says, stopping next to me. "You work here?" She doesn't remember my name—if she ever knew it in the first place.

"Yeah," I say. "How's it going?"

Massy stops next to us. His gaze swings over to my face for two seconds. Then he blinks and stares at the shelves behind my head.

"Not bad." She pauses and leans into Massy. "We're just taking it easy."

Massimo's about as animated as a cardboard cutout next to her, and I wonder, for the first time in months, what lies Adam told him about Audrey and maybe even about me. At the time, Audrey said she didn't care what it was, that it was only Massy's reaction that mattered, but she must have wondered too. She just didn't want me thinking about Adam any more than I already was.

Even now, ten months later, I'm so itchy in my own skin at the thought of him that I could scratch right down to the bone.

"Hi, Massy," Nishani says from behind me. "You still working at Sobey's?"

"Yeah." Massy squeezes Kaitlynn's waist as he eyes Nishani. "How's your sister doing?"

"Good," Nishani says.

"Good." Massy's lips curve up, but they never quite make it into a smile.

"Come on." Kaitlynn bumps her hip against Massy's leg. "Let's check out the video games."

"Yeah, right." Massy's head jerks like she just woke him up. "Have a good summer, Nishani." His dark eyes leap over to me. "See you later, Finn."

That's the first thing he's said to me since last fall, and it makes my stomach twinge. "See you," I croak.

"Bye," Kaitlynn says.

I watch them move down the aisle, Kaitlynn tottering away on her honey-colored legs and Massy's hand around her waist. It's so stupid. They're actually together, just like Audrey predicted. And after ten months Massimo finally feels like he can say three meaningless words to me.

Is that supposed to make me feel better? Like I'm finally finished with this thing because Massy decided to start speaking to me again?

I don't feel better. I feel like maybe nothing ever really changes, and that's so unfair that it can't possibly be true. The thought loops around in my head for the rest of the day, and when Mom comes to pick me up later, my head is throbbing with the weight of forgetting all over again. I want to climb into bed, pull the sheets to my chin, turn up the air-conditioning, and listen to Our Lady Peace.

"Did you take your vitamin this morning?" Mom asks, eyeing me sharply.

"I don't remember," I mumble. "I have a killer headache."

"You look white as a ghost," Mom says. So what else is new?

After dinner I put on my scruffy old track pants, drink ice-cold chocolate milk out of the carton, and almost trip over Samsam in the hall. The phone rings on my way upstairs. Mom answers it from her bedroom. I begin to eavesdrop from the hall and then stop myself cold. What difference does it make who she's speaking to or what she has to say? What can I do about any of it?

So I dive under the covers with my earphones, and soon there's only Raine Maida's voice, a relentless beat, and my lungs filling up with oxygen. I'm not sleepy but I shut my eyes. I just want to *be* and not have to think about it for once.

Mom has other ideas. She touches my shoulder, scaring the shit out of me. My eyes pop open as I tear off the earphones. "Jesus, Mom, you shouldn't sneak up on people like that!"

"I didn't know you were sleeping," she says. "Do you have any uniform shirts for the wash?"

"I wasn't sleeping," I grumble. "I was trying to sedate my headache." I get up and shuffle across the room like an eighty-year-old woman. My closet door's half open, revealing an inside-out Play Country shirt lying under a black bra. I surrender the shirt and collapse back onto the bed.

"Anna invited us over for a barbecue on Sunday." Mom smiles. "The three of us. You're not working, are you?"

"No, I'm doing Saturday this week." I shove my feet under the covers, and suddenly it hits me that a barbecue at the Mikulskis' will probably mean seeing Jersy. I don't know if I'm ready for that. Last time was so weird that I haven't fully recovered yet. Showing up at his place Sunday could make things even stranger, and where will I be then? "This weekend?" I repeat.

"This Sunday," Mom replies. "Anna and I have been meaning to get together for dinner, and she thought this would be just the thing."

"I was thinking of maybe getting together with Jasper or Maggie on the weekend," I lie. "I haven't seen them since school let out."

"You can see them on Saturday night," Mom points out. "Or some other time this week."

I'm not quick enough to reason my way out of that one. My defense mechanisms need work.

"Okay then," I tell her. Maybe I'll get lucky. Maybe Jersy won't be home anyway. Even if he is, we'll all be hanging out by the pool eating burgers. There won't be any time for weirdness. Besides, Mom really needs to get out and enjoy herself. I don't want to drag down that operation. I'm sure Dad will do that soon enough.

"Good." Mom nods. My inside-out Play Country shirt is folded over her arm, and her hair looks tidy enough, but all traces of makeup have been scrubbed from her face. She looks like a "before" picture from a makeover contest.

"I'm seeing Dad next weekend," I say suddenly, watching Mom's eyes. "I told him I couldn't go for the weekend but that we could hang out on Friday night before him and Daniel drive up to the cottage."

"He'll be pleased." Mom's eyes crinkle up. "He really wanted to spend more time with you last time he was down."

Last time I didn't want to see him. I still don't. I don't want Mom staring down at me with small eyes either, like she's glad I've decided to make my father happy. I'm sick of feeling sorry for everyone. Why can't they take care of their own problems and leave me out of it?

I fake a yawn and tug my earphones on.

Mom takes the hint and moves towards the door. "I don't know how you can listen to that with a headache," she says, grabbing the doorknob.

It's better than aspirin. I switch the music on, close my eyes, and let it carry me away.

twenty-one

○　○　○

SATURDAY IS THE busiest shift of the week, which means Nishani and I barely have a minute to talk on our last day together. People keep tapping us on the shoulder, asking us where they can find party goods, Easy-Bake ovens, and Play-Doh sets. Nishani, in a good mood, on account of her imminent transfer to cash, does most of the PR work while I rush in and out of the stockroom on overdrive.

One of the stock guys, Sebastian, left halfway through his shift with food poisoning. Courtney says it's more likely alcohol poisoning. Either way, the result is me running around pretending to be stock girl of the century. If I didn't have those extra hours' sleep last night, I'd be done for. As it is, I've had to pee for the past fifty minutes but haven't had time.

It's next on my list, right after I get more copies of the latest Disney DVD everyone's been asking for back on the floor. I load another box of movies onto the cart and throw some bagged candy on top for good measure. Last I looked, we were nearly out of gummies.

"Finn-oolala," Kevin croons, striding up to me out of nowhere. "Where've you been all day? You trying to avoid me or something?"

You can take that as a given. "I'm busy, Kevin," I snap. "Way too busy to worry about avoiding you. I gotta get this stuff on the shelves."

Kevin grabs his chest like I've mortally wounded him. "You never have two minutes to talk to me. How's that supposed to make me feel?" His Chiclet smile's eating up half his face, so I guess he doesn't feel too bad. Anyway, I don't have time for this.

"Later, Kevin," I say. I grab my cart and begin to steer it out of the stockroom.

"Come on now." Kevin plants his hands on my shoulders from behind. I jump back as I swing around. "Relax," he says, snatching his hands back. "What do you think I'm gonna do?"

"I'm going." My words sound anorexic thin. I'm trembling like something newborn.

"You think I'm gonna kiss you or something?" he asks, taking a step towards me and leaning his head in near mine. His breath smells like sour milk and garlic, and he hasn't stopped smiling. My chest's thumping like a racehorse. My lungs won't take in oxygen.

Suddenly my hand's hurling towards him, slapping him across the face so hard that I can make out the angry red imprint of each of my fingers on his cheek.

His smile crashes. His left hand flies to his cheek. The red fades to pink as I watch, stunned. "You're crazy," he spews. "What was that?"

"Leave me alone." This time my voice is pure rage. "Just leave me the fuck alone."

I turn slowly back to my cart, breathing hard. Blood's rushing through my arms and legs and I want to push Kevin's Chiclet teeth in and run until I can't take another step.

"You're a fucking wack job," Kevin says to my back.

"You got in my face," I shout, winding my fingers around the cart's handle to steady them. *"What was that?"* Why did he have to push me? What is it about me that makes these things happen?

I keep my eyes on my hands as I pull the cart forward. My head's spinning and my stomach's rolling over like it's not attached to anything. I could be sick if I let myself. I could throw up in the stockroom and make the customer-service-booth girls call for cleanup. It'd give them something else to talk about—one more reason to think I'm freaky, because after Kevin leaves the stockroom you better believe he'll be spreading the word to everyone.

"You're crazy," Kevin repeats, taking his hand away from his cheek. "I never even touched you. You think you can walk around slapping people in the face for nothing? That's assault."

"Why don't you tell Suzanne then?" The tears well up in my throat and I hold them there, scared that once I start I won't be able to stop. "And I'll give her my version." I'll tell her that Kevin stands too close to all the girls and says something stupid nearly every day but that I was never afraid of him before. I'm not even sure I'm afraid of him now. My sleeves are long enough to hide the goosebumps on my arms, but I can feel them. I'm shaking too— angry, confused, and scared. Because what if Kevin's right? What if I'm just crazy?

"Why are you doing this?" Kevin says incredulously. His hands are at his sides, palms forward, imploring.

"I'm just sick of your shit, Kevin." I turn and face him. "If you try anything else, I'm going to Suzanne and Gerald." I'm shivering, but I mean it.

I can't go through all this again, but I know by the expression on Kevin's face that I won't have to. He doesn't understand, but he believes me about telling. "I hear you," he says in a low voice. "Just haul your crap outta here. I'll put my hands behind my back and turn around. Will that make you happy?"

I tug my cart forward, wrestling with the weight of invisible tears. I walk as fast as I can so that all the customers and staff will know I don't have time for them. Then Nishani passes, and I hand over the cart and shuffle along next to her. "Are you okay?" she asks.

"I had a fight with Kevin in the back," I confess. "I have it under control."

Nishani steers the cart around a woman with a stroller. "What'd he do now?"

I don't know what he did; I just know what I did. "He's an idiot," I say with a shrug. The doubt's deeper now that I'm out in the open, but if I explain I won't be able to hold back the tears. "Typical Kevin." Maybe he didn't mean to scare me. Maybe I slapped him for nothing.

I don't know what to believe.

"I'll catch up with you," I tell Nishani. "I need a pee break."

I rush into the empty staff washroom and slam the stall door behind me. The tears are stuck halfway up my throat. They burn, but they won't come out. Not even when I give them permission.

I pee and then wash my face and hands with sickly-sweet-smelling liquid soap. The person who looks back at me from the mirror is different than the one I saw this morning. I've never hit anyone before. I never even thought of fighting Adam. I was too scared to think.

I haven't lost that fear. It's in the room with me now, whispering things about Adam, Kevin, and me. I don't know what to do.

The one thing I'm sure of is that I'm not sorry about Kevin. Maybe he was never really going to kiss me, but if I let him I'd feel worse. It'd be like living last September all over again.

And I can't do that.

I wait, but the tears never come. In the end I wipe my face dry and go out to find Nishani. Kevin doesn't come within ten feet of me for the rest of the day. In fact, he avoids most of the girls, and when I catch him glancing in my direction from the end of the action-figure aisle, he turns his head slowly away, giving me a clear view of his cheekbone. But there's no point looking for traces of the red marks I left there. I already know I won't find any.

Mom makes me carry the wine and hands Daniel her homemade mixed-pepper salad. That leaves her in charge of a bag of nachos and a jar of salsa. It's a perfect day for a barbecue—white-hot and not a cloud in the sky—and Anna called this morning to remind us to bring our swimsuits. I'm already wearing my tankini top and black-and-red-striped bottom under my clothes, but I don't intend to unveil them until I'm ready to get in the pool. My boobs may be small, but I don't want them wobbling around for everyone to see.

It could be my imagination, but I think they've grown a little lately. Or maybe Mom's just shrinking more of my clothes in the wash.

Daniel's got his swimsuit on too. Mom's wearing tiny sandals and a cotton wrap dress that comes down to her bare knees. She looks like a movie star going casual at the Cannes Film Festival, and today she's not doing it for Dad. I smile proudly at her and catch a puzzled look darting out from behind her sunglasses.

"I haven't been swimming in ages," I tell her. "Not since last summer."

"I go all the time," Daniel brags from the backseat. I guarantee he'll still be the first one in the pool—and the last to get out.

Mom's not much of a swimmer. She does a very delicate breaststroke and keeps her head above water at all times. She's so confident in most other things that it's almost funny to watch, and I smile again at the thought of it.

"You're all smiles today," Mom observes, sweeping her fingers through her hair.

"It's good to be off work." I haven't figured out how to deal with Kevin when I see him again. Anxiety wells up inside me, making my arms twinge.

Audrey said she was proud of me, even if I misjudged the situation. She wants me to call later tonight so we can talk it over properly. Maybe I'll feel better afterwards. Maybe a day by the pool will help too—especially if Jersy's not home.

I search for signs of his presence as Anna opens the front door. "Come on in," she says with an energetic movement of her arm. She doesn't look like somebody who's especially worried about her absent daughter. She's smiling and motioning us on towards the kitchen like life is an endless summer barbecue.

Mr. Mikulski's sitting on a patio chair in the backyard, his sunglasses reflecting our image. "Gloria," he says, pulling off his shades as he clasps her hand. "Good to see you." He nods at Daniel and me. "You'll have to reintroduce me to your youngest. He really takes after you these days."

Daniel endures a formal introduction and then points eagerly at the pool. "Can we go in?"

"Daniel, we just got here," Mom admonishes. "Have a seat."

Mr. Mikulski smiles widely. "It's fine. He can go in. I haven't even started on the food yet." Mr. Mikulski switches his gaze to me. "You too, feel free. Jersy will be down any minute."

My stomach drops. "I'll go in later."

Daniel pulls off his T-shirt, tosses it at Mom, and dips his right foot in the pool. Satisfied, he plunges himself into the water. I turn impatiently back to Mom and Mr. Mikulski, who are complaining loudly about gas prices. The conversation's so boring that it makes the suspense worse. "Back in a minute," I tell Mom.

I rush into the kitchen, where Anna's assembling plastic yellow glasses on a matching tray. "Is there anything I can do to help?" I ask. Where the hell's Jersy? I just want to get this over with.

"Thank you, Finn," Anna says graciously. "I was going to start with some lemonade and the nachos your mom brought. You can take that out for me."

"Sure." I watch Anna grab a pitcher of lemonade from the fridge and pour out five glasses. "Is Christina around today?" I ask, although I know better. Why can't I leave things alone?

"No, she's away with friends for another week." Anna quick-scans the kitchen. "Where did I put that salsa?" We spot it next to the toaster at the exact same time. "Ah." She scoops the salsa into a serving dish and empties the nachos into a bowl. "Perfect."

Anna beams up at me as we load the tray. "I'm glad you could all come today. I've been meaning to see more of Gloria since we moved back, but we've both been so busy."

Jersy strides into the kitchen just as I'm picking up the tray. He gives me an easy grin and says hi. For a second I think he's going to lean over and kiss me on the cheek like we're Europeans.

"Hi." My face burns as I say it back. Of course he's not going to kiss me. This isn't Italy.

"Get the patio door for Finn," Anna instructs, diving back into the fridge with the bottle of wine Mom brought.

Jersy grabs a pile of nachos from my tray as we edge towards the door. He drops them in his mouth and crunches away.

"I didn't think you'd be here," I tell him.

"You never think I'm going to be here," he points out. "This is where I live."

Between work, partying with friends, and riding his dirt bike, there are probably twenty minutes of non-sleeping time left in his day. "I just didn't get the impression you were around much." I'd shrug, but I have the tray in my hands.

Jersy slides the patio door open for me and watches me step outside. I hand out the drinks like a cocktail waitress and set the salsa and nachos down on the table. On my way back in with the tray, I pass Anna coming out with a plate of shrimp. If we're not careful, we'll all bloat up before the main meal.

I put the tray on the counter and take in Jersy standing in front of the open fridge. "I called my dad," I announce. "I'm seeing him next week."

"How was it?" He turns to look at me.

"Sucky. It's like it's never going to be any better." I lower my voice. "He says he's probably going to get his own place, but I don't think he's told my mom that yet." Jersy scratches his head vacantly. He's probably sick to death of hearing about my parents' separation. He only came over last time because he was worried about his sister. "So what'd you do last night?" I ask, abruptly changing my tone. "Or do you even remember?"

Jersy rolls his eyes, exactly the same way my brother does when I piss him off. It makes me feel old. "If we were together you'd be ragging on me about that all the time, wouldn't you? You'd be one of those girls who's always texting her boyfriend to check up on what he's doing."

No, I wouldn't. I want to tell him that I wouldn't be his girlfriend in the first place, but I don't. I get real quiet there in the kitchen, and then I start thinking maybe it's better to go outside and be with everyone else because with him, I'm lost.

"I talked to Christina a couple days ago," he says, tucking his hands into his armpits. "She thinks she's going to come back next week."

"That's good," I tell him. "Does that mean you can relax?"

"I guess." His head tips to the right as he looks at me. "What about you? How do we get you to relax?"

I remember the smell of his sweatshirt and how I pressed my face into his neck like a kitten. It's the best thing that's happened this summer, and it's horrible. "Pharmaceuticals," I joke. Then I shake my head at him. "Nope, I forgot. I'm the control-freak type."

"You are, you know," Jersy says, but he's smiling.

I'm not in control of a single thing.

"You coming out to the pool?" He cocks his head.

"Yup." I go outside with him and peel off my shorts and T-shirt as unobtrusively as I can. Once I'm in my swimsuit, I don't waste a second getting into the pool. I make a clean dive into the deep end and watch Daniel try to impress Jersy with his own Aquaman routine. I want to tell the kid not to knock himself out, that he'll never be able to outdo Jersy, but I'm having too much fun watching him try. Mr. Mikulski comes in and does lengths. After a long while Anna and Mom ease themselves into the pool and Mr. Mikulski climbs out to start the food. "Sausages or burgers?" he shouts.

"Both," Jersy replies.

Everyone else starts to answer at the same time, and Mr. Mikulski takes a count. "Give me a hand, Jersy," he calls.

Jersy glances expectantly over at me, his body submerged below the neck. He dips his chin into the water and then pulls the rest of his head under with it. When he comes up ten seconds later, his eyes find me and then veer swiftly away.

I watch him pull himself out of the pool. He makes it look so effortless that I almost believe he has superpowers. He grins when he catches me looking. He knows. I know he knows, and I should feel worse than I do.

But I don't. And that's all. After two minutes I climb out of the pool and go after him. He's handing over the burgers and sausages to his father, and his eyes hang on me as he says, "Are you taking a break?"

"Yeah." We move away from the barbecue. My swimsuit's sticking to me, keeping me cool in the sun, and Jersy keeps staring at my shoulders.

"It's really warm out here today," he says, stealing a look at my face. "You want to go inside for a while?"

"Sure." The fact is, I can't get there fast enough.

We go down to the basement together and sit on the couch, soaking wet because neither of us thought to bring a towel. The door's ajar because it has to be, and drops are rolling off my hair and down my back, making me shiver now that we're in the air-conditioning. "Won't your mom be upset about the couch?" I ask, tucking my hair back behind my ears.

"It's not the good couch," he explains. "They always sit upstairs."

When I glance down, I see cleavage. My belly button's peeking out from the bottom of the tankini, and my bottoms are bikini briefs. There's nothing to cover myself up with and my heart's speeding, but it feels good.

I want to tell Jersy to touch me. I want to lean over and press my wet self against him. If we keep sitting here staring at each other with hungry eyes, I'll die.

"Jersy," I say, my lungs collapsing.

His eyes take me in, but he doesn't answer. He puts one hand on my knee and curves the other around my shoulder. His fingers coast slowly up my neck. I want to scream at him and make him hurry. I want to take his hands and put them other places, but this is too sweet to rush. He nestles his face into my neck and licks at it like I'm sugarcoated.

I melt next to him on the couch. It sounds corny and stupid, but I do. This is what people mean when they say something "just happened." It's not that you couldn't stop yourself if you tried; it's just that you're all wrapped up in something that feels too good to be true, better than you even would've let yourself imagine.

I pull away from him, and his face sinks like he's done something wrong. Then I'm pressing my lips against his, tasting his tongue and winding my hand around the back of his head. His hair's so short that my palm itches. One of his fingers works its way into my belly button, making me giggle. He spreads his hands possessively around my bare waist and drops his head to study my skin.

When our eyes meet, he kisses me fiercely on the mouth, twisting a hand into my hair. I don't want to think about the last time someone touched me like this. Jersy isn't anything like Adam. I can stop this anytime. I break away to prove it, and Jersy hunches over, cups his hand around the back of his neck, and says, "I know. It's Audrey."

I nod at him, burning all over. I've pushed Audrey to the back of my mind, but I haven't forgotten. I don't have any excuses for myself. My nod's a lie. It's Adam and the way he changed me that's holding me back. Maybe I trust Jersy but I don't trust myself. I don't know how long this good feeling will last. It could mutate any second now.

"I slapped this guy at work in the face yesterday." I swallow hard and look away. I never meant to tell him this. "I thought he was trying something, but now I'm not sure." I hate the way my swimsuit feels on my skin suddenly, cold and stale.

Jersy's arms are folded over his knees. He looks up at me, his hand reaching up to cradle his face. I could stop talking and lay my hands flat against his chest. It'd be easier than talking.

"I get nervous sometimes. I don't mean with you." I'm shivering again. My hands grip my knees. "Do you remember how you asked about Adam Porter?"

Jersy's head snaps up. His eyes are wary and he nods slowly.

"He tried to do something to me." My teeth are chattering. I never should've started this. It's too big to say. "At a party last fall."

Jersy's face is grim. He wants me to be a normal girl, like Audrey; he doesn't want to deal with this shit. "It's not Audrey, is it?" he says quietly. "It's this."

"Yeah." The word slashes. It's like that night with Adam just happened.

"Why didn't you let me smash his stupid fucking face in?" he asks. He's angry, but I think I hear helplessness too.

That makes me sadder still, and I shake my head and hide my eyes in my hands. My arms shake but I won't let go. I'm silent as a stone.

Jersy doesn't touch me. He's probably afraid to now. I could slap him in the face or think bad things about him.

When I look up, he's staring at the wall, stroking his scar. "Does anybody know?" he asks. "Your parents?"

"No," I whisper. "Just Audrey."

"And she's not here," he says to himself. He turns towards me, looks into my eyes, and brushes his hand against mine. "The guy at work. What happened?"

I tell him what I remember. I don't even care what he thinks anymore. I just need to tell somebody, like when my dad left. "I don't think he's going to be a problem anymore," I confide, wrapping my arms tightly across my belly to fight the cold.

Jersy slides his arm protectively around my shoulders. "Do you want me to get your clothes?" His skin feels as warm as sunlight. "A towel?" he suggests. "A sweatshirt?" It's as though he has to get something for me, do something.

"I'll get my clothes in a minute," I tell him.

"Okay." He squeezes my shoulder reassuringly. Nothing sexual's going to happen anymore. He's my second best friend again. "I didn't mean to scare you. I thought it was okay."

"I thought so too," I say truthfully. "I'm sorry."

"No," he says quickly. "That's okay." He stares straight ahead. "I just thought it was about Audrey."

"It should be that too." I'm like a truth machine. I can't help it. "I miss her so much, and then I go and do this." I peer into his eyes. "I'm here and she isn't. That's the only reason this happened, isn't it?"

"No. That's not the reason." Jersy frowns and lifts his arm off my shoulders. "I liked you first. Before Audrey." His eyes shine as they stare steadily back at me. "You acted like you weren't interested. I let it go."

That's not how it was. The truth is that I'm damaged. I don't know how to be with anyone.

"It's okay," Jersy says, sympathy in his eyes. He folds his arms slowly around me and holds me gently, like he's afraid I might shatter. "I'm sorry."

"It's okay," I whisper. I'm not sure what he's sorry about, but it doesn't make any difference. I hold my breath and think of Audrey missing him from three hundred miles away. This is finished before it started. It has to be. I'm not afraid of Jersy; I'm the problem. I'm burning up, even as I shiver. I'm thinking about him and me and how it'd be. He's the most Beautiful Boy I've ever seen, and the image keeps flashing inside my head, making me crazy. "I'm all right," I add. "I should get my clothes."

I draw away from him and look at his chest and arms, golden brown. Except for his underarms he's nearly as hairless as me. His blue-green eyes are so pretty that my chest aches, and when he curled his hands around my waist a few minutes ago, I wondered where he'd put them next.

My brain goes wild, looking and remembering and imagining. If I don't stop soon I'll go blind.

twenty-two

○   ○   ○

I TALK TO Audrey for about forty-five minutes. She's super supportive about the Kevin incident, but neither of us mentions Jersy. When my voice gets hoarse, she thinks it's because of Kevin, and I let her. She says she dreamt about her and me walking past the St. Mark's track field together. We were laughing so hard she thought she'd wet her pants, and when she woke up she couldn't remember what was so funny—just that we were happy.

When we hang up, I feel like Judas. How is it possible to feel so close to someone and lie to her?

I'm still thinking about that when I get into bed, but the next morning at Play Country my brain latches back on to Kevin. We pass each other in silence all day long, and without Nishani to distract me the hours drag on endlessly. I'm a bundle of nerves, guilt, and terrible customer service skills. I jump when someone asks me a question and take too long to answer.

Then, when my shift's finally over, I run right smack into

Kevin outside the staff room. He averts his eyes like I'm some kind of leper and mutters, "I didn't see you."

"Me neither," I tell him. "Sorry."

"Yeah." Kevin holds up his hands like I'm about to steal his wallet. "Whatever. Just don't get excited."

"Whatever," I repeat, walking calmly by him like I don't give a shit what he does as long as he stays out of my way.

And he does. He's quiet around me for the entire week. The couple of times we're forced to communicate are awkward, but we survive. He doesn't stand too close to me and breathe into my face, and I don't smack him and call him a pervert. Courtney says there's a rumor going around that we hooked up. In one scenario I dumped him. In the other we're stupid-crazy for each other like one of those soap opera couples who act like they hate each other.

"I can't believe people would think that," I tell her.

"Oh, I know," Courtney chimes. "I don't think most people do. It's just something to talk about. Like when Suzanne and Gerald have an extended meeting in his office and people say they got stuck in a sexual position they couldn't get out of."

I've joked about that too. It's hard not to. Play Country isn't what you'd call intellectually scintillating. Our undernourished brains need some kind of stimulation.

Nishani and I make another movie date, and while we're there she asks me about Kevin too. Aneeka's on a secret date with some Jamaican guy her parents would never approve of, so it's just the two of us, and for a second I consider telling her the whole truth. "You remember that day we had a fight?" I begin.

Nishani nods and stuffs her face with popcorn, and I want to say it, I really do, but I haven't known her long enough to get that personal. "Well, I freaked out on him for getting in my face all the time—you know how he does that." Nishani nods keenly. She sees it every day too. Everyone knows what he's like. "And now he won't talk to me, which is fine by me."

Nishani opens her mouth, but I cut her off. "Can I trust you?" I continue. "If I tell you something, will you keep it between us?" My heart's racing like it was that night with Jersy. I thought telling him would be enough. Now I feel the words chafing against the back of my throat, begging to be set free.

"You can trust me." Her coal-black eyes zoom in on mine. "I won't tell anyone."

It's exactly what I expect her to say, and the words are already forcing themselves out. "I slapped Kevin in the face." I tap my fingers nervously against my watch. "I thought he was going to try to kiss me in the stockroom. His face was like this." I hold my hand up in front of my face to demonstrate. "At the time I really thought he was going to do it. I didn't mean to hit him. It was like an automatic reaction." Nishani's listening intently, waiting for me to get it all out. "But right afterwards I wasn't sure anymore. It was like he was as shocked as I was, and he asked me why I'd hit him and said it was assault."

Nishani tilts her head thoughtfully. "You must've been really angry," she says, "to react like that. Maybe it'll make him think twice next time."

She's right, and most of me is glad I did it because what would Kevin have gone and done if I hadn't? "Maybe." I scratch my arms. They're still peeling from the barbecue. I forgot to put on more sunscreen when Jersy and I went back into the pool; I wasn't thinking straight. "I just can't tell if I overreacted or what." I wish there was some way to know for sure.

Nishani reaches down and sets her popcorn on the floor. "He's creepy. I probably would've done the same thing." She folds her hands in her laps and adds, "Aneeka kicked someone in the balls once. This guy on the beach kept bugging her. He was like thirty or something; it was disgusting. He grabbed her ass, and she kicked him right in the nuts. He was practically crying."

I can totally see her doing that. I bet she doesn't take shit from anyone. "That's cool," I say. "What an asshole."

"They're everywhere." Nishani nods as if to say it's the same thing with Kevin and me. I'm not sure it's as black and white as that, but the important thing is that I have to be positive; being the regular me isn't doing any good.

Nishani's dad picks us up at the end of the movie, and when I walk through my front door Samsam jumps on me like I've been gone a week. Mom's still up, haunting the kitchen in her silk pajamas, and my heart leaps. She's only gone to bed at eight once so far this week.

"How was the movie?" she asks.

"It was okay." I dig into the cupboard for a late-night cookie fest as Mom sips her diet soda. "Did you walk Samsam?"

"Oh." Mom's voice sinks. "I forgot." She stares at me with penitent eyes.

No wonder he was extra excited to see me. "I'll do it." I don't like walking him alone at night, but it's not the first time.

"I'll get changed," Mom offers. "We can go together. Just a short one, okay? I'm exhausted, and I don't want to leave Daniel too long."

So we walk Samsam briskly around the block together. A couple of kids are skateboarding at the bottom of our road, and they make me think of Jersy. Everything makes me think of Jersy. I almost told Nishani what happened between us at the barbecue, but it's not the kind of thing you should reveal to a new friend. Slapping Kevin doesn't make me a bad person, but kissing my best friend's boyfriend does. The worst thing is that I'm not over it. I know it was a mistake, but I keep playing it back in my head, adding bits on.

"What're you thinking about?" Mom asks, keeping pace with me.

"This summer's weird without Audrey." The air smells like freshly cut grass and flowers. It's a good summer smell.

"But her absence is giving you a chance to make new friends and spend some time with other people," Mom points out.

My head snaps around to look at her. Classic Mom. She must be feeling better. Dad obviously still hasn't mentioned his fall plans. "New *friend*," I correct. "Just the one." Two if you count Aneeka.

"Jasper and Maggie?" Mom says. "Didn't you say you were going to see them too?"

"Maybe." I hand the leash to Mom as I bend to tie my running shoe. "I haven't called them yet."

I look up at Mom, waiting for her to spur me on to action. She hands me back the leash and says, "We should hurry back. I don't like to leave Daniel alone in the house."

"I know." No directions on owning my height or struggling against my natural instinct to live like a quasi-hermit. I'm almost disappointed.

We scurry back to the house, and Mom gives me a good-night kiss. She pauses on the stairs like she has something else to say. Then she turns and waves goodbye over her shoulder. The phone rings just after she disappears. It stops after two rings, so I know she must've picked up. A second later it rings again—and rings and rings. Finally I answer.

"Finn, it's me," Jersy says. "Your mom said to hang up and call back." She was too lazy to come downstairs and get me. I don't blame her. This is a late night for her.

"We were walking Samsam." Now that we have that out of the way, I'm all shy and stupid, like the new kid in kindergarten.

"Mm," Jersy hums. "I tried to get you on your cell earlier. I was just wondering how you were doing, you know, after Sunday." He pauses like he's giving me a chance to answer, only I don't. "I didn't know what to say when you told me about Adam," he adds.

"It's okay." My stomach's up in my throat. I'm a giant-sized frog that used to be a girl.

"I shouldn't have said that about liking you before Audrey," he continues. "That was probably the last thing you wanted to hear."

"I liked you too," I confess. It feels so good to say it that I could cry. "I've just been really messed up."

Jersy's quiet for so long that I jump off the couch and start to pace. "Are you still messed up?" he asks.

My heart's bouncing under my rib cage like a rubber ball. "Yeah," I say truthfully. My skin's tingling in amazement and I can't breathe. "And I still like you." My words are so low that they seem to take on added depth. I'm in awe. I've never heard my voice sound like that before. I tug at my ear and pace wildly.

I am still messed up and I still like you.

I feel tremendous and terrified. What am I doing?

"Me too," Jersy says. "So what does that mean?"

We haven't even mentioned Audrey. "I don't know," I tell him. "Do we have to know that?" Samsam's watching me. I see him out of the corner of my eye. All my pacing's making him nervous.

Jersy laughs lightly. "I don't know. I was hoping you'd tell me."

"I'm the one who's messed up," I say, smiling uncontrollably into the phone. "How am I supposed to know?" I slapped Kevin's face, kissed my best friend's boyfriend while she was three hundred miles away, and still don't want to speak to my father—who I'm having dinner with tomorrow incidentally. I don't have one single thing figured out.

"I'm messed up too," he says. "Just in different ways."

It's awful the way we're avoiding Audrey's name, but I can't make myself say it. Things are complicated enough. "So can we still hang out at least?" Jersy asks. "In this weird gray area?"

"When?" I shiver. My voice is doing that magic thing again.

"Tomorrow?"

"I'm seeing my dad tomorrow," I remind him.

"Right." He pauses. "Saturday?"

"I'm working Saturday, but I can do Saturday night."

"Okay," Jersy tells me. "Hey, your situation at work—is that under control?"

"We're not really speaking. He thinks I'm a freak."

"Who cares what he thinks," Jersy says. "He's a loser."

"You don't even know him."

"Anybody who would think you're a freak is a loser," Jersy says confidently.

If he were here, I'd crush my lips against his and breathe in the smell of his sweatshirt. A tickle's snaking down my chest and budding between my legs. It's been so long since I felt like this. Jersy's so sweet and beautiful that I don't care about anything else.

I don't trust myself to speak. I'm frog-girl. Crazy-happy frog-girl with a crazy-happy tickle.

"So should I come there or do you want to come here?" Jersy asks.

"Come here," I tell him. My brain's doing its dirty translation bit again. I blush into the phone and add, "It doesn't really matter."

"It's all a gray area, right?" Jersy says. "I'll be there around eight."

"Cool, I'll see you then." I hang up and do a little spin. My face is warm and I tickle all over. I don't want this feeling to end.

Dad snares Daniel and me in a three-person hug outside the front door. He's tanned and clean-shaven, and he turns to wave goodbye to Mom, aiming a generous smile at her. "What's everybody in the mood for?" he sings, so happy to see us that nothing could get him down. "Italian? Chinese? Greek?"

"Swiss Chalet," Daniel yelps. Hand the boy a plate of fries and he's happy.

"I could go for that," I say. My stomach rumbles its approval. For once I'm on the same page as the Anti-Me. I could drink the Chalet sauce out of the bowl. Pure delicious.

"If that's what you both want," Dad agrees. He passes the local Swiss Chalet in favor of the newly renovated one across town. This get-together is supposed to be something special. It's a reunion, after all. "Any movies you guys want to check out after?"

My brother mentions the Aidan Lamb action flick. It's PG-13, but my father would agree to anything today. "Sound good, Finn?" Dad asks.

"Yeah, fine." At least we don't have to talk during the movie. I don't want to hear any more about how much Dad misses us and how great it'll be when we can sleep over at his new place in the fall. I don't want two bedrooms, two Thanksgivings, and two birthdays. I don't want to worry about how Mom will keep herself busy while we're with him or whether he'll be lonely when we're with her. How can any of that be great?

In the restaurant Daniel talks nonstop about camp. I play with my straw and soak everything in Chalet sauce—chicken, french fries, and bread. Every now and then Dad cuts in and tries to draw me into the conversation. He's so obvious that it makes me cringe. He wants to know what's going on with me, but things have changed so much in the past month that he can't even get the questions right.

When Daniel excuses himself to go to the bathroom, the conversation grinds to a complete halt. Dad and I glance at each other over our sauce-coated food. He swallows ice water and anxiously touches his chin. I spear soggy fries and let them melt in my mouth. I can go longer than him any day. Talking doesn't help anyway.

"You know," Dad says quietly, "I was hoping this was going to go a little smoother." He wipes his mouth with his napkin. "We've always been close, Finn. I don't want that to change. These past few weeks have been tough on all of us, but—"

"This was your choice," I tell him, anger thickening my voice. "None of us had a choice. Mom didn't want you to go. I didn't want you to go. Daniel didn't want you to go. You got to decide for all of us, and now you're trying to tell me that not only did you get to decide but that I have to like it!" I dig my fingernails into my knees and glare at him. "I don't want to hear about how you want things to be. What about what I want?"

Dad presses his fingertips into his cheek and stares at me, bewildered. "What do you think?" he says. "Do you think I haven't tried?" I stare back at him, my face falling. He sounds lost and lonely. This isn't my father talking. "Do you think this is what I had in mind for my life? Starting over at thirty-eight?"

I push my plate away and chew my lip. I can't listen anymore. I won't feel sorry for him. Mom's lonely too. I don't know if she can do it all without him.

"You have to trust me on this one, Finn," he pleads. "I have tried; *we've* tried. Staying together would be worse for all of us. I'm not trying to take the easy way out here. I'm not going anywhere; I'm not leaving your lives." He leans towards me over the table, his eyes bloodshot. "I know this is painful for you. I know how hard you take things and I'm sorry it has to be this way, but there are some things I can't change."

Dad stares at me until a lump forms in my throat. I couldn't speak now if I wanted to.

"I'll always be around for you guys," Dad says. "I hope you know that."

He repeats himself as Daniel slides back into his seat. My brother looks embarrassed and grabs a chicken leg. He munches on it zealously, avoiding everyone's eyes.

Dad and I keep watching him. It's easier than looking at each other. When our eyes finally connect, I don't look away. The look hurts so deep that I blink double fast. "I know," I whisper. "But that doesn't make it easy."

Daniel glares at me from across the table like I'm ruining everything. Dad nods gravely and says, "I know." I want to blurt out everything about Mom's marathon sleep schedule, her unplucked eyebrows, the horrible thing I'm doing to Audrey, and how I slapped Kevin so hard that his cheek turned red. "But we'll all be okay," he promises.

I want to trust him. I do. But you can't make yourself believe something just because you want to. I put my elbows on the table, fold both hands around the back of my neck, and swallow the lump, again and again.

Across the table Dad clamps his hand on Daniel's back. The Anti-Me stares at his half-eaten chicken leg like he's going to bawl. His bottom lip quivers and he swipes at his sweaty forehead with one hand. If he picks this moment to lose it, I'll kill him, I swear.

I shovel mushy fries into my mouth and concentrate on the top of his head. His hair's blonder than it was only three weeks ago, but his arms are dark. He's stock-still in his chair, Dad's hand glued to his back, and I can't take the silence a second longer.

"Daniel," I say, kicking him under the table.

His cheeks are shining red like a little kid off a baby-food jar, and he pouts at me as he looks up. "What?"

"Are you gonna eat those?" I point at his fries.

Daniel eyes me cautiously from across the table. He divides the remaining fries into two piles with his knife. "You can have those," he says, pointing to the smaller pile. He sets his knife down, picks up his chicken, and bites slowly into it.

I sit up straight in my chair, owning my height. Relief flows through me as I reach for my fork and dig into my pile. I catch a grateful look from Dad and without a second thought begin to tell him what this summer has been like without Audrey. I tell him about Nishani and Aneeka and what I hate about stocking shelves. I tell him that sometimes I hang out with Jersy, even though we don't have a lot in common. The waitress brings free refills of our drinks, and then Daniel starts talking about the Mikulskis' pool and I don't have to speak so much anymore. It's my turn to listen.

twenty-three

○   ○   ○

I DON'T NOTICE Kevin much at work the next day. I'm too hung up on eight o'clock and what Jersy and I are supposed to do at my house later. He's used to people and noise on Saturday nights, and I spend my weekends e-mailing Audrey, downloading MP3s, and redesigning my Web site.

By the time my shift's over, I'm convinced tonight is a mistake. He'll be bored. We won't have anything to say to each other. I'm a temporary distraction while Audrey's away. I'm a Judas and a moron and I hate it when I think like that. Other girls don't blame themselves for things and think they're freaky. They get their ears pierced with six holes, have their pubes pulled out by the roots, and hook up with whoever they want, even if that happens to be their best friend's boyfriend.

Anyway, if tonight is a mistake, I'll find out soon enough. Because I'm not phoning him to cancel. Maybe that means I'm like other girls after all.

When Mom picks me up, I make her drive me to Blockbuster for DVDs and popcorn. At home we cook frozen salmon with canned asparagus, and she tells me that Daniel called earlier and said he was having a great time. "He wants to go back for another weekend in a couple of weeks," Mom says with an uneven smile. "Maybe you'll want to go too."

"I already told Dad I can't. Not with my hours at work." I frown at her. "Are you trying to get rid of me?"

"Of course not." Mom pinches her earlobe as she watches me. "But I know you must miss him."

"I'm fine." I'm not doing this two nights in a row. She can say whatever she wants, but I have other things to think about—like Jersy coming over in an hour. "I'll see him when he's around. It's not like he's moved to New Zealand or something." That's what Dad said about Audrey. I could've used the line on him last night, but he got to me; all that stuff about being around for Daniel and me worked like magic. Sometimes I'm so easy.

"He told you about finding an apartment," Mom says quietly. "He told me he mentioned it."

"He told me," I confirm. "It sucks." It's easy to be mad at him when he's not around. Especially when I'm choking on Mom's sad vibes.

"It does." Mom smirks. She guides a forkful of asparagus into her mouth and chews mechanically.

"Does that mean we'll have to move out too?" We've lived in this house since I was five. I can't imagine the three of us someplace else. I never thought I'd live here forever, but I assumed this house, and my parents, would always be around for me to come back to.

"Maybe." Mom rubs her eyes. "I don't know, Finn. I don't have any answers." She pats my arm affectionately. "I'm sorry I brought it up. Nothing's been decided yet for sure. I don't want you to worry."

"That's reassuring," I say sarcastically. "Thanks."

Mom clenches her jaw and throws her right hand into the air. "I don't like this any better than you do. I'm doing my best, Finn. I don't know what you expect."

"You act like everything's falling apart and then tell me not to worry. I don't know what *you* expect!" I'm sorry as soon as I've said it. I watch Mom carry her plate over to the sink, square her shoulders, and face the window.

"Jersy's gonna be here around eight," I say. I'm not angry with her anymore. I just want her to turn around.

"I remember," she says to the window. "Do you want me to stay out of your way?"

"No." I can't believe she just said that. "What's that supposed to mean? We're just hanging out." My cheeks are burning.

Mom turns to face me, only I don't want her to look at me anymore. "Does every single thing have to be a battle?" She sighs loudly, turns on the tap, and begins washing her plate. I bring mine over along with the glasses and cutlery.

"I'll dry," I offer.

Mom shakes her head. "Go on. Get ready."

For what? My stomach lurches as I walk away. The guilt is worse now that she knows. Months ago she would've asked me for details, stuck bamboo under my fingernails until I confessed, and then salivated over the specifics. This is what she's been waiting for. Some guy to stroll into the picture and make me a regular girl.

In my room I switch on the stereo and brush my hair. My skin's pretty clear at the moment, and if I put on some eye shadow and foundation I could look okay. I could do lipstick, mascara, and the whole bit, but then Jersy wouldn't recognize me. It'd be like that night in September all over again. I still have Kaitlynn James's purple pill buried in an old backpack in my closet. I could give it to Jersy to prove I'm not a control freak. We could get out of our heads together, and then I wouldn't have to worry about what we're going to do tonight.

Shit. My legs feel like they're going to buckle underneath me. I'm sweating like a pig and stomping around my room like a rabid elephant. It's ten to eight. Why didn't I go to the cottage with Daniel? This is wrong.

And it's worse at eight and worse still at ten after. Then, somewhere between twenty after and eight-thirty, I start to get mad. Maybe Jersy went to a party with his friends and forgot all about me. Do I need this kind of shit in my life?

"Finn," Mom shouts, knocking on my door, "Jersy's here."

"Coming," I call. No makeup after all. Plain old me in a sleeveless red print T-shirt and scruffy jeans.

I hurry downstairs and into the family room, where Jersy's sitting on the carpet, petting Samsam. "Hey," he says, looking up at me. His eyes are greener than I've ever seen them. I love the way they change color with the light. My breath catches in my throat. Every ounce of irritability melts away in an instant. "How was work?"

"The creep, you mean?" I sit down on the couch.

"Everything," Jersy says with a shrug. His tan knees are poking out from under his long shorts. I can't stop checking them out.

"Boring," I tell him. "The usual. How about you?"

He only works weekdays, but from what he told me before, it's exhausting manual labor. "It's okay." Jersy smiles. "I won't miss it. I can tell you that. The guys I work with make me look like a genius."

"Me too." I smile back. "Only I feel like I'm losing brain cells by the hour while I'm there." I pull my legs up onto the couch with me and cross them, yoga-style. "What was my mom like at the door?"

"Normal." Jersy stretches out sideways on the ground. "Why? Something going on?"

Something's always going on. I tell him about our dinner conversation. The last part's the hardest, and I hesitate before adding, "She thinks something's up with us. I can tell."

"What'd you say?"

It's my turn to shrug. "Not much. I mean, there's nothing going on, right?"

Jersy squints at me like he's trying to read the fine print. "I don't know. That depends on you." I shake my head like I don't know either, and Jersy gets to his feet and says, "Do you drink coffee?"

"Sure."

"You want to check out the new coffee place down by the lake?"

"Yeah. They have tables outside, right? We can bring Samsam." That way I won't have to walk him later.

I knock on Mom's bedroom door, and when she opens it I surprise her by throwing my arms around her neck and hugging her. "I'm sorry about before," I tell her. "We're going for coffee. We'll be back later."

Mom hugs me back. When she pulls away, I see that her eyes have softened. "So it's safe to come out?" she jokes.

"It was never unsafe." I force myself to smile. "You have an overactive imagination, is all." Mom shakes her head at me but she smiles.

Jersy, Samsam, and I set out for the lake, and it's so humid that my hair instantly sticks to the back of my neck. "No wonder you shaved it all off," I tell him, pushing my hair off my face. "I wish I could do that."

"No, you don't." Jersy lightly cups the back of my head. "You're a long-hair kind of girl." It's hot as hell, but I shiver anyway. I can't believe we can be like this together, that he can make me feel like a better me by doing the simplest thing. "Sorry." He sinks his hands into his pockets. "I didn't think."

"It's not that," I tell him. If anything, it's the opposite, but my conscience steps in and adds, "You're still with Audrey. This is just one of those summer things. It wouldn't stick." It's not fair that the person I can feel like this about belongs to Audrey. It's not fair on any of us.

"You think so?" Jersy sounds so sincere that my stomach drops. "I haven't been able to stop thinking about you since Sunday, and I haven't even e-mailed her this week. I think I knew when she left that it was only a matter of time until we broke up. It felt . . . like it was ending."

"That's crazy." The part of me that's Audrey's best friend is upset on her behalf. "You guys liked each other so much. Being apart for two months shouldn't change that."

"It's not just about the two months." His eyes sparkle in the sun. "It probably would've ended this summer anyway." He pauses to search for the right words. "I think we ended up liking each other more because we weren't supposed to. All the sneaking around and stuff, it keeps things interesting." Jersy looks past me like he wishes he could take that back. "I don't want to say anything bad about Audrey."

"So it's only fun if there's drama?" I say quickly. "What does that say about you?"

"That's not what I meant." Jersy stops in the middle of the

sidewalk. "And what does kissing me say about you?" He sounds angry, and that makes me mad too. I speed up, not sure whether I want him to follow, and he matches my pace and adds, "Look, I really like you, and it's not about drama or Audrey being away. I don't know where this is going, and I know it's not going to be easy, but if you tell me . . ." He stops walking again. "If you tell me what we can do and when and I promise to listen, don't you think we could work things out?"

"Maybe," I whisper. "I don't know." There's a big difference between kissing someone on his couch once and really being with him. "Sometimes I just don't feel right," I confess. "It's like . . . I don't know how to be like I was before."

Jersy bows his head towards mine, so close that they're almost touching. "You could talk to someone. It could help." His hand brushes against my arm.

"You don't know that."

"Yeah," he says under his breath. "I do. It's like with Christina." His eyes are so near that they're out of focus—just splotches of shining black. "A really bad thing happened to her in Kingston." He touches his forehead and folds his arms in front of his stomach like he's going to be sick. "It was bad," he repeats. "And it made things bad for all of us."

It's still bad. I can feel it off him the same way I felt it with my mom, and I drop Samsam's leash and fold my arms instinctively around Jersy's neck. He puts his arms around me too, and we stand frozen in a knot in the middle of the sidewalk, breathing and holding tight, and I think that if I can be with anybody, it must be him. I don't even think I know how to do without him anymore.

"I'm too attached to you already," I complain. "I thought cutting your hair would help, but it didn't."

Jersy smacks his lips against my forehead. "You were killing me in that swimsuit on Sunday. Fuck." He shakes his head. "Sorry."

"No, tell me." I want to hear this. Already his words have transformed me into liquid sunshine.

A slow grin creeps across Jersy's lips. He looks so good that I'll never be over it. "No," he says decisively. "I'll sound like a pervert." He scratches his neck and adds, "I don't even think you know how beautiful you are."

With my frizzy hair, scruffy jeans, and albino skin. Ha. I almost laugh at him, and he touches my arm again, leans forward, and says, "Can I kiss you?"

It's funny to be asked, and a laugh escapes as I lean forward to meet him. We kiss soft. Like he's afraid to hurt me, and I wish it didn't have to be that way—that I could be normal for him—but this is me now. This is how it is.

Samsam waits for us all the while, and I reward him with a dog bagel from the pet bakery when we get downtown. The new coffee place has two seats left on the patio outside. It's like fate or something, and Jersy goes in to order our iced cappuccinos.

He smiles as he sits down next to me with the coffees, and I want to smother him in kisses and tell him how amazing he is. Instead I sip my iced cappuccino and stroke Samsam's ears. Jersy watches me in silence, until I can't take it anymore and burst into an enormous grin. "So what're your friends doing tonight?" I ask, cheeks puffing out like a chipmunk.

"Nothing special," he says. "Hanging out."

"Billy's cool," I tell him.

"Yeah, he is. They're all okay. You just don't know them that well."

"You think we'd get along?"

Jersy flashes an incomplete smile that seems to concede my point. "Probably not, you're just different types of people." His hands swim through the air as he searches for the words. "You're focused. You know exactly what you want to do and what you don't." He looks down at Samsam. "Audrey's like that too." He takes a sip of his coffee and touches my hand under the table.

Neither of us has ever mentioned what we're going to do about Audrey. It's eerie. I let Jersy thread his fingers between mine, to test out how it feels. I've never held hands with anyone except my family. It's such a weird feeling that it blocks out everything else.

"How was the thing with your dad last night?" he asks.

I tell him about the Anti-Me almost crying and how my dad wore me down in about three seconds with his cheesy speech. "It kills me that I'm so easy," I groan. "He gets to have everything his way."

"Not exactly," Jersy points out. "You didn't go to the cottage with him."

"That's true." I nod. "And I'm not going to."

The sun sets while we're finishing our coffee, and afterwards Jersy, Samsam, and I walk back to my house. I put on one of the action movies I rented and sit next to Jersy on the couch. He's yawning already and I hit him on the arm and say, "Don't you ever sleep?"

"Not as much as I should," he admits. I wonder if that has anything to do with Christina and what happened to her back in Kingston, but I don't want to drag the conversation back there again. "Where's your mom?" he asks, twisting his neck so he can glance into the hall.

"Probably asleep already." We haven't seen her since we got in. "She goes to bed early."

"She's okay with us alone here like this?"

"She doesn't seem too concerned." I could get away with murder at the moment. No one would notice.

Jersy smiles that easy smile of his. "That's a change."

It's more freedom than we can use. Sitting next to Jersy on a Saturday night with no one around is a definite temptation, but I know we have to go slow. So we watch the movie and then sit on the floor and play with my brother's Xbox, Jersy instructing me in the fine art of destruction. I feel like Vin Diesel with estrogen and more facial expressions, and I can't believe I can lounge around shooting things with him like we're buddies while inside I'm sparkling like a thousand constellations.

But that's one of the things I like about him too. It seems like maybe we don't have to just be one thing.

In the end it's me who starts to nod off around two-thirty. My head bobs as I grip the joystick. "I think I'm done," I say.

"Yeah," he says with a massive yawn. "Me too."

"I'll drive you home," I offer. Whoa. Completely spontaneous. I didn't see that one coming.

"You're not even sixteen yet." Jersy's eyes pop open, and the fact that it's so easy for me to surprise him makes me want to fling my arms around him.

"No one will know," I tell him. "Your house is like two minutes away." I'm not especially worried about getting caught. Mom would consider this normal teenage behavior. She'd pretend to disapprove, but I bet she'd almost be proud.

"Exactly." Jersy scratches at his brown knee. "And I have my board."

"You worried I'm going to get us killed?"

Jersy munches on his grin as he sits back on his elbows. "I'm not worried," he says. "It's cool." His gaze rushes up to meet mine.

"But if you change your mind, I got my G1 two weeks ago, so I'm good to step in." Technically a G1 means he has to spend the next eight months at the wheel with a licensed driver next to him. Last time I looked, I'd had one brief illegal lesson in a school parking lot, but I wasn't about to change my mind.

"You won't have to," I tell him, standing up and heading for the hall.

"Okay then," Jersy says. "At least bring the dog for company on the way home in case the car breaks down or something, okay?"

I'm pretty sure the car won't break down in the short time it takes me to drive back, but it's another one of those things that make me want to kiss him, so I agree. I grab Mom's keys from the hook in the front hall, and the three of us head into the yard. Getting Mom's Mazda out of the garage is the hardest part of the operation. After that I'm cruising no problem.

I shift into park in front of Jersy's house, and he says, "Not bad. You really only had one lesson?"

"Yup." I nod and look over at him, feeling my whole body tickle in the darkness.

"You're a natural." He stares out the window and back at me. "Tonight was cool."

"Yeah. Weird but good." Is this the part where we're supposed to kiss goodbye? I stare at his lips and plant my hands on the steering wheel.

"The gray area's always weird," Jersy says, his hand on the door handle. "We should do this again sometime during the week." He runs his other hand swiftly over his head and swings the door open. "Call me, okay? We'll set something up."

"Wait!" I call.

Jersy turns in his seat. I lean over and kiss him fast on the mouth. Our tongues glide together as his hand cups the back of my head. I could do this forever. I press my hands against his chest and kiss his chin. He squeezes my thigh and slides his mouth back against mine. We push back and forth, taking it deeper, and I slip my hands up inside his T-shirt and feel him tremble. "You should get home," he says, pulling back. Beads of sweat dot his forehead. He wipes them off with the back of his hand and steps onto the grass. I smile again as I hear it squelch underneath his feet. I must be setting some kind of personal record for corny grins.

"Be careful," he says, staring down into the car.

"You too," I tell him. Given the context, it doesn't make much sense, but Jersy nods anyway.

I drive slowly off into the night, Samsam pressing his nose into the air from the back window—totally in the moment. Tonight I know just how he feels.

twenty-four

○　　○　　○

MY e-mails TO Audrey are full of holes. No mention of Jersy coming over on Saturday night, his plan to call in sick on my day off so we can spend it together, or of me hijacking Mom's car for my own evil purposes. As far as she knows, I'm expending all my energy lugging around toys and fighting with my parents. I'm such a traitor that a brick settles into my stomach every time I sit down to write her. You'd think that would make me change course or at least own up to what's going on, but I don't want to do either of those things.

I can hardly believe it myself. How can I be so selfish?

The excitement and guilt battle it out daily, threatening to crack me down the middle. One evening I can hardly stand it and almost confess to Mom over dinner. Another afternoon I get within an inch of telling Nishani during break. For a couple seconds I even consider spilling it to Courtney at the customer service booth.

Then Thursday, my day off, hits and I still haven't told a soul.

Jersy said he wants to sleep late and that I should come over around noon. I'm supposed to bring my swimsuit. Samsam is optional, and this time I decide to leave him at home. If this thing with Jersy is really going to happen, we have to be alone sometime.

I put a two-piece on under my clothes and walk over to his house. I'm not nervous, just buzzed, and when I get there the doorbell seems to ring forever. I jump when Christina appears in the doorway. "Hey," I say breathlessly. "You're back." I feel weirdly close to her since Jersy confided in me. I'm so glad to see her that it's an effort not to smile too wide.

"Yeah." Her unpainted fingernails lose themselves in her white-blond hair. "Mini-vacation."

"I should take one of those." Jersy must be relieved to have her back too. It's weird how you spend more time thinking about someone when they're not around. I guess it fills the space.

"Start now," Christina advises, standing aside to let me pass. "They're on the back patio."

"They?"

"Billy and my friend Nikki," she elaborates. "We're about to barbecue—you like chicken burgers? That's all that's left in the freezer."

I nod, feeling dazed. I had the idea Jersy and I would be alone. Now it seems like a pool party. "Hey," Billy calls as I step into the backyard. "How's it going, Finn?" He's wearing dark brown shorts, no shirt, and gulping back a beer.

"Hey, Billy," I say, scoping wildly around for Jersy. He's pulling himself out of the pool, walking swiftly towards me, looking too incredible for words.

"Hey," Jersy says, catching me around the waist. No mistaking where we stand now. Everyone here will know. "How're you doing?"

"Great," I tell him. *A little, uh, surprised.*

He points to the girl next to the barbecue. "This is Christina's friend Nikki."

"Hi," she says, smiling. She's wearing a white tank top with a denim miniskirt and is nearly as tall as me.

"Hi," I say back.

"I hope you didn't eat," Jersy says. "We're making chicken burgers and salad."

"Christina told me." He could've mentioned it before.

"Right." Jersy takes a sweeping look around the patio and motions for me to follow him inside. Once we're there, he leans against the counter and says, "Billy's air conditioner broke down. He's leaving in a couple hours."

I nod patiently, which is a complete lie. Two hours is forever. "I didn't know Christina was back."

"Yeah, just got in last night," he says cheerfully. "Nikki drove her." I'm full of questions, but I don't ask them. I stand in the kitchen across from him, listening to the laughter spill in from outside. "Come on," he says, grabbing my hand and guiding me back through the open sliding door. "I'm starving."

Soon Nikki, Christina, and I are in the pool. I catch Jersy checking me out from the barbecue and feel self-conscious in my two-piece. Billy offers me a beer when I climb out, and my face warms up as I will him not to look at me. "No thanks," I tell him. "I hate beer." My last taste was ten months ago. I don't need another.

Billy makes a face like I'm loco, and Jersy comes over and hands me a Coke. "Thanks," I tell him. I grab a seat and pull my T-shirt over my bikini.

The five of us eat and then Christina, Nikki, and I do the cleanup. Billy takes off while we're finishing up, and Jersy sits at the kitchen table, refusing to help because he cooked the burgers in the first place. I stay out of it and let him and Christina argue. I've never heard them fight before, but once they get going they sound just like every other brother and sister. Christina points out that she made the salad, and Jersy says all she had to do was tear open the bag and sprinkle on some croutons and, anyway, there are already more than enough people to do a few dishes.

By the time they quit arguing, everything's done and Christina and Nikki go back out to the pool. I sit down next to Jersy, and he drums his fingers on the table and asks if I want to hang out upstairs. "Sure," I tell him, my voice husky.

I follow him up and eyeball the half-eaten bowl of cornflakes on his dresser. Aside from breakfast his room is surprisingly neat for a change. Jersy moves to close the door behind me, then changes his mind and leaves it open a crack. "Do you have an elastic or something?" I ask. "For my hair?" It's frizzing up like a tennis ball as we speak.

He ransacks his desk and pulls out the world's biggest rubber band. "Thanks," I tell him, twisting it hastily around my hair to form a ponytail. My fingers are clumsy with excitement. We're finally alone again.

Jersy plops down onto his bed in his swimsuit. I sit on the chair across from him in my T-shirt and bikini bottoms, determined not to shiver. "You're a good swimmer," he says.

"Thanks. I didn't know there were going to be so many people around."

"Me neither. But then we're not really in a hurry to be alone, right?" It's a funny thing to say with his bedroom door all but closed and the house empty—but he sounds serious. "There's the whole gray-area thing." Jersy stares at me, his hands on his knees. "Have you said anything to Audrey?"

My jaw drops at the sound of her name. What kind of friend am I? "No." I wrap my shaking fingers around my ponytail. "Have you?" I already know he hasn't. She would've said something.

"No. But I think we should."

"She's my best friend," I say in a low voice. "What am I supposed to tell her? That the minute she was out of the picture I swept in and stole you?" I can't do that. I'm crazy to be here. Whatever this is, it can't go anywhere. I've been in denial since the barbecue—even before that.

"You didn't steal me," Jersy says indignantly. "This isn't anybody's fault."

Of course it is. "This is so shitty." I bite my lip hard. The words aren't strong enough, but anything I can think to say is an understatement.

Jersy reads the feelings in my face and takes a long breath. "We can wish it happened differently all we want, but that won't change anything, Finn." His little finger bends as he says my name. "Audrey's great, she is, but it's not like being with you." He studies his kneecaps. "There's nothing I can do about it."

"Nothing serious has happened between us," I tell him. "We can still stop this."

"You can stop if you want." Jersy's chin drops. "I'm still breaking up with her." He stares boldly into my eyes, waiting for me to contradict him. Then he lies back on the bed and squeezes his eyelids shut. "This is fucked already, and we haven't even started."

I stare at him and feel a shiver tear through me. I don't want to stop before we've started. I want the chance to find out what this could be—even if it doesn't last past summer. "Maybe it's better. We never have to screw it up."

Jersy groans across from me. "That's such bullshit, Finn. Don't even, okay?"

It's bullshit, he's right. It's not better; it's just sad. I bow my head and think of Audrey. She trusts me like a sister, and I like him so much. "She's my best friend," I repeat. "I can't do this, Jersy."

For a while he just lies there, gritting his teeth, and when he finally says "Okay," it's one of the saddest sounds I've ever heard. He sits up, his eyes back on me, and I cross over to the bed and sit next to him. My legs feel wobbly and I'm shivering like crazy. Jersy rests his hand on my thigh and leans his head in near mine. He's waiting for me to make the next move, and I do. It's like I don't even have to think about it. Before I know it my lips smack into his and then his hand's fitting itself around my ponytail, pressing against my back, stroking my arm.

We lie down together and then I'm shivering more. My hands are on his skin, gliding up and down his back. Our tongues swirl slowly around each other. I want to lick his neck and his ears and slide my finger over his lips. I want to whisper things in my new secret voice.

Jersy slides on top of me and kisses my neck. He fiddles with my T-shirt like it's in the way, and I yank it over my head, feeling brave and wild. Jersy stares at my bikini top and kisses the exposed skin between my breasts. Then our mouths connect again and he's pushing down on me, stealing my breath, wanting something else. I slow down, trying to get back to where we were just a few seconds ago, but I can't. That place is gone.

I tug my mouth away and say his name. He stops instantly, his face crumpling. "Are you okay?" he asks.

"Yeah." I hide my eyes. "You didn't do anything wrong. It just felt like too much suddenly. I'm sorry." I hate that I'm embarrassed.

Jersy rolls off me and touches my shoulder. "Don't say that. It's okay." He lies next to me, only our arms touching. "I don't even know what Adam did to you and I want to kill him," he says quietly. "I should've known. Whenever he was around—"

"I don't want to talk about him, okay?" I roll over on my side towards him. My head lands on his chest, and next thing I know we're lying like puppies, all curved into each other, almost airtight. Jersy pulls the blanket over us and hugs me close. We're hushed and warm and I could stay here forever, my left leg caught between his and our arms snugly around each other. "You're falling asleep, aren't you?" I whisper.

"No," Jersy says, and this time I know he's telling the truth. He pulls his head up and gazes down at me in a way that makes my chest ache. "You can't tell me you don't want this." He balances his weight on his elbow and blinks his beautiful brown lashes at me. "We can't leave things like this."

"I know." I can't even stop looking at him. How would I say goodbye? I'm kidding myself all round. I can't do this to Audrey, and I can't stop. I'm doomed.

"Talk to Audrey," he continues. "I'll tell her myself if you want."

He means it. He'll do it himself if I give the word. He wants to try with me—despite everything.

"I should be the one who tells her." My voice cracks.

"When?" Jersy's eyes are fixed on mine, and the feel of our legs tangled together under the covers is so amazingly natural that I can't believe it's us. We're warm and wonderful and right. How did this happen?

"Tonight," I tell him. I must be crazy, because this time I·mean it too. "I'll call her when I get home."

Jersy's eyes are shining like stars. He holds my hand and smiles like everything's going to be okay. For a minute I think I actually believe him.

twenty-five

MOM AND DANIEL are in the middle of dinner when I get home. I tell Mom I ate at Jersy's, rush up to my room, put Snow Patrol on, and lie on my unmade bed with my eyes closed. I don't want to change out of my bikini or take down my hair. I want to stay the girl I was in Jersy's bedroom. Then "Chocolate" comes on, and it sounds so undeniably bittersweet, so us and Audrey, that I snatch up the phone and dial before I can break and change my mind.

"*Allô?*" a man's voice says.

Fifteen seconds later Audrey's in my ear, happy to hear from me, killing me with every word. "I have to tell you something," I cut in. Panic rushes through my veins, transforming me into someone I don't recognize. *I would never do this to Audrey. It's not possible.* "I've been seeing a lot of Jersy lately," I go on. "Since you left and my folks split up—and things have been changing." Dread swallows me whole, but I keep talking, spitting out clichés that I don't know how to make sound true. "We've been getting closer the past few weeks. It's like he's really been there for me, and I know you'll be upset but if you could just try to understand it." I choke back the knot in my throat. "I told him about Adam and everything and . . ." I clutch at my T-shirt and scratch my arms. The skin on my face is stretched tighter than a drum. "I told him everything." It's a plea. I don't know what else to say.

"What're you talking about?" Audrey asks. "What do you mean 'getting closer'?"

I breathe silently into the phone, shaking under my skin.

"*Oh my God,*" Audrey whispers. "I can't believe this. I can't believe you'd do that."

"We haven't done anything. It's just . . ." I dig my fingernails into the receiver. "It's the way I've been feeling. For a while now."

"For a while now?" Audrey repeats. "You know how I feel about him. How can you do this?" Her voice lashes out at me. "And him? Does he know how you feel?" She laughs bitterly. "He does, doesn't he? *You told him everything.*"

"Audrey, please." Tears gush out of my eyes. "It's been so hard with you away. You have no idea."

"I have no idea?" she cries. "You know exactly what this summer has been like for me, Finn! You know how terrible I felt being apart from him all this time. I can't believe you'd do this. You of all people."

"Don't," I beg. "Nothing's happened."

"You're lying."

She's right and I don't protest. I swipe at my tears with one hand as I grip the receiver.

"So what is it?" she asks. "Are you sleeping with him?"

"No!" I cry, my voice raw.

"Is that a lie too? Tell me the truth." I hear her disappointment and it makes me wince. "Go on," she urges. "The least you can do is tell me the truth."

So I tell her everything, stumbling over the words, and she listens quietly until there's nothing more to hear. Thirty seconds pass in complete silence. "I'm sorry," I rasp finally. "I'm so sorry. Say something."

"I don't think I want to," she says. "What did you think? That I was going to tell you it was all right? I'm not going to tell you that, Finn. It's not all right and it won't be. I don't have anything else to say to you."

I'm losing her. It's the worst thing that can happen, and I'll do anything to stop it. "I won't see him anymore," I promise. "I'll do anything you want." I give up Jersy so easily that it breaks my heart. It's a joke to think it ever could've been otherwise. He never stood a chance.

"Too late, Finn," Audrey says blankly. "Don't call me again."

Then she's gone and I'm pulling my hair out of my ponytail, tugging off my clothes and my swimsuit, doing my best to reverse the damage. My hair smells like Jersy's pool, and I tear into the bathroom, climb into the shower, and coat my skin in floral soap.

I could call Audrey back this minute, but she wouldn't talk to me. I know the way she thinks as well as I know myself. I've been worse than an enemy. Nothing can change that. Probably not even giving up Jersy, but I have to try.

I remember the day, not long after Audrey's mom and Steven were married three years ago, that they decided to buy the house they all live in now. Audrey didn't really want to change houses, but things weren't the same since Steven had moved in with them anyway. Audrey and I walked over to her new place so she could check it out without them. The owners had already moved out west, and we jumped the backyard fence and sat on top of the wooden monkey bars they'd abandoned there. Our legs dangled over the sides as we sat six feet off the ground, talking about anything that came into our heads, until a gray-haired guy with a Bluetooth in his ear stared over the fence and said we shouldn't be there.

"She's going to live here," I called back to him, pointing at Audrey.

"It doesn't feel like I'm going to live here," she said after he'd disappeared behind the fence again.

It didn't feel like it to me either, but I said, "That's probably just because it hasn't happened yet. You'll have so much more room—it's going to be way better."

When my parents first stopped getting along, I didn't want to admit it to myself, but Audrey knew something was wrong with me and guessed it was about them because she could see the difference too. I wondered why they didn't worry about me or Daniel noticing. "They'd worry about it if they thought about it," Audrey said, and I knew what she meant, but neither of us could figure out why they wouldn't *make* themselves think about it to begin with.

And now . . . now I can't stop crying. I close my eyes and tilt my head up to the shower, wishing I could take this summer back, even the best parts, if it would mean Audrey wouldn't hate me. My eyes are pink when I come out of the bathroom, my scalp too. I smell like an English garden, and when I stumble out of bed for work the next day the aroma's still leaking out of my pores. "You smell like an old lady," Daniel complains in the car.

I ignore him and face the window. I'm me but not me. I'm the girl who did this to Audrey and the one who looked on, perplexed. My boobs bounce along in my Play Country T-shirt, and I don't even care. I don't care about the awkwardness with Kevin. I don't care about anything. Nishani grabs my arm halfway through the day and asks me to take break with her, but I don't.

I don't care.

When I'm back at home later, Jersy calls my cell and I tell him I can't talk to him anymore. Simple as that. "What'd she say to you?" Jersy demands.

I sigh into the phone and disconnect because I don't care. I can't.

He calls back on the home line and I won't pick up, so Mom has to answer it herself. She knocks on my bedroom door and swings it open before I have a chance to answer. "That's Jersy on the phone for you," she says irritably. Heaven forbid she should ever have to answer the telephone for herself. Isn't that what offspring are for?

"I don't care," I tell her. "Tell him not to call me anymore."

"What?" Mom plants her hands on her hips like some demented little teapot. "I'm not going to tell him that."

"Why not?" I scowl. "I'm not going to talk to him, and there's nothing you can do that will change my mind."

"Finn." Mom fixes her oh-so-concerned eyes on mine. "What's going on with you two?"

It's the conversation she's always wanted, but we're not going to have it now. "Absolutely nothing," I say. "That's the whole point. He's Audrey's boyfriend." *Was Audrey's boyfriend. Just like I was Audrey's friend.*

"He's still waiting," Mom says, pointing to my phone.

"I don't care!" I shout. "Don't you get it? I'm not going to speak to him—no matter how many times you say it." My lungs are exploding. I fasten my arms around myself like a straitjacket, but I can't hold it together. "You don't understand! You never do.

Can't you just listen to me and do things my way for once? Would it kill you to hang up on him?" The words scald my throat, but I don't care. I'm crying so hard that I can hardly feel anything else.

"Honey." Mom's voice is tender. She pets my hair like I'm three years old. "What is all this?" She sits next to me on the bed, one arm around my shoulders, waiting for me to explain.

Her hand in my hair makes me blubber more. It's like I'll never be able to stop. It's like everything I was and everything I am. And it's Jersy too. And Audrey and Dad. I'm losing all of them at once, and for the first time I try to tell her.

It already hurts so much—saying it out loud doesn't make it any worse. The truth about Adam is different. That would hurt her more than anything I've said so far. It's an invisible line I can't jump over.

"Your dad," Mom says firmly, "he loves you so much, Finn. He'd do anything for you and Daniel. You're not losing him. He'd never let that happen. If you picked up the phone right now and said you needed to see him, he'd drive down here tonight. You know that."

"I know," I croak.

"And he'll be closer come September," she reminds me. "You can have your own room at his new place too."

"I know." My nose is a snot factory on overtime. It makes the syllables come out muffled. "I just don't want anything to change." It already has. That's the reason I've gone into a state of collapse.

"I know," Mom says. "You miss him."

I sneak a look at her as I nod. My hair's hanging in front of my eyes, and she brushes it aside and tries to smile. "You told me there was nothing going on between you and Jersy. That's what you said when he was here that night."

"I lied," I admit, fresh pain slicing into me. "I lied to everyone except him. Audrey's never going to forgive me."

"You don't know that," Mom says sympathetically. "This just happened—give her some time." I stare at her with my eyes streaming, and it's the first time that I haven't felt like I should be hiding my tears in I don't know how long. It makes me angry with my dad even as I sit there missing him. Does he have any idea what he's giving up? Why does Mom have to get left behind?

"Wouldn't you be mad?" I ask her. "Wouldn't you hate me?"

Mom spreads her hand across my back. "I'm sure she's hurt, but you two are so close—I don't know that I've ever had as close a friendship as you do with Audrey."

"You and dad?" I ask, because isn't that partly what marriage is supposed to be? Before she has a chance to answer, I add, "Was it ever really like that?"

I want her to tell me that it was, but not only that—I want it to be true.

Mom presses her lips wistfully together as she straightens her shoulders. "I don't think that it was ever quite like that," she admits. "But we were in it together. We had a lot of good years."

I rub my eyes and nod at her. I guess the truth will have to be good enough. The doorbell rings as we're sitting there, and Mom stares into the hall and adds, "I told the papergirl I could pay her tonight."

She gives me an apologetic look, and I say, "It's okay. Go pay her." I'm all cried out anyway. I want to sneak down to the kitchen and down a dozen Popsicles. Maybe that would smother the fire in my throat.

"Okay. Won't be a second." She blinks and pats my knee. "I'll take care of the phone too."

I watch her rush into the hall, but I don't hear her pay the papergirl or get rid of Jersy; I don't bother to listen. Then she's back, leaning against my doorframe like we've had some kind of breakthrough. "Jersy's downstairs," she announces. "He really wants to see you."

My breath catches as I get up. Why can't he leave it alone? Why do I have to do this?

"Do you want me to tell him to go?" Mom offers.

"I'll tell him." I'm already halfway there.

Jersy's waiting for me out on the front step, his face pale and his tan hands working their way inside his sweatshirt sleeves. I swing the door open and stare at him like he should know better than to come here. Everything has changed.

"Okay," he says hollowly. "Just tell me to my face."

"You already know," I say. "I'm sorry."

"You didn't think she was going to make it easy, did you?" His blue-green eyes stare accusingly into mine. "It was never going to be easy."

"I don't know what I thought." I grab my sides as I hunch over. "She doesn't even want to talk to me."

"Then we don't have anything to lose," Jersy declares, his finger tracing the outline of his scar.

"Maybe." My teeth scrape across my lips. "She's still my best friend. I have to do something." I raise my head and look him straight in the face. "I'm really sorry."

Jersy stares back at me, all lips and eyes and Beautiful Boy, and shrugs heavily. "What about me?" he asks. "Am I still your friend?"

I can't do this. Any other time I'd dissolve. But I can't. I've already hit bottom.

I stand on my front step watching Jersy watch me. He's waiting for something that won't happen, and at some point he'll figure that out and disappear and I'll feel so sad that I'll wish I could call him back and do it right.

"You were a really good friend," I tell him. "I wish everything could be different."

"Yeah, me too." Jersy's hands slide slowly out of his sweatshirt. I watch his chest rise and fall as he stares at me. It's like we're trapped. Like the moment will never end. Then he tilts his head and takes a step back.

It's over. We never even say goodbye.

twenty-six

○   ○   ○

THAT'S HOW SUMMER changed everything, not in a single moment that neatly divided before and after, but in a series of little ones that altered life incrementally until I couldn't deny the differences. I went back upstairs and sat with my mom for a long time after Jersy left, until the Anti-Me trudged into my bedroom with his face dragging along the carpet and asked what we were doing. I think he was afraid something else was going wrong—or about to. He'd had enough family drama lately, and so had I. Enough drama all round. So I went to the cottage with my dad after all, and we did boring things like canoeing, throwing a Frisbee around, making homemade barbecue sauce, and listening to the radio, but it was a good kind of boring, the kind I really needed.

When I got home, I tried to call Audrey again. She wouldn't come near the phone, and I ended up e-mailing her a long apology instead. No excuses—I was wrong, I'm sorry, and it's all over with Jersy.

I knew I wouldn't hear anything back. I wouldn't have forgiven me either, not right away. Before summer the thought of not having Audrey as a friend would've torn me to pieces. A big part of me still didn't want to do anything other than hang out with Samsam and wait for her to change her mind, but I forced myself to call Nishani and tell her about Audrey, Jersy, and me. Nishani said it sounded sad and messed up and like something we really needed to talk about in person. We arranged to meet at that same coffee place Jersy and I'd gone to, and she bought me an iced cappuccino and listened while I blabbed most of my summer secrets. The weirdest thing was that it wasn't hard to tell her. I could've kept going all night, and when Mom picked us up at eleven, I felt like I was just getting started.

A few days later Nishani and I tagged along when Aneeka and her friends went clothes shopping in Toronto. Another time I ran into Maggie by the mall food court with her mom and humored her by comparing notes on the Aidan Lamb flick. I even invited her over to watch a movie, and we had a pretty good time.

I was busier those last weeks of summer than I was all year. At heart I'm as much of a social outcast as ever, but something had to change. I couldn't wait until I hit New York or London to talk to people, especially now that I didn't have Audrey or Jersy.

Losing them both at the same time is beyond hard, and Aneeka's asked me more than once if I've been tempted to call Jersy or even see him. Of course I want to talk to him, but what I want more than anything is for Audrey to be my friend again.

Two days before school started I walked over to her house and apologized in person with a scratchy throat and my eyes burning. She said I wasn't being fair, asked how I'd expected her to react, and told me to go home. When I didn't budge, her top lip started twitching and she yelled at me to go cry on Jersy's shoulder.

Some girls would've done that, but how I'd acted with Jersy seemed even worse once I saw the damage I'd done to Audrey up close. Getting in touch with him would've felt like sticking a second knife into her back. I couldn't do it.

When school started up again, I saw him in the hall at St. Mark's and he nodded at me as he passed, but he didn't look happy. Audrey was in my biology class and sat in the front row with Teresa. For the first couple of days, the force of her injured vibes flowing in my direction overshadowed everything else. Then, on the third day of class, Billy Young showed up in a pair of severely creased uniform pants, skimmed my sleeve, and motioned that we should sit in the back. He wasn't mad at me because of Jersy or Audrey; he wasn't taking sides. He'd just spent a day and a half stuck in a car with his dad while driving back from Florida and said he still felt claustrophobic, like he wanted to find the world's biggest open space and run until he collapsed.

"But what would happen after that?" I asked him. "Wouldn't your dad show up to give you a ride home?"

Billy laughed and stretched his arms out above his head. "That's exactly what would happen. I guess it's a good thing I didn't follow through with that plan."

We sat together in bio every day after that. At lunch I mostly stuck with Nishani's friends, but I still hung out with Jasper and Maggie during the classes we shared too. A couple of times Maggie and I went to the mall together, and I had to make a conscious effort not to roll my eyes when she squealed about how cute some reality-show chef guy named Michael was.

I missed Audrey. I missed Jersy. I missed places I'd never been.

But there I was in Glenashton, helping my dad pick out wallpaper and place mats for his new bachelor pad. Okay, he says he's not interested in dating anyone, and I hope that's true, but he could change his mind at any minute. *Anything is possible.*

Anything is possible is still something I'd rather not think about, and one morning in late September I'm rushing through the upstairs hallway at St. Mark's when I think I spot Adam Porter's athletic frame leaning against a locker in the distance. My fingers turn instantly to ice. The flavor of rust crawls into my mouth like it had never left and will never leave.

When he turns to walk away, I see that it's actually some sophomore guy who shot up half a foot over the summer and doesn't even look that much like Adam from the front. I'm so relieved that the relief makes me dizzy. Why can he still do this to me when he's gone?

Why?

Maybe Jersy was right about talking to someone. I've been wrong about other things. I could be wrong about that too. I don't think I could do it in person, but maybe over the phone, anonymous, so no one will have to know. It's not like I'll call the cops or anything. It's not like I'll tell my parents or see a shrink, but maybe I'll do something just for me.

At the time, it felt like telling Jersy helped, but the thing itself is still there, like a microscopic flaw inside me that functions like a domino. Sometimes I don't think about it for days at a time . . . and then I do. Like with the fake Adam spotting that flashes me back to last year's panic. I don't want to feel that way anymore— I want to forget for real—so later that day I make up a test for myself, the way I used to force myself to think of Adam just to prove to myself I could.

After school I head for HMV with some of my hard-earned Play Country cash in my knapsack. About forty seconds after I walk into the store, a girl with streaked blue hair lopes over to me and wants to know if she can help me find anything. A guy with a Celtic tattoo and impeccable taste in music, I think anxiously, and just then Record Store Guy strolls in with a bag of Japanese food. He stands next to me and flashes me the most amazing full-on smile.

"Hey, you," Ryan says. "I thought you'd given up on us." By "us" he means the store, of course.

"I've been around," I lie. "I guess you just haven't been here at the time."

Ryan nods, his eyes twinkling. His fingers are nail polish free, and his eyeliner is so smudged that you can barely see it. Audrey would almost approve of him like this. "You know, we had a job going here in the summer," he says. "I was going to mention it in case you were interested."

But I never came in. Ryan is taller than me, and I have to look up at him a little. I'm not sure if it's because of some of the things that happened between me and Jersy during the summer, but somehow being around him seems easier than before. I mean, he's as Belgian-chocolate edible as ever, but that doesn't seem quite as scary as it did for most of last year.

"That would've been cool," I say. "I wish I'd known." We've talked lots in the past, Ryan and me, but always inside these walls, and suddenly I feel like this test needs to be bigger. My heart's jogging a little faster now, but I tell myself I can handle this. "Are you on break?" I point at his Japanese food. "I was just thinking about grabbing a wrap or something."

I can't believe I just asked Record Store Guy if he wants to spend his break with me. Audrey would be impressed. I want to share this with her so much; it's impossible for me to imagine that she wouldn't want to know.

"I'm not really a fan of the food court," Ryan says. "It's a warm day. How about we hit the park in front of the civic center?"

I buy a vegetarian wrap, and we head out across the parking lot together. The civic center's on the west side and has a public library, day care, art gallery, and a bunch of other offices in it. At first I'm nervous, wondering if we'll have anything to say to each other now that we're outside HMV, but then Ryan starts talking about a folk-punk Norwegian band I've never heard of and a New Zealand singer/songwriter that I've been listening to a lot lately.

The park's more of a parkette, and we sit there eating our food. Ryan has chopsticks and knows how to use them. I stare at his lips as he eats, and I can't help but want him the way I used to, but the feelings around the want are more complicated. I feel guilty about Jersy for even thinking about Ryan, and then the Jersy guilt makes the Audrey guilt flare too. My brain short-circuits as I try to follow the thoughts through to some satisfactory conclusion, and I end up just watching Ryan slide pieces of shrimp into his mouth.

I wonder what it would be like to kiss him, to go home with him and maybe lie on his couch with his weight on me. Would I get scared? I don't think so, but that's probably only because I know it would never happen.

Ryan stops chewing and holds his chopsticks aloft. "Are you okay?"

I swallow the bit of zucchini in my mouth. "I think I'm coming down with something. I've had this start-of-a-headache feeling all day." That's pretty close to the truth, except that my headache's not what was making me stare.

Ryan sets his chopsticks down in the cardboard container on his lap and lays his right palm against my forehead. I'm sure that it's the kind of thing tons of people would do when someone says they're not feeling well, but now instead of jogging my heart is outright racing.

"You feel warm," he confirms, withdrawing his hand. "We have some Tylenol back at the store if you want." Ryan smiles to himself. "Now I sound like my girlfriend—she's always trying to feed people drugs."

Once upon a time hearing that he had a girlfriend would've put a lump the size of a quarter in my throat, but now it only fazes me for two seconds. Then I start to tease him, my heart beginning to slow back down to normal. "Your girlfriend is a drug pusher?"

Ryan laughs. "She's a nursing student, a big believer in modern medicine."

I nod like that makes much better sense.

"C'mon," Ryan tells me. "You really look like you need that Tylenol." He reaches out to touch my arm before getting to his feet, and it's at that exact moment that I see Jersy striding towards the civic center in a plain white T-shirt, his navy uniform sweater tied around his waist. He stares at us for two long seconds before wrenching his gaze away. His jaw has dropped, and I instantly sense that he thinks there's something more than Tylenol going on between Ryan and me.

I see Jersy round the corner at school or walk into the cafeteria all the time, so I should be used to it, but the sight always feels like a shock of longing chased with a lingering, aching sadness.

This time it's even worse, because of the way his eyes zero in on mine and then jolt away, like I've hurt him all over again.

In a flash Jersy disappears inside the front doors. Meanwhile my guilt alarm is beeping loud enough to wake the entire state of Alaska. *It's not true, Jersy. Don't believe it.* I send him urgent telepathic messages while Record Store Guy and I trek back to HMV. Ryan gives me two Tylenol tablets, and the girl with the blue-streaked hair offers me her water bottle to chase the pills down. "Grab an application now," Ryan advises, handing one over. "That way we'll have it on file when we're hiring again."

I take the application, still thinking about the look on Jersy's face. I know I'd look that way if I saw him with some other girl. Audrey probably looked that way when I told her about us.

Whatever they had is over; I've heard it through the grapevine, but I can see it for myself too. They don't let their eyes land on each other. The three of us are like a natural disaster, a hurricane or avalanche that can't be undone. I don't know how to fix it, and then there's the invisible domino . . . the thing that never happened but that I haven't entirely left behind. Later that evening I lie on top of my bedspread, thinking and thinking and thinking, with my almost headache burrowing into the right side of my skull and Samsam curled up beside my bed.

There's no escaping the fact that there are three conversations I need to have as soon as possible. Maybe none of them will really change anything, but I have to try.

First I call Audrey. That she even picks up is good news, I guess, but my nerves make me frantic. "Don't hang up," I plead. "I have to talk to you."

"I think we've already had this conversation," Audrey says. "Please don't keep doing this."

Once I hear her voice, the thought of telling her about my conversation with Ryan seems ridiculous. From her point of view, there's nothing new with me that matters.

"I'm not going to bug you anymore after this," I tell her. "I'm sorry, Audrey. I'm so, so sorry. *Tell me what I can do.*"

Audrey sighs, and she sounds nearly as sad about it as I feel. Maybe sometimes there's nothing anyone can do to change things—the bad feelings catch and stick. "Do whatever you want," she says finally. "It has nothing to do with me."

"Audr—" I begin, but she's already hung up. If I want to tell someone about Record Store Guy or anything else, from now on it will have to be Nishani, or maybe even Maggie or Billy. Somehow I still can't believe this is where we stand, but I can't let it stop me in my tracks. I give myself a few minutes to detox from my depressing call to Audrey, and then I sit hunched over on my bed with my stomach fluttering and dial the very number I'd sworn weeks ago that I wouldn't.

On the third ring, I start debating with myself about whether I should leave a message. After the fourth, Jersy says hello. We haven't said anything directly to each other since summer, and the sound of his voice makes me flinch. I can't say who I miss more, the Jersy who was my friend or the one who pulled the covers over us and hugged me tight. Maybe the reason I miss him so much is that I've never been able to separate the two.

"It's me," I tell him, sucking back my nerves. Can I still be a *me* after all these weeks? "It's Finn."

Jersy's voice deepens. "Yeah . . . hey."

"Hey," I say back. "I know this is . . . probably weird." Jersy leaves me hanging and forces me to continue. I can't blame him, but it's hard. "I just . . . you know . . . I saw you outside the civic center earlier, and I didn't want you to get the wrong idea."

"Don't worry about it," he says. "You don't have to explain anything to me."

The emptiness between us sounds like regular old silence, and maybe that's all it is. Maybe I read him wrong earlier and he doesn't care about me anymore. "I know. I just . . . I didn't want you to think I was with Ryan."

"Is Ryan the guy from HMV?" Jersy asks.

"Yeah."

We both go quiet again.

I get scared that he won't say anything else, and I mumble, "I think you were right about talking to someone about what happened to me last year. I think I—"

Jersy interrupts me. "Finn, are you okay?"

Considering the mess the three of us have been through, I think I'm actually pretty good, but I could be better—and I want to be. "Don't worry," I say. "I'm fine. I just want to get some things straightened out in my head." There are details I'm still scared to say out loud, but I've already looked up a number for a twenty-four-hour help line. I'm not positive that I'll make that third phone call tonight, but I'll do it soon; that's a silent promise I make to myself while I'm on the phone with Jersy.

"Okay." I hear him exhale into the phone. "That sounds good."

"And what about you?" I chew my lip and dig my fingers into my front pocket. "How're you doing?"

"I'm okay."

"And Christina?" I ask. It's impossible to get him to say more than two words at a time, but even hearing those few words makes me ache. I don't know how to switch the feeling off.

"Yeah, she's good too. She asked about you."

"What did you tell her?"

"What could I say?" Jersy asks. "I told her the truth about us."

"I'm sorry. I don't know what to say."

"Me neither," Jersy says quietly.

He's wishing he wasn't on the phone with me, I bet. It seems I didn't need to call him and let him know about Ryan after all. I'm just making things weirder. "Do you want to go?" I ask. I ache all over, even though I'm the one doing the talking.

Jersy takes a couple of seconds to answer. "Not if you don't want to," he says slowly. "We can talk."

"Yeah?" I let myself breathe.

"Yeah," he repeats, and he sounds like he means it. I haven't had an excuse to take a good look at him in so long that my mind has to make up for it. I picture him in jeans and the same white T-shirt he was wearing earlier. He's not frowning but not smiling either. Maybe he doesn't know what to think. "So what happened with your dad?" he asks.

I tell him about going to the cottage with my father, how his new apartment is nice but feels small with the three of us there, and that I'm not really mad at him for leaving anymore. My words feel clunky, like I'm just starting to remember how to talk to him. Jersy says it's cool that things are starting to work out, and I ask him how the rest of his summer was. I feel bad just using the words "the rest." They make me think about that moment at my door when he realized that I wasn't going to change my mind. Jersy sounds okay, though. He says that he spent the last week of summer in Kingston with his friends. They saw something weird in the sky while hanging out in his friend's backyard late one night, and he asks if I believe in UFOs.

"I think there probably are some real ones, but I bet most of them are fake." It's so good to be talking to him again, about any-thing, that I'd stay on the phone spinning UFO theories with him all night if he wanted.

"Or experimental military planes the government doesn't want us to know about," Jersy goes. I open my mouth to agree, but he says, "*Shit.* My cell's beeping a low-battery warning. Hang on, I have the charger somewhere . . ."

I picture him rushing around his room, searching under his bed and pushing crap around his desk in the hope of uncovering his missing charger. He told me a long time ago that he's always losing things, and I wonder if that's because of his insomnia (or whatever he wants to call it) or if it's just how things are.

I know our conversation has to end sometime and that Jersy probably won't find his charger before his cell flatlines. My brain has been so consumed with the immediate situation between Audrey, Jersy, and me that I haven't projected beyond our phone call, and even if I had, I'm sure I wouldn't be able to predict what will happen to us after we're disconnected. I haven't been able to predict anything up until now. Why should this be any different? Adam Porter, my parents' breakup, Jersy, Nishani, Record Store Guy laying his hand along my forehead—for better or for worse it's all been a big surprise, and I brace myself for a dial tone, any second now . . .

I can't hear anything from the phone. Maybe it's already happened and I'm just listening to dead air. The silence sounds claustrophobic, but I don't hang up just yet. I hunch over more and spread my left hand visor-like over my eyebrows, feeling the separation anxiety in advance of the dial tone.

One–one thousand. *Hush.*

Two–one thousand. *Hush. Hush.*

Three–one thousand. *Hush, hush, hush.*

"Got it!" Jersy declares triumphantly. "You still there, Finn?"

I wonder if he can feel the weight of my smile over the phone line. My gaze lands on Samsam stretched out beside my bed. His paws are twitching joyfully in his sleep, like he's dreaming he's sprinting after squirrels with no one to stop him. The sight makes me smile deeper still.

"Still here," I confirm. I hug my knees, feeling so good that I almost want to laugh.

Yes, Jersy, I'm most definitely still here.

C. K. KELLY MARTIN lives in the greater Toronto area with her husband. You can visit her Web site and blog at www.ckkellymartin.com.